PF

EMPIRE'S
END

A ZOMBIE NOVEL BY
DAVID DUNWOODY

"A powerful new chapter in an epic series of zombie thrillers. Endlessly entertaining."
—Jonathan Maberry, author of *Patient Zero* and *Rot & Ruin*

"Everything a sequel should be—bigger, faster, gorier, and the zombie characters are the creepiest yet. It's a fantastic return for the Reaper."
—Peter Clines, author of *Ex-Heroes* and *Ex-Patriots*

"More than just a solid sequel to an excellent zombie novel; it surpasses its predecessor with a deeper look into a world filled with dark magic and vivid characters, both living and dead. Dunwoody somehow manages to make Death a sympathetic character and his zombies are some of the scariest around."
—Patrick D'Orazio, author of *Comes the Dark*

"Let the reaper be your guide in this epic entry in the *Empire* series. David Dunwoody once again delivers the goods with this post apocalyptic masterpiece."
—Timothy W. Long, author of *The Zombie Wilson Diaries*
and *Among the Living*

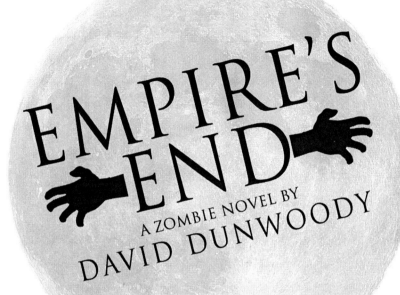

EMPIRE'S END

A ZOMBIE NOVEL BY

DAVID DUNWOODY

Permuted Press
The formula has been changed...
Shifted... Altered... Twisted.
www.permutedpress.com

A PERMUTED PRESS book
published by arrangement with the author
ISBN-13: 978-1-934861-73-8
ISBN-10: 1-934861-73-1

Portions of *Afterdead: A.D. 2007* previously appeared in
*The Undead* (2005) and *The Hacker's Source* magazine (2005-08).

... AND HELL FOLLOWED WITH HIM

# PROLOGUE / LADIES AND GENTLEMAN, CHILDREN OF ALL AGES

"It doesn't hurt?" Christmas asked. It was the answer that most disturbed him.

Luis shook his head, cracking a smile that split the great wound beneath his empty eye socket. Fissures opened in the sinew over his cheekbone and bled, yet he never lost his grin. Despite the mutilation, Luis had insisted on applying his makeup. His remaining flesh was painted bone-white, his lips black; a corpse clown. A velvety top hat sat at a jaunty angle on his head, baring part of his ragged scalp.

Christmas helped Luis button his jacket. It was difficult for the performer to do so himself, what with his missing fingers. Turning to peer through the tent flap, Christmas said, "Full house." Luis snapped up his cane and used his teeth to tug at the gloves on his hands, half of their fingers empty and dangling.

"Of course," he replied, his voice a hoarse croak. It amazed Christmas that, when standing before an audience, Luis was still able to command the room, bringing the crowd to an awed silence so that they could hear him speak. He was a mere shadow of the man he'd once been; as his body wasted away, he'd given himself over completely to the performance, withdrawing from the others, withdrawing from Christmas, his mind gradually slipping away as he became one with his circus persona.

"I'll announce you," Christmas said. Luis nodded, and Christmas stepped through the flap, raising his arms into the air as he strode toward the center ring.

1

"Your attention please!" he shouted. The audience immediately sat up and stared at him, jittery with anticipation.

"It's time for the man of the hour! The dancer among the dead! The King himself—Eviscerato!!"

Christmas gestured toward the tent flap. He waited. They waited. All was silent.

Then it began.

\* \* \*

He started out juggling heads in Mexico City. Standing brazenly in the middle of the street, the twenty-year-old Luis heaved severed skulls into the air, bystanders gasping as the heads' rolling orbs and gnashing teeth plummeted toward Luis' open, fleshy hands. He'd deftly catch each one by its hair, swinging it back up, smiling at his audience. He never looked at the heads. He never looked for the police. The police, in fact, often stopped to watch the show, sometimes handing Luis food vouchers and patting his shoulder. It was the same for them as it was for everyone else: Luis' illegal performance stirred their spirits more than did any singer or puppeteer. He braved the reality they were living in, unlike the government, which hid within the city walls and pretended that the world had not changed in a hundred years.

A hundred years since the plague had struck—early in the twenty-first century, a virus had erupted in the southern U.S. and hitched a ride with fleeing immigrants into Mexico. A virus that, some believed, was supernatural in nature. They called it the Lord's judgment. They called it Man's sin. They called it the end.

Yet a century later, Man was still here. But running, and hiding, while the undead roamed free.

Luis didn't believe in running or hiding. He juggled. He danced. He captivated his audiences. Then he'd met Christmas, an American, and together they'd conceived the idea of a traveling show.

There was no money to be made. The occasional food vouchers, perhaps, but mostly they dealt in bartered goods—and they set their sights on *los Estados Unidos*. For there, many cities still stood, protected by the military. And in the badlands, the fallen states, stubborn people still lived amidst the packs of ravenous dead.

In those people Luis saw the spirit he himself possessed, and indeed, the badlanders received him with great enthusiasm. Word spread quickly of Eviscerato and his caravan of performers. Word especially spread of the animals used in the act. The dead ones.

The U.S. strictly enforced a law that prohibited making any sort of profit off of human rotters. Animals were another story, and so Christmas and Luis set about gathering a host of creatures from the badlands: wolves, horses, even bears. The shambling beasts were netted and dragged back to the camp, to be placed in hastily erected cages. Then, before a packed house, Luis danced among the creatures, taunting them, stabbing at them, riding their backs and severing their noses and plucking out their eyes while cheers shook the tent.

The dead animals generally posed little threat. They fed only on their own kind—a common trait among each infected species—and were sluggish in defending themselves. Besides, not even a *live* bear could win against a chainsaw. It was Christmas who came up with the notion of sewing a midget performer inside the bear's gut, then slicing the animal open so that the midget somersaulted through a hail of blood into the center ring. It became one of their most popular acts.

The dead animals generally posed little threat. But, as Christmas warned time and time again, there was always a risk.

It was a risk that Luis did not fear.

So, one night, when he'd stumbled and a ragged wolf had clamped down on his arm, flaying it to the bone, the great Eviscerato had done nothing to fight it off. Instead, he rose and swung the animal through the air on his arm, playing to the shrieking audience, whose horrified cries turned into applause as he knelt and bit into the wolf's hide, tearing loose a rotten strip of meat and spitting it onto the ground.

"You're infected," Christmas whispered after the show, kneading his hands and pacing in circles. An outsider might have thought that the circus manager was fretting over the loss of his biggest act, but Luis knew that he was mourning the inevitable demise of his friend.

"It might be weeks. Months," Luis said in an attempt at being reassuring.

Christmas shook his head. "Days. Maybe hours, Luis! You can never tell with the plague!"

"My spirit is strong," Luis said firmly. "It only depends on the strength of one's soul, and I know I—"

"You always wanted this, didn't you?" Christmas snapped. "You always dreamed of becoming one of them. You think there's some mystery there that must be solved, some goddamned revelation to be had. There isn't! You're going to die, and the virus is going to take over and you'll be no more."

"I've seen rotters who remember," Luis protested, clenching his fists. "I've seen them try to drive rusted-out cars. I've seen them use axes. I've seen them try to swim in the Pacific—even though they didn't *need* to keep themselves afloat, they tried. They try!"

"Memory and spirit are two different things." Christmas slouched on a wooden stool and looked toward a distant fire, where the others were roasting a freshly killed deer. "You, the Luis I know, will die."

"But you'll live on," Luis replied. "And you'll have everything you need. Because my new act is going to sweep across this country like the plague itself."

"New act?" Christmas looked warily at him.

"We'll have to restrict ourselves to the badlands," Luis went on, as if he already had the entire plan mapped out. And he did. "We won't be able to perform in the cities, but that's just as well. People there still trade money like it has value. You and the others will be able to retire after I'm gone, living off your reputation alone—I promise."

"What is this act?" Christmas said. "Are you talking about parading your undead body around the ring?"

"No, no. I told you, I still have plenty of time left. I haven't died yet, John."

"What," Christmas repeated, fear creeping into his voice, "is this act?"

"Rotters.

Human ones."

* * *

Luis was right.

The show was a runaway success.

Christmas could only cover his eyes in horror as Luis danced among a group of chained undead, passing within inches of their jaws and hands, laughing all the while—and then giving himself to them. Letting them bite his shoulders, his arms. And he bit them back. The audience always reacted to that. They saw it as a last act of defiance against the plague. Eviscerato became a hero.

Before Luis' performance, there were others. Spinner, the tightrope walker, would traverse a taut rope suspended over a cage full of hungry dead. The mute Fire Juggler would hurl his torches toward the tent ceiling while the Strongman, with his massive hammer, crushed the legs and bodies and heads of attacking rotters.

Christmas appointed Nickel to be the zombie handler. It wasn't common to refer to the undead as "zombies", but Luis felt it spiced up the show. When it was time, Nickel would slip a noose over the neck of each rotter and lead it to its place in the act. Chained to a rolling platform for Eviscerato, or caged beneath the tightrope, or trussed and blindfolded to be released into the Strongman's playground.

The rotters were easy to find in the badlands. Ferals usually hung around ghost towns. They often gathered in packs, following one another as if someone had a clue as to where the meat was. They were usually underfed and in bad shape. Simple to catch.

It seemed all too easy, all too convenient, that these aberrations of nature now provided the means for John Christmas and his employees to live. It sickened him how they had shattered their values and cut out their souls in order to fit the undead into their wretched existence.

Spinner fell from his tightrope into a pit of rotters. Nickel was savagely bitten. The Strongman lost his footing one evening and was trampled before the others could clear the undead away; his eyes and mouth filled with tainted blood, he'd stalked without a word from the tent and never spoke again.

And Luis...

Luis only smiled.

* * *

"Your attention please! It's time for the man of the hour! The dancer among the dead! The King himself—Eviscerato!!"

Christmas gestured toward the tent flap. He waited. They waited. All was silent.

Then Eviscerato leapt into the tent, throwing his arms in the air, eliciting a deafening roar from the crowd. He danced toward the center ring, waving gaily.

"My dear, dear friends!" He cried, still smiling, blood dripping from his chin. "Tonight I have such a special treat for you."

As the performer gave his spiel, Christmas glanced outside the flap. He saw the Strongman there, waiting, but oddly postured in the shadows, his great hammer dragging in the earth behind him.

Nickel was closer. The light revealed his face.

He stepped into the tent and pulled the flap down, and he was dead and Christmas saw it and the audience saw it, then the canvas began to blacken as the tent was set aflame and the Strongman stormed into the seats for his meat.

And Eviscerato danced, and danced, and danced. Through the fire and the smoke and the blood he performed, in his mindless, gleeful reverie; he danced until all the colors swirled together and swam, together, in chaos.

# ONE / DEAR MOM

**February 16th, 2109**

It's only the third week of the tour and I've already learned so much—about everything, not just the badlands and the war but the plague itself. I've even learned some things I never knew about the Great Cities. I don't know if you've heard it back home but they've taken to calling the safe zones the "Great Cities" now, not just because most of them are on the Great Lakes (save for our Cleveland) but because the Senate is trying to raise morale among the people. The message is that America is still here. We still have something to fight for.

You wouldn't know it from touring the badlands. Our convoy has passed through at least a couple dozen ghost towns. Not a soul in sight, not even a rotter. But I don't guess the undead would have any use for an unpopulated city, would they?

We've seen a few badlander communities. They're shanty towns set far back from the highway and the ghost towns. No one has approached the convoy at any point. They don't trust the Senate. That's why Gillies has come out here. He's a brave man, Mom (divorced too, FYI) and it's an honor to be his aide. I've spent most of every day with him. That's how I've learned so much in such a short while.

He says that the Great Cities region will be expanded to include St. Paul to the west and Lansing to the east. They've decided that Chicago will be the capital city. All in all, parts of seven former states will be inside the Wall when it's complete. Senator Gillies says there are big plans in the works for Cleveland, too. I don't know what, so don't ask! Maybe I'll know by the time I get back.

I'm putting as much as I can into this letter because there's no postal service beyond Utah. Can't trust that a lone rider will be safe any further south. We're rolling through the Utah desert as I write this. The Army commander says there's a large group of badlanders out here, and Gillies wants to stop and talk to them about the Great Cities.

Why would anyone choose this wasteland over civilization? That's what I'm going to ask them. Maybe they just don't know about the work being done.

Gillies said that the withdrawal could begin as early as 2111. The Wall won't be finished then, but that's actually a reason why he wants to pull the troops out of the badlands. The Wall's completion would be safeguarded by the military, and then I guess it would become their job to patrol it. The withdrawal is just another reason why everybody should be heading north now.

The most interesting discussions we've had, though, have been about the undead. They supposedly only outnumber us by five hundred to one now, but that's because the human population has dropped so sharply. However, the Senate maintains radio contact with Europe, and they say things might actually be worse there than here.

The plague virus isn't just a virus. It doesn't behave that way. Gillies believes there's more to it, something otherworldly. Some people turn only hours after being bitten while others take weeks. There's no real proof that it has anything to do with biology. It could just as well depend on one's spiritual constitution, and that's what he says it is. You know what? I believe it, too.

That's why Gillies calls the plague God's judgment. Even though it began on an Army base what, 102 years ago—he says that their tampering with nature is what brought on the Lord's wrath. He's a very spiritual man. I think most of the Senators are, but especially Gillies. His father was a religious teacher at a place called Seminarium Vita. He told me that his father died trying to minister to the undead.

It's also because of the virus' otherworldly energy that the rotters have a sort of aura about them. I'd never heard about that before but I know now that it's true. I've seen dead insects rise in a rotter's wake. Sometimes, at night, the soldiers hang bags of fireflies around the perimeter of our camp. I've seen the bags light up and start thrashing seconds before a stray rotter walked into camp and into a hail of bullets. Yes, even though bullets don't kill rotters, the troops still use guns. They shoot out the rotters' knees and then torch them. (Sorry if that seems morbid. I thought it was interesting.)

You remember when I read Darwin to you? His observations are present in the undead. Not just undead animals, but people too. See, if a rotter feeds often enough, it can "regenerate" tissue. Anything from skin to bone to brain matter, they can grow back. Those undead lead the packs and get stronger, while the others rot away... Senator Gillies says that some rotters have the potential to relearn things like speech! Wouldn't it be awful if a rotter looked and sounded like a healthy human being? Luckily that's only in theory.

Those rotters that run like the wind... I've seen them. "Alpha zombies," as the commander calls them. I've only seen a few, and they didn't last long against our troops, but Lord they were frightening.

I guess that's it for now. I want you to know that I am safe and I am happy. Believe me when I say that our men and women in uniform are up to the challenge, and only the best of the best were handpicked to protect the Senate President's convoy. I think we're going to make a real difference out here. We're going to save the badlanders.

I love you, and I'll see you in a month's time.

Todd

\* \* \*

Mom never got the latter.

It was lost in the ambush. An ambush by rotters.

Heavy with stains of blood, the letter fell into the Utah sand and was forgotten in the unfolding chaos. Then, eventually, it was buried, and finally the elements claimed it and erased the words that a naïve young man had written to assuage the fears of his worried mother.

# TWO / THE NEW FLESH

**October 18th, 2112**

Every Main Street in every town in the badlands looked the same. The leaves had turned and fallen from the trees encroaching on empty businesses; plants grew in smashed windows and uprooted the sidewalk. The sun bleached crumbling brick and cracked asphalt, The rust-eaten skeletons of cars sat in the street, now home to small animals, the entire city slowly being reclaimed by Nature; the last signs of human life nothing more than scars fading in her flesh.

This particular Main Street in central Colorado had only a few cars in the road. There was a minivan that had run up onto the sidewalk, and a police cruiser abandoned in the middle of the street. At the end of the street, however, blocking off a municipal plaza, was a barricade of vehicles scorched by fire

And at the other end of the street, hanging from a traffic light, was a man in a noose.

He'd hung himself that very morning, and the rotters scattered throughout the area had begun to take notice. Raspy moans issued from desiccated throats, and creaky joints made scraping sounds as the dead started to move.

The moans increased in volume, attracting rotters from nearby streets. It wasn't long before a mob of several dozen shuffling corpses was advancing inch by inch toward Main Street, most of them with no idea why; they just followed the sounds.

Rotters who would have once growled menacingly at their competition could now only gurgle on the rotten paste filling their windpipes. They hadn't fed in perhaps years and had just stood, silent, patient; waiting for food to come along as they decomposed. The virus could only fight off the elements for so long. The dead in this Colorado city were nothing more than shambling husks. But most of them still had arms, and fingers, and most important of all, teeth. And they all had the hunger.

They closed in on the hanged man from all directions. The man wore a dark suit. He was pale and hairless and thin. A pleasant breeze carried the odor of decay through the air, though none of them could smell; had they been able to, they might have noticed the lack of any odor coming off the hanged man.

Closer, closer. Thick saliva gathered behind swollen lips. Hands groped through the air. The moans all came together in a maddening crescendo.

The hanged man had one arm behind his back. Strapped to it was a blade: a long, curved implement made from fused bone, sharpened to a razor's edge on both sides. Its tip rested against the noose around the man's neck.

His eyes opened. They were dark and lifeless, doll's eyes. They stared coldly down at the undead.

A shoulder sling and wrist straps secured the enormous curved blade to his right arm. A leather thong bound around his hand, he simply flicked his wrist; and the noose was severed.

The man came down in a tight crouch, sending plumes of dust into the air with his impact. Before any of the stupid, shambling dead had a chance to register what was happening, to even hazard a guess at what the man really was—he rose and thrust the blade out and spun with a battle cry that killed the dead's senseless conversation, as if he were an unwelcome guest; and he most certainly was.

As he spun, rising, the blade cutting upward in a sweeping arc— heads flew off of shoulders and rolled through the air. And those slashed across the torso opened up and rotten gray guts spilled onto the street. Stomachs burst and vomited their contents onto the man's feet. He threw the blade out again, spinning in the opposite direction, and cut down a dozen of them at once.

They were dead, the ones he'd struck—dead and deader. They would not rise again.

The others came at him. He planted the tip of the scythe blade in an emaciated rotter's gut and ripped through his sternum and skull, halving the bastard. The blade turned and tore downward, through the legs of another undead, then reversed course and decapitated a hissing female. Her open throat continued to hiss as foul ichor spayed into the air.

The man barreled into a line of rotters, lifting one off its feet and divorcing its legs from its torso with a mid-air strike. He whirled to knife through the kneecaps of the others, and they fell limp, never to get up again. Every blow with the scythe blade was a death blow. The blade seemed cursed; no, *enchanted.*

He had forged it himself, binding and shaping the bone with dark magic, then endowing it with the power to kill the unkillable— to reap the undead. Such a task had been his burden, as he had once been the Reaper himself.

For thousands of years little more than a silent record-keeper, marking the passage of souls from one plane to the next, the Reaper had felt obligated to take on a new role with the rise of the undead. It was more than just a plague on humanity; they upset laws and balances set before time began. With every fiber in his being he'd hated them... and with that, he himself had begun to change, even as death had.

He'd found will, and righteous anger. And when he'd found *her*—the one he dreamed about, the child from the swamp-house— that had been it. He had relinquished his role as Death and bound himself to the mortal coil upon which shuffled Man himself.

He was still a supernatural being, yes, but so much more fragile than he had once been. Unharmed, he might live for an eternity, but if the undead were to overcome him, and tear him apart, he'd simply be gone. No afterlife awaited the pale man with the black eyes. He was a spirit made flesh, and this was his *only* life.

But he had accepted all this without hesitation because it meant saving *her.* Lily, the child who, once he found her, helped him to find himself. She had been forced to live among the undead in the swamp-house by her mad brother, forced to treat the cadaverous predators as kin. And the Reaper had—

*You simply lost it. You lost it.*

But what he'd gained had been worth the price. He was *alive* now. And he had begun to sleep, and to dream, and in his dreams he saw the little girl and he knew he had to find her again. To ensure her safety, of course, but more than that. Their bond seemed beyond his understanding.

Upon entering this strange new life, the former Death had chosen a name for himself: Adam. And it was as Adam that he spun like a grim dancer through this sea of severed limbs and putrid gore.

He'd already cut down a third of the mob; the end was near, at least for today.

Leaping atop the police cruiser, he vaulted off the roof's edge and took down a row of rotting fiends before they could flinch. Some of the undead had begun to slow in their approach, but the lure of the flesh was too great. None would flee, making Adam's job all the easier.

*And I am not a man of flesh. They could not consume me. Although some have tried...*

He climbed the barricade of vehicles at the end of the street and ran onto the municipal plaza to make his last stand against the horde.

When they came at him he spun right into their midst, cutting a crimson swath through the center of the mob, ripping it apart at the seams and scattering the shell-shocked remnants across the plaza; he then flew at those stumbling about the edge of the plaza and slew them with surgical precision. A pair of rotters attacked from behind. He turned on his heels and skewered them both. Their guts churned as they struggled, fluids spilling down their threadbare jeans, and then both fell still. Adam yanked the blade free and watched them drop. They were the last. It was done.

His own clothes were soaked through with gore. He'd taken this nondescript suit off of a corpse after shedding his reaper's robes. A spongy mold was beginning to grow inside the jacket, feeding on the blood that suffused it. He figured it was time to trade up. Maybe this time he could find a pair of pants that felt less awkward, since he didn't have a—

Movement to the left. He spun and saw a shadow disappeared into the old town hall.

Uncommon for a rotter to run; then again, this one had just seen dozens of its contemporaries mowed down by a single man. Maybe they were getting a little smarter. Adam wasn't really interested in the reason for it, though. It only made his mission more complicated.

Stealthily he crept up the steps of the town hall building and peered through the open doors. He saw a lobby, littered with debris and dimly lit by the sunlight spilling through a fractured ceiling high overhead. As he entered, the floor creaked loudly beneath his bare feet. It felt like the whole thing might come down on his head at any moment.

Somewhere in the building, footsteps creaked in response to his. From upstairs. Up the grand staircase, past the soiled American flag and the faded photos of city councilmen. Adam padded across the floor like a tiger after its next meal. Another creak led him down a narrow hallway lined with empty offices. The windows were all shuttered, allowing only a few slits of light into the corridor. Any moment now he'd find his prey cornered in one of these rooms, and he'd pounce.

He passed a doorway, just barely registered a silhouette standing in the room, and stopped short.

It might've had its back to the doorway. Maybe not. He had to strike.

Adam leapt into the room, and the rotter swung something at the shutters and they came crashing down, flooding the room with light, temporarily blinding him—

But he saw enough.

It was a thin-haired, stocky rotter in coveralls. He was holding a shovel. He was the one from Jefferson Harbor, Lily's town. The one with the shovel who had separated him from the girl—and who was supposed to be dead—but now he was here and he was bearing down on Adam with the shovel pointed at him like a spear.

No time to think. Adam deflected the shovel with the scythe and threw an elbow into the side of the rotter's head. It stumbled right into a wall—through it—and into the next room. Adam followed through a shower of sawdust.

The floor groaned as the rotter rose to face him. Shovel met blade again, and this time it was Adam who was knocked off balance. He fell on his back and rolled aside just in time to avoid being impaled. The rotter caught his ankle and hurled him across the room with inhuman strength.

This was much more than just a zombie. Something had changed, and Adam knew why. When the bastard had ambushed him in Jefferson Harbor, he'd done something that defied all undead instinct: he'd *tasted of the Reaper's flesh*, swallowing a pound of Adam's otherworldly constitution before collapsing on the ground. Adam had revived to find the rotter lying inert and assumed he was finished. Wrong.

What had his false flesh done to the rotter? And had he actually followed Adam all the way here from Louisiana?

Again, no time to think, and Adam paid the price for his hesitation. The shovel bit into his side and he felt himself propelled through the air like a rag doll, crashing through a paper-thin wall and into a railing and nearly toppling over it to the lobby below.

He turned, ducking as he did so, and the shovel whistled over his head. He thrust the scythe at the rotter. No purchase. He had to get closer. But that damn shovel was beating him back with every effort, and he felt the railing pressing into his back, then he heard a sharp crack and suddenly there was nothing at all supporting him.

Adam dropped through space, through beams of light and dust motes, down down down to the floor where he landed on the shattered railing and felt a sort of pain he'd never felt before. It knifed through his spine, from his neck to his buttocks, and he arched his back with a cry of pure agony.

He had no bones, was only God's clay, but his new life had blessed him with a knowledge of suffering, and he felt now as if he'd been snapped in half by the fall. And the rotter was thundering down the stairs.

Thunder. The entire chamber was rumbling. It was all going to come down.

As the rotter crossed the lobby toward him, Adam forced himself into a kneeling position and swung his blade into a nearby column. It bowed and exploded outward, and a balcony dropped from the upper levels with a boom that shook the foundations of the town hall.

Adam rolled out of the way of falling plaster and wood, landing right at the rotter's feet. He swept the undead's legs out from under him.

The rotter hit the floor with a solid thud. He was all meat, wasn't he? Healthy as a living man but with the appearance of a cadaver. Bloodshot eyes glared at Adam from skeletal sockets. The thing fumbled for its shovel, but Adam got it first and he brought it down on the rotter's face with a wet crunch.

The staircase crumbled. The roof was sagging. Time to go.

Adam dove out the front doors and was followed by an eruption of debris as the building fell in on itself. Dust blanketed the plaza, and Adam pressed his face into the ground and covered his head while hunks of wood and marble skipped across the concrete like wayward missiles.

At last the world settled. Adam looked up and took in the scene. A work of classic architecture, centuries old, a testament to Man's spirit, now dust; for the sake of one rotter. And Man would not rebuild. Not today. Such was the plague.

\* \* \*

By twilight, the man with the scythe was gone. There were only the voices.

*You feel him in your bones. You taste him in your mouth—quickly now, before he's gone too far and you lose him!*

*Get up! Get after him!*

*You are the end of him. You are the Omega. It is what you must do.*

*Aren't you aching for his flesh? Isn't your black blood on fire? What's keeping you? GET UP!*

A cacophony of disembodied voices crowding out the rotter's own animal thoughts. These voices, spitting and howling, arguing with him and with one another—they were his conscience, or had at least taken its place. Voices young and old, speaking in all tongues yet perfectly understandable to him. It was their rage that made it all so clear, more so than any of their pleas or threats. He felt their collective rage in his rotten core, like flames rising to warm the walls of a broken-down furnace. It was the rage that drove him, and the lingering taste of the Reaper's flesh—the memory of it sending chills through his bones even as his black heart fluttered to life.

The Omega clawed his way out of the rubble where the town hall had stood. Using the recovered shovel to pry his legs free, he climbed down from the ruins and surveyed the plaza.

A few other rotters were standing around the site, swaying slightly as their blank stares turned toward the Omega. He approached the nearest one, a female with sagging breasts and belly, and he raised the shovel.

It cleaved into her heart with a brittle snapping of ribs. She staggered, arms swinging at her sides, face expressionless. She tried to turn and walk away.

The Omega sank the shovel into the tough meat of her back and wrestled her to the ground. Then he fell upon her.

*Yes!*

*Devour her, all of her! Take her energy into yourself. We'll need all we can get.*

*Cleanse your body! Drive out the rot!*

He fed. Pus was spat from the lips of abscesses in his legs and back. Writhing maggots were forced from his ears and hair. The fungus in his innards boiled away. As his body grew stronger—as *they* grew stronger—all impurities were driven from him, and his latest wounds began to scab over. He felt the broken bones in his face being manipulated and healed together; and he ate ravenously.

They knew how to use the virus' dark energy. He was a mere animal, maybe less, dead and dumb; but they took care of him. And they drove him across the badlands after the scent of the other. Soon would come the inevitable, the final feast... the Reaper.

*Fill your gullet to its brim. Then go after the other ones. Feed!*
*When next we cross paths with him, it shall be our last meeting.*

# THREE / NORMAL

More than five months had passed since the exodus from Jefferson Harbor, and Voorhees still didn't know what had become of Lily.

As he boarded a bus on the outskirts of Chicago, someone caught his arm. It was Killian, a young officer he'd met during his orientation. "I found her," Killian said.

They got a seat together near the back and waited until the bus got moving. "I can't believe buses run between the cities like this," Voorhees muttered. "All those miles of lonely highway..."

"And not a rotter to be seen," Killian said. She nudged his arm and smiled. "So, do you want to know where your girl is or not?"

"She's not my girl." Voorhees frowned out the window. "I don't know if I want to know. She was the last living citizen of the Harbor... I was supposed to protect them all, and I got one little girl out. Then she's taken from me the second we enter the Wall. Who knows what's happened."

"Well, do you want me to tell you? It's nothing bad, Voorhees."

"Tell me."

"She's in Gaylen, the same city where we're headed. A young couple took her in. They're seeking permanent custody."

Voorhees let out a long, tired sigh. "So she's safe, then."

"She's safe."

"Now I can start worrying about what's going to happen to me."

"You'll be fine. I've got your back."

"You're half my age."

"Really? I didn't think you were *that* old." Killian smiled again, leaning toward him. "It's a joke, Voorhees. When's the last time you had a laugh?"

"I don't remember what my laugh sounds like," he replied.

She saw he wasn't kidding and whistled. "That's gotta change. You're *okay* now. You've come a long way from that place. You're in the Great Cities now—and you're gonna be a real cop again. Did they not mention that to you, repeatedly? You're gonna be a Gaylen P.O.—of course that means Peace Officer here, not Patrol Officer—but it's the same thing."

"I was a senior officer in the Harbor."

"Nothing I can do about that, buddy." Killian patted his arm. "Look at it this way. Being a beat cop means less time filling out reports and more time doing the job."

"Paperwork *is* the job—"

"Oh, you're hopeless." Turning from him, Killian stared ahead. Feeling guilty, Voorhees tried to think of something to say. "Hey, I'll be getting paid again. That'll be nice."

"Social Services explains in orientation that you earn credits, but what they don't tell you is that, as a P.O., you don't have to pay for everything like the rest. Explaining that is my job." She had been in the Great Cities for a year, and had only been in Chicago to help run orientation. With a sideways glance toward the other passengers, Killian slipped a card from within her jacket and handed it to Voorhees. "It's a forever pass for medical services. Any hospital, any time. Everyone else has to spend their credits on day passes and hope that the line for the doctor isn't too long."

"What about emergencies?"

"They still bill people's accounts. Costs a lot more too. But not for you."

"How many emergencies do you think go unreported as a result of that?" he asked.

"People can afford medical care, it's not like they're being paid minimum wage. Hell, minimum wage isn't even minimum wage anymore. You know full-time parents with multiple kids earn as much as a Senate aide?"

Voorhees pocketed the medical pass. "Any other perks?"

"Discounted food and entertainment. All the food in Gaylen is grown or raised on farms. Beef is expensive as hell."

"You said entertainment?"

"Sure. You know the live music in Chicago? They do that in Gaylen too. And he rugby teams are always looking for new players if you think you're up to it. Plays, too, chosen by the Senate. Our city admin, Senator Cullen, writes some himself. Really fucking boring unless you're stoned, but that costs an arm and a leg—"

"What?"

"Nothing. Anyway, all the P.Os live in the same building, a refurbished hotel on West Avenue. They'll put you on the top floor. You think it's a steal but then you find out the heating is shot. Course, they'll still dock your pay for it"

"Yeah, back to the drugs."

"C'mon, Voorhees. Everyone needs a break once in a while. It's just pot."

"Yeah, I've heard of it. Do you smoke on the job?"

She glared at him. "Of course not."

"Good."

"Which reminds me, Gaylen's a dry city. We do still have some moonshiners underground but we usually just let that go. Alcohol's not as much of a problem when no one drives."

"I was about to ask. These buses travel between cities though. And run on ethanol?"

"Yeah, and so do the generators in town, but the good news is Gaylen's hydroelectric plant came back online last month. They've been working to keep that thing alive for the last fifty years. Not a bad investment. Technology, industry may have stagnated in the last century, but we didn't. We're surviving."

Surviving. That seemed to be enough for most. Voorhees grimaced. "And is the water as clean as Chicago's?"

"Cleaner." Killian's smile had returned. It was probably contagious in most circumstances. Voorhees had forgotten what it felt like to smile. Every waking moment since he'd been born had been a losing war against the undead. Every day was the end of the world. And now he was supposed to believe in this walled paradise, this new Eden, established by the same government who'd left everyone in the badlands to die?

Of course they would say it was one's own choice to remain in the badlands. But it had been hard to swallow the radio broadcasts about a rotter-free safe zone.

*Well, here it is. Right outside your window.*

Gaylen, on the southern tip of Lake Michigan. His new home. He tried to focus on that, rather than the nightmares of the past with their strange characters and unanswered questions. He especially tried not to think about the cloaked specter of Death, astride a pale horse, charging into the undead hordes.

*Life is normal now,* he told himself.

"We celebrate holidays, too," said Killian. "Halloween is coming up. You know what that is? On that night..."

Voorhees shut his eyes and tried to block out the rest of her words. He tried to think about health benefits and utilities and neighbors but he simply hadn't been bred for such a life. There was no *after the apocalypse* in his mind. All they had here was the Wall, and he couldn't wall out his memories.

# FOUR / DEAD LIZARDS WITH BELLS ON THEIR FEET

They were dangling by strings from the lowest branches of the trees surrounding the rock quarry. Adam peered into their lifeless dark eyes and saw his own soulless gaze, doll's-eyes blinking curiously.

They were alarms to announce the presence of afterdead. *Afterdead...* he hadn't called the rotters that since he'd shed his robes. It seemed so long ago. Strange, when he had existed for ages; as Death, every moment had been the same, and time without meaning. A thousand years or a day, it had mattered not to him. But now he marked hours, days, weeks. He rose with the sun and would observe the changing of the seasons. He bore scars on his hands and feet, and in his reflection he saw not a being frozen in time but a man living his life.

In his reflection, in the lizard's eyes, he saw torchlight, and spun to meet the young woman climbing out from the sea of shadows that filled the quarry.

She stopped short, gaped at his face. "Is it you?" she asked, blue eyes shining. "Are you the angel?"

He frowned and took a step toward her. "I—"

THWACK! An arrow planted itself in the tree beside him. "*Don't move!*" barked a man's voice.

Another man, old and frail, stepped out from behind the girl with a bow pulled taut in trembling hands. "Do as the boy says, friend."

"*Are you alone?*" A third voice called.

"Yes," Adam replied.

"*Are you Army?*"

"No."

"How could you be out here by yourself?" stammered the old man. "Better tell the truth before you get hurt!"

"It's the angel," the girl breathed. What did she mean by that?

Gravel crunched beneath boots as a man approached, a man with a hard face, shirtless body slick with sweat. He had a camouflage tee tied around his waist. Combat fatigues. Maybe Adam would have been better off saying he *was* Army.

The man saw Adam studying his clothing and grinned. "They're stolen," he said. "We used to raid Army camps back before the withdrawal. It's a lot tougher finding something to eat these days, I'm sure you know that—but at least we're warm."

The man extended his hand. "I'm Thackeray," he said. "You look like you're an albino. Must be brutal for you out here."

Adam nodded quickly, shaking the man's hand. "Stand down!" Thackeray shouted over his shoulder.

"Come down into the crater. I don't want our torches visible up here too long." Thackeray patted Adam's back and led him past the old man and girl; she looked woefully disappointed.

\* \* \*

"Must've taken a lot out of you to get here," Thackeray said. "How did you hear about us?"

"I didn't—I was just passing through."

"Now that I find hard to believe." Thackeray smiled. "I know the welcome wagon was a little rough, but you're in good hands now. Matter of fact, some people around here call me the boss. Not a title I much care for, but it seems to stick."

He pointed toward the top of the quarry and the darkness beyond. "Tons of rotters in the cities around here. They tend not to wander off in our direction, though. If they ever thought to come a-hunting, we might be in trouble. But for now all we have to deal with is the occasional feral."

The camp at the bottom of the crater was comprised mainly of Army tents. Small fires burned here and there, but nothing that would attract attention topside. In fact, even as he came down the slope of the quarry Adam hadn't seen any light at all; the fires were each concealed behind boulders.

The people there were families of all ages, and mother and child alike tensed when they saw Adam; but relaxed when they saw Thackeray at his side.

A large rodent turned on a spit in front of Thackeray's tent. "Hungry?" he asked. Adam shook his head.

"It's been overcast the past week," Thackeray remarked. "Guess it's a lot harder for you when it isn't."

"Yes." Adam sat on a rock beside the fire. Thackeray stabbed a fork into the rat. Blood ran, sizzling, into the flames.

"We always have to make sure they're not undead before we eat 'em," Thackeray said. "What have you been living on?"

"Uh... mostly berries." Adam silently begged for the questions to end. He tried to avoid badlanders, and had he not been mesmerized by the lizards with their tiny bells he would have turned and gone in the opposite direction. As much as he yearned for companionship—

*(Lily)*

He didn't expect all people to be as accepting as the child had been. The man who'd helped to get Lily out of Jefferson Harbor, Voorhees—he had regarded the former Death with more than a bit of apprehension. But he'd been a good man. Adam had watched him for a long time to make sure of just that.

"You're lost in thought," Thackeray said. He chewed an ear off of the rat's blackened head. "I don't think you heard a word I just said."

"I'm sorry. What was it?"

"I said the berries around here are deadly poisonous."

"Oh." Why was the man telling Adam that? He was forgetting his own lies.

"Let me try something," Thackeray said through a mouthful of rat meat, and sank the fork's tines into Adam's shoulder.

They both stared down at the handle of the fork. It had gone clean through the new suit Adam had taken from one of the rotters back in town.

"This is where you would express some sort of discomfort," Thackeray said.

Adam looked across the fire at him. Tentatively, he grasped the fork and pulled it free. "I... it didn't..."

"I know who you are," Thackeray said softly. "Josie was right. You're the angel. The angel of death."

He reached out and took the fork back. "Sorry for the whole 'stabbing you' thing. I'm a little eccentric, they say. Maybe that's why I can sit across from you and keep a straight face. If the others knew..." He shrugged and took another bite of his dinner.

"How do you know of me?" Adam demanded.

"Most badlanders in these parts have heard of you. I mean, you've saved so many lives, cut the undead down right in front of them—did you really think no one would tell?"

"I've appeared to many in the past," Adam said. "I didn't think anyone would believe them."

"Well, in a world where the dead walk, nothing seems impossible. I've heard old folk say they saw you killing rotters seventy, eighty years ago. Were you?"

"I have been hunting them since it began," Adam said. "But things are different now. You have to understand—I'm no longer the Reaper."

"I guess that explains the suit. Sorry for ruining your jacket, by the way."

"It's fine."

"So what's been strapped to your back all night?" Thackeray asked.

Removing his jacket, Adam loosed the ropes securing the scythe blade to his pale torso, and handed the weapon across the flames. "Jesus, that's heavy," Thackeray whispered. "So this is it."

Adam nodded. "You don't talk to a lot of people, do you?" Thackeray asked.

"I've not had much need to," was the reply. "There was one, but..." His face brightened with hope. "Maybe you've heard of her. Maybe she told you her story. Her name is Lily."

Thackeray shook his head. "Sorry friend."

"I shouldn't have thought so."

"Where did you know her?"

"Somewhere far away. A man took her north. He said she'd be safe there."

"Maybe he meant the Great Cities?"

"I don't know them."

"It's the place where the government's hoarded away all of our country's resources." Thackeray's expression grew dark, angry. "It's where they've consolidated America—leaving Americans like us here with nothing. And now all the troops are there too. They're walling themselves up in there and going on as if the rest of the world doesn't exist, as if the plague doesn't exist. They're wrapping themselves up in a blanket of ignorance and trying to sleep through the apocalypse. As for the rest of us—the people who choose to keep fighting for this land, the people who are actually *living*—we're condemned along with our homes. But make no mistake, the Great Cities aren't going to last. Unless something's done, the bubble is going to burst, and then no one will have any resources to use against the undead."

He spoke with a fervor that drew onlookers from the shadows. People murmured in agreement and clenched their fists as his voice rose. "Either we can watch the Great Cities fall to the rotters or we can do something ourselves, to give all of America a fighting chance!"

He lowered his head. "I'm sorry. The anger is always there— anger and helplessness. The outrage at what they've done! That's what drives me."

The people around them had begun to drift away. "I understand," Adam said.

"Do you?"

"I feel the same way about the undead." Taking the scythe from Thackeray, Adam added, "But not helpless."

Thackeray nodded grimly. "There is still hope. We can still... but the rotters, some of them, are getting smarter. I suppose you've seen that too."

"From time to time." In his mind's eye Adam saw the ones Lily's mad brother had trained, like dogs. Only those dogs nearly behaved like living, breathing humans.

"The King of the Dead," Thackeray whispered. "Is he real?"

"I don't know of whom you're speaking."

"Oh. Never mind then."

"They're beasts. They have no king," Adam told the man. "Whatever you've heard is likely just a story people tell."

"What do you call yourself?"

"Adam."

"Well, Adam, you were just a story people told, not long ago," said Thackeray, and he disappeared into his tent.

# FIVE / FREEDOM

"I can point you toward the Great Cities, but that's all I can do," Thackeray told Adam the next morning. "We're moving east."

Adam had dreamt of Lily again. This time he saw her huddled in shadow, shivering, as thick flakes of snow settled in her long dark hair.

These were more than just dreams, he was sure. Once, he could have held her life's flame in his very hands; now he could only guess at what fate had in store for her. He had to reach these Great Cities.

The girl, Josie, set about drawing Adam a map using charcoal on sackcloth. She paused to whisper something into Thackeray's ear. He nodded at her, and the girl beamed at Adam.

*The angel.* It had been one of many personas he'd adopted over the years in order to deal with mortals. But it was this form, that of the pale man in black, that he was most comfortable in. Perhaps that was why he'd been reborn with this look. Perhaps he himself had willed it. So hard to remember. Day by day he was forgetting the details of his service on the other side.

"Before you go there," Thackeray said,

"let me tell you why we're not going with you. Let me tell you what I know about the men who built the Wall.

"A few years ago, I lived there. I trusted in the Senate, and even worked for them—I was an aide to the Senate's President-for-life. Gillies. God-fearing son of a preacher. He really believed—still does—that it's his calling to rebuild the world. For who, Man or God or both, I can't tell ya. But he truly believes that what he's doing is good, and *right*—and that's the problem.

"When we came out here to try and sway the badlanders, I was on his side. Even when rotters swarmed the convoy in Utah and half of us were left for dead—still I was on his side. I shrugged off the badlanders' offers of food and shelter and trekked back to the Great Cities with my colleagues. Back to Cleveland, where my mother lived.

"What happened there is beyond reprehensible. What they've done, in the name of what's good and right, is depraved—and these atrocities are bred by ignorance, not evil."

Adam listened, and Josie drew, while Thackeray told him everything.

"Here we are free," he said when he was finished. "Here we take the good with the bad and we face our problems. We share grief as well as joy, and it makes us appreciate the joy all the more. I understood that, for when I came back to Utah, back to the badlanders, grieving, they took me in with open arms."

He placed a hand on Adam's shoulder. "You know what Man is capable of. You'll see, and then you'll understand too."

Josie handed over the map. It was simple and straightforward: northeast until he hit the fabled Wall.

"We're headed for the East Coast if you ever want to look us up. Maybe you'll join us out there someday. Someday things will be right again. Trust me."

Thackeray said those two words with such dead certainty that Adam wondered what he *hadn't* been let in on.

"I'll keep that in mind," he said, rolling the map up and placing it inside his jacket. "I wish you the best, Thackeray."

"Please. Todd." Thackeray shook Adam's hand for the last time. "Take care of yourself. And her."

"I will."

\* \* \*

Thackeray and a couple other men walked Adam to the edge of the quarry.

"Listen, I have to ask you something," Thackeray said. "You probably get this all the time..." He looked expectantly at Adam, who stared blankly back.

"About... the nature of things. God. Afterlife."

"What about them?"

"Are they real?"

The other two men stopped, the same yearning in their eyes. It was almost childlike... and what good would it do them, really, to know?

Adam didn't have to wrestle with that particular quandary. "I don't know," he said. "You have to understand that it was never necessary that I know such things as God's nature, or where people go... so I never did."

"Well, what do you *think?*" Thackeray pressed.

Adam forced a smile. "I think it's all in what you believe. There's no knowing."

He had sensed high beings before. He knew there was *something* out there, that he'd come from *somewhere*... but whether or not that something gave a damn about humanity was another story.

"So who's the 'King of the Dead'?" he asked Thackeray. They were both glad, as it turned out, to change the subject.

"He used to run a traveling circus in the badlands. I know people who saw it—he would perform tricks with undead animals. People too. They say he was infected, and he'd let the rotters take bites out of him One night he kissed one and it tore his lips off. That's what they say.

"They say that he eventually turned, but not alone. He talked his performers into turning with him. They were *willingly* infected—most of them anyway. I've heard of people committing suicide by infection but this was different. They celebrated their deaths. And when they came back, they kept traveling—kept performing, kept entertaining, audiences none the wiser until the next morning when the circus was gone and so were their children."

"I don't think such a thing is possible," Adam said. "I've spent more a century among the dead. I've seen undead capable of frightening, lifelike things—but for ferals to work together, like a pack? That's beyond their grasp. Their only drive is self-preservation."

"Fair enough," Thackeray replied. "Just remember that things change. You changed."

"I did," Adam said, "but by choice—and they have no will."

He passed under the lizards hanging from their branches and gave the men a wave. "Be safe."

"The East Coast!" Thackeray called. "Remember!"

Adam didn't look back.

•

# SIX / THE WALL

"The Wall" actually referred to the security wall surrounding the entire Great Cities region. In addition, each city had its own type of barricade set up around its perimeter. In the event that the outer Wall was breached, citizens could rest easy while troops swarmed the "dead zone" between cities and cleaned out the rotters, be they man or animal. But such an incident was thought impossible by most, because the Wall was the pride of the Cities.

The work of two generations of Senators, it was three stories tall and five feet thick, concrete poured over a steel skeleton with roots buried deep in the earth. Every thousand yards there was a guard post, where soldiers would ascend a ladder or stairs to the walkway atop the Wall and monitor the badlands. It was understood by all that if badlanders approached the Wall seeking asylum, they could be taken in. But if they refused to undergo the standard quarantine procedure, they were assumed to be infected and would be shot.

There were two or more men for each guard post, and more at the gates that appeared every few miles; but there was one section where only one man kept watch. Neville Dalton preferred his solitude and made no secret of it. He had lobbied the brass for weeks to allow him to work with his dogs instead of other soldiers.

Rottweilers, the dogs had been trained privately, by Dalton, for months prior to his Wall assignment. They could sniff out a single rotter hiding in the night. At least that was what he told the brass. All he knew was that the dogs were simple, straightforward companions who knew their place and didn't complicate everything the way people did. They would walk the Wall inside the dead zone from dawn to dusk while he sat perched atop it, sniper rifle in his lap.

Most of the other troops were scared of his Rotties. Even Major Briggs had refused the opportunity to meet them, although they fell into rank at the sight of him. So Dalton had finally gotten his way, and the arrangement was quite comfortable until the afternoon when he heard a Jeep pull up, and the nagging cough that could only mean Tuck Logan.

"How're you doing all by your lonesome?" Logan asked with a filthy grin as he ascended the ladder. "They just wanted me to come out and check on ya. Don't worry, I won't tell 'em anything. But you should know that Senator Gillies might be coming out to see the dogs."

Dalton arched an eyebrow. "That might be interesting." He tried to ignore the flies buzzing around Logan.

They both had been part of an elite unit known as Hand of God. Led by Ian Gregory, a stalwart Christian, the unit had exclusive membership requirements that would've raised a shitstorm if any limp-wristed civilians had known about it. Yes, even Logan was a God-fearing Christian, though he behaved like an apostate these days. Ever since the withdrawal he'd become more and more... unusual. The flies were evidence of that. He was on one of the burn teams that were called in to put down rotters, once they'd been marked and paralyzed by a sniper's bullet; and he seemed to enjoy most the responsibility of carrying the charred remains off to be buried. Dalton suspected that Logan spent a little extra time with those remains. His greasy, unwashed hair and darting eyes were overlooked by his supervisors, but Dalton had a keen eye, a sniper's eye, and he saw into Logan and knew that he was *fucking* them, wasn't he, rutting in a pile of ash and rotten meat like some sort of animal. Worse than an animal. Logan meant trouble.

"So," Dalton muttered, "they sent you to check up on me."

"For the Senator," Logan said. "They want to know that your dogs are as well-trained as you say."

"Well, climb down."

"What?"

"Climb down and I'll call them in."

Dalton plucked a whistle from his shirt pocket. Logan started down.

Dalton watched him standing there at the bottom, staring dully; he almost wished he had the guts to sic the Rotties on him. He blew soundlessly into the whistle

They came running from either direction, keeping a tight formation alongside the Wall. They saw Logan and quickened their pace. The man fidgeted, glanced up at Dalton. "Are they—?"

They surrounded Logan and stood frozen, staring up at him. He saw their legs trembling, saw them fighting to restrain themselves. They smelled the dead on him. He was terrified.

"Break!" Dalton called.

The dogs settled on their haunches and let their tongues hang from their jaws. Logan was still too scared to move.

"Let him go, boys," Dalton said as he came down. The dogs sat about him and waited patiently while he checked each for injury. Satisfied, he sent them off to play.

"The Senator ought to be impressed," Logan said breathlessly.

"I should think so," Dalton said. He gave Logan a smile. It was chilling.

* * *

"Sergeant Gregory?"

Gillies was ruggedly handsome and fit for his age. A man of sixty, he carried himself well, and his pressed suits made him look like he was from another time—he didn't belong in the living Hell of this world. But here he was, talking with Ian Gregory atop the Wall like it didn't mean anything.

"My entourage is down below, touring the facilities," Gillies said. "The reason I'm up here, though, is to make you an offer."

"Me?"

"Absolutely. You studied at Seminarium Vita, didn't you?"

"Yes sir."

"As did I. Glorious institution. Tragically, I hear it's burned to the ground. We are its legacy, men like you and I. Do you remember all you learned there?"

"I believe so."

"And you implemented those teachings in a rather controversial way. Hand of God."

"I did what I felt was right."

"Of course you did. I admire that. Too many men forget their faith the second they step onto a battlefield. You never did. Even though you, yourself, lost men out there."

Gregory lowered his head. Not just men.

32

Barry had been a devout believer and a woman whose beauty was not diminished by her tough demeanor. They had fallen in love quickly, and he might have proposed but for the fact that she would have been forced to leave his unit. So they lived in sin for a while, but those were the circumstances they had to live in. God wanted them together, both were sure of that.

And he'd sworn to himself that his love would never interfere with the unit's operations. And it never did, until—

"I'd like you to lead my personal security detail," Gillies said. "What say you?"

Gregory didn't know what to say. He didn't know what he wanted. He spent most days atop this wall just staring down, wondering what it would be like to fall and never wake up.

But, again, he knew what was right, and he saw the Lord at work in this situation.

"Yes. Yes sir."

# SEVEN / THE BEAT

"I'm assigning you to the lake district," Senior P.O. Casey told Voorhees. "It's blocked out in red on the big map."

The hotel which had been converted to a living quarters for Gaylen's Peace Officers also housed the department itself. Killian had explained that Gaylen's original police precincts were all destroyed during the original outbreaks. Overrun by infected and people looking for shelter or arms, most police stations and military installations were lost early on; same for hospitals and airports. Of course there were no airports anymore. Every nation in turn had closed its borders and grounded all flights, domestic and international, in hopes of slowing the plague. Like everything else, it proved pointless.

Voorhees followed Casey across the squad room to the "big map" plastered across the wall. Casey was in a wheelchair, both legs gone below the knees. He probably hated his desk job. And here Voorhees was being put out on the street again after a decade as a senior officer. He'd done plenty of beat work in his S.P.O. role, but he'd also had control and respect with whomever he interacted.

He supposed that he had failed in Jefferson Harbor, and maybe he deserved to start back at the bottom.

"Social Services sent over your cleaver," Casey said, "but we're going to have to retire it for the time being. God willing, you'll never have to use it again."

He meant Voorhees' widowmaker, a military-issue blade used in close combat against rotters. He'd decapitated more of them than he could count. The weapon an extension of his arm; now he was going to have to settle for a baton. Not even a gun. The Great Cities kept guns out of the hands of *all* civilians. He wondered how long that would last.

Another officer walked over and introduced himself as Blake. "I'm Killian's partner."

Up until that point, Voorhees had thought he might be paired with her. She had a mouth on her but was easy on the eyes. Voorhees didn't look forward to another male partner.

"You'll be with Halstead," Casey said, reading Voorhees' expression. "She's out until tomorrow, as is Killian, so you and Blake'll patrol the lake district this evening." Casey turned his chair to face Blake. "Be sure you talk to Meyer about those kids he roughed up the other day."

"Ready to head out?" Blake asked. Voorhees grabbed his overcoat from the back of his chair. "Why not?"

\* \* \*

It was cloudy, as it had been for days, and the city was a hundred shades of gray. People's faces were hardened slate. As they passed him by they looked away, some at their feet, others at the sky. One muttered something about rain, but she was only talking to herself.

Lots of people in the street. Everyone walked. Shuffled past one another without so much as a word. Patrons in a vegetable market rummaged quietly through bins. It was like a citywide awkward silence.

Blake slapped Voorhees' arm and led him into the market. "My girlfriend owns it," he said. "Her brother-in-law runs the biggest farm in Gaylen."

A petite brunette smiled and stepped away from her counter to hug Blake. "Becca, this is Voorhees." He looked to Voorhees as if expecting a first name. The man was silent.

"... Well, he's Emily's new partner, and I'm giving him the grand tour."

"Call me Becks," the girl said. "This one keeps forgetting. Oh, Blake, you oughta take him by the amphitheater. Jeff Cullen's got a new play for next month. I just started reading it."

"So you're in it?" Blake leaned against Voorhees. "My girl's an actress."

"It's just something to do," she said, blushing, "even if Cullen thinks it's high art."

"What are the plays about?" asked Voorhees.

"Life before the plague," Becks said. "So who knows whether it's accurate or not. But I guess it's how we're supposed to live now, now that we're safe."

*Safe. Normal.* None of it rang true to Voorhees. If this was normal—everyone just going through the motions and trying to forget about the real world—he didn't want any part of it. He was starting to feel claustrophobic and imagined that the living zombies in Gaylen's streets felt exactly the same way.

Zombies. There was a fitting metaphor. *Gee, I'll bet no one else has thought of that.*

Soldiers... Soldiers carried guns and widowmakers. Soldiers dealt with the undead. Maybe that was his new calling?

"We'd better get going," Blake said. "You heard what Casey said about Meyer."

"Who?"

"Finn Meyer."

* * *

"They weren't kids, they were grown men," Finn Meyer said in his thick Irish brogue. "And they knew what was gonna happen if they crossed me."

He was a stout man with a pudgy scarred face and sausage fingers grasping at the lapels of his suit. It was a nice suit, the sort no one made anymore. And he was talking to P.O. Blake with such unbridled arrogance that it took all that Voorhees had in him not to knock the bastard upside his head with that baton.

"Seventeen-year-olds aren't men, Meyer," Blake said, "and besides, I thought we had an understanding about the hands-on business."

The tone of this conversation made no sense to Voorhees. Blake had told him that two boys with a laptop were running a dice game near the lake district. Players were able to wager credits, provided they could prove said credits existed. And the losers were billed for what they owed, by all appearances a legal transaction. It was a legit practice, although the kids were hacking the network to transfer credits. The real problem, however, was that Finn Meyer claimed exclusive rights to the game. So he'd had a couple of thugs smash the laptop and knock the kids around a little. "That's business," the Irishman said.

"You're liable for the cost of that laptop," Voorhees snapped. "And I don't know why you aren't in cuffs already, but at the very least you're going to be cited for assault."

Meyer had a shit-eating grin plastered across his face. "Mister Blake, maybe you oughta educate the new guy about how we do things." His glassy eyes fixed on Voorhees, Meyer added in a low growl, "You know what happened to the gentleman you replaced?"

"All right, enough of that," said Blake. "If I have to come down here again because of you pushing people around, we're going to have a conversation with Cullen, you and I. Because that's how we do things in Gaylen."

Meyer raised his hands in mock surrender. "Whatever you say, boss. Just trying to make a living."

Voorhees started to say something, but Blake pulled him away from Meyer and out into the street.

"What in the hell was that?" Voorhees yelled.

"There are some things you don't understand," Blake said grimly. "Our job is to maintain a balance in Gaylen—there are some elements that can only be contained, not cut out."

"Are you saying—"

"I'm saying, let's go grab some dinner and I'll lay it out for you."

It was probably going to rain soon. Voorhees' sixty-year-old joints were aching, and he didn't feel like arguing any longer so he shut his mouth and went along with his partner.

# EIGHT / LILY

"How come you get to drive a truck?" the girl asked.

Jack Calvert looked away from the road and said, "It belongs to the company. Sometimes I have to haul materials out to the job site."

Sitting in Molly Calvert's lap, Lily twisted to make the seat belt fit more comfortably. "Are you allowed to take us into the city?"

"Of course," Jack replied. He was a man of thirty with bright eyes and a lopsided smile that meant he knew a lot of jokes. He was good at making Lily laugh, even if some of his jokes were too silly. But she was only thirteen—or fourteen, she wasn't sure—and it was excusable.

"Anyway, I'll drop you two off downtown, then I'm gone until four in the morning," Jack was saying to Molly. "You'll make it home okay?"

"So long as it doesn't rain," Molly sighed. She was pretty, with long dark hair just like Lily's. She really could have been the girl's mother, except Lily knew her parents were dead.

"Did you have a nightmare last night?" Molly asked Lily. "I heard you saying something in your sleep."

Lily couldn't explain to her new guardians that they weren't nightmares—that Death was her friend, that he'd saved her life more than once. He had a kind, gentle face. His doll-like eyes made her think of a baby, innocent and unformed. In a lot of ways, he was like a child; he didn't seem to understand a lot of things, like feelings.

But he and Lily had still gotten along. He'd held her while she wept for her parents, and he'd saved her from the house in the swamp where her brothers and sisters were undead. She longed to see him again, and somehow knew that she would—that he was searching for her right now, at this very moment.

"What are you building today?" she asked Jack. Sometimes he was reluctant to talk about his job, but other times he had funny stories. This time he only shrugged. "I can't say, exactly. I can tell you we're laying a sort of asphalt right now. We hope it doesn't rain either."

He couldn't tell her about the airfield project—hell, he wasn't even supposed to tell Molly, but he had. It was a secret that only the Senators knew about.

The firm he worked for had restored most of downtown over the past five years. It was a huge company, but only a select handful were chosen for the airfield. He had no idea what they intended to use it for—did they even have planes?—but he was starting to form a theory.

If he was right, then he would have to do something. It might mean a real future for him and Molly. And, well, Lily...

Thunder rumbled overhead. Molly cursed, and Jack tightened his grip on the steering wheel, his knuckles already bone-white.

# NINE / BEGINNING OF THE END

At dusk, Thackeray sat on a rock and whittled arrows from kindling. The evening fires were being lit, and the day's purchase—rats and other small vermin—were being cleaned for supper. To almost anyone it might seem like a dismal life of poverty. But he knew better. He'd seen what was on the other side. And he knew that, soon, the Senate's empire would fall.

Somewhere far off, at the very edge of his hearing, a little bell began to ring.

A few others heard it too. They looked to the west end of the quarry. The jingling increased in volume as other bells were triggered.

Then, to the east. More ringing. And the north.

Thackeray snatched a bow off the ground at his feet and peered into the trees on the quarry's rim. Didn't see a damn thing. Ringing to the south now.

Panicked exclamations split the air. Women grabbed their children and ran for their tents. Others took up torches and bows and watched the woods above. The ringing was almost deafening, every single lizard kicking its tiny legs as they were bathed in the aura of a presence massive, something huge and unseen watching the humans from the trees.

Then came the scream, the most godawful thing Thackeray had ever heard—a ragged, high-pitched banshee's cry that seemed to come from all directions. It was in that moment that Thackeray realized all of them were about to die.

The rotters surged forth, all runners—*all of them*—cascading down the sides of the crater in a wave of gray flesh that swept over the men standing at the camp's edge. Thackeray stared in abject horror as he saw his men torn limb from limb in seconds, ripped apart and simply thrown aside—fresh meat discarded while the undead went after the others!

He ran for the nearest fire. Fire, that was all they had. And fires were being stomped out right and left by the feet of the dead as tents collapsed under the weight of ravenous attackers and then the screams of the women filled Thackeray's head, women grieving and dying all at once. Still the rotters kept pouring in.

Thackeray spun, a torch in each hand, and saw a pair heading right for him. He ran at them, flames thrust forth, ready to beat them both to pulp with the goddamned things if he had to—

They weren't two. They were one.

Siamese twins, rotters fused at the torso and scrambling along on three legs like some sort of giant insect. Its heads snapped and slavered and both stared Thackeray dead in the eyes. He dropped the torches and fell to his knees. God in Heaven, it was them—it was *him.*

A shadow towered over him from the back. Turning he saw, framed in firelight, a great hulk of a man, covered in obscene tattoos and wielding a massive hammer.

Thackeray saw the hammer coming down and couldn't even close his eyes. He was trapped in this waking nightmare, forced to see the death blow as it rocketed toward his face; and then

\* \* \*

*Kill. Then eat.*

He'd taught them that taking down the entire herd at the onset left more meat for each of them. If they were to stay strong, to stay fast, they needed to eat well. To increase their chances of survival, all of the pack needed to stay healthy—and each of them understood that.

That said, Eviscerato was the alpha, and he always fed first.

All of the night's kills had been dragged into the open, out from beneath bloody canvas and away from the heat of those campfires still burning; stripped naked and laid out before the King of the Dead, for him to select his morsel.

The young girls were soft and fatty. He grabbed one by the bracelet on her wrist, letters chained together. He couldn't read them, and cast the item aside. J-O-S-I-E.

Pulling her away from the others, he knelt over her, lifting her to his mouth by her little ponytail—then tore into her. And the pack leapt at the remaining meat, spitting and gnashing in a frenzy of blood.

Eviscerato still wore his old suit, the crimson vest and top hat, even his cane—a handy bludgeon—and he hadn't lost his showman swagger either. The dancer among the dead, they'd called him. He still moved with a sort of grace uncommon in thee dead. There were no memories of his former life, at least not in his mind; but his muscles remembered that peculiar gait with which he walked, and a certain instinct told him to smile grandly in the face of a large crowd. So he often came at his victims with an ear-to-ear grin, lipless and rotten, cane swinging in the moonlight.

They were animals, the lot of them; but preserved in each member of Eviscerato's circus was a sense of identity. The Strongman and the Fakir and the Geek each knew his place.

And they all followed Eviscerato—who, in turn, had been following the withdrawal, the human convoys heading north. With those convoys long gone he pressed on, guided by am intuition which told him that there was a great nest of living flesh at the end of this long and bloody road.

There, they would feast until their bellies burst.

# TALES FROM THE BADLANDS / THE RAT KING

The joke was that they called it Old New York. Some people didn't get it, some people didn't know history and didn't care to know about the world before, and that was fine. But for those looking for a little light in the world after, for a little humor in the burnt-out labyrinth, the dust-swept amphitheater of silence, the concrete-and-steel canyons of the dead island—they called it Old New York and maybe cracked a smile.

101 years or so out from the Year of the Plague, the Last Day, End Time, Old New York was a sun-bleached husk of a city. Nature had reclaimed what it wanted, but it had left a lot of the skyscrapers and sewers and streets to themselves, a decaying spectacle bespeaking an ancient fallen empire. The skeletons of monolithic business enterprises and government concerns loomed over ruptured veins of asphalt and seas of dirt and glass. Loomed over nothing.

"So what are we looking for?" asked Keane. He was perched on a rusted-out hulk that had once been some piece of construction equipment. It was now host to an ecosystem of plants and insects that had infested its limbs and guts and built kingdoms of their own. It was almost like a little hill, this so-called "Caterpillar" entrenched in earth somewhere in the former Manhattan.

"Anything," answered Alex, balancing his axe on his right shoulder while trying to sort through the torches under his left arm. "Anything we can use."

"Or eat?"

"If you want to hunt, let's hunt. I don't know if we'll find anything edible in these streets, but let's hunt."

"Well, I am hungry."

"Why'd they only send three of us?" asked Jarrett.

"Because this is pointless. All of this," said Keane, gesturing to the ghost city around them, "and there ain't shit worth taking. Not anymore."

"At least it's empty," Jarrett said.

"We don't know that," warned Alex.

"If there are any rotters here, they're starved down to fuckin' skin and bones. They gotta eat just like us, and just like us, they don't eat." Keane held an aluminum bat, a relic from a time when there was play. It was caked with rust, and other things rust-colored, and he wielded it like an extension of his arm. "All right. Look, Alex, we know this city's been stripped bare... If there's anything here, it's under."

"Under?"

"Ol' New York is supposed to have a whole other city beneath it—train tunnels, sewers, basements and connections that ain't on any of our maps. There might be some real worthwhile stuff down there. Stuff locked up even before Plague Year. Hell, there could be a goldmine down there."

"We're just looking for basic supplies—"

"Yeah, I know," Keane snapped. "We're just trying to get by. Make it to the next day. Is that livin'? C'mon. What if we could bring back more than some goddamn salt and paper? What if we brought back books? Booze? Fucking juice! I don't needa get drunk, if I could taste apple juice just one more time—"

"Don't start," Alex shook his head. "Just don't."

"Yeah, you hate to think about it, but what if it's really fuckin' down there? What if, Alex? C'mon, we're otherwise basically wastin' our time in this ghost town, why not just go look? Jarrett, whaddaya think?"

The smallest and youngest of the three, Jarrett stared at the dead city with wonder. He still had dreams, Alex knew, he still had an idea that life was more than breathing and eating and outlasting the rotters. He had a concept of the future.

"I wonder what's down there," Jarrett said.

Keane slapped his knee and held the bat up. "Let's just poke around this block, huh? Just see what's under this block. Under this hill here, Caterpillar Hill. If we find somethin' interesting, we'll head back to camp and they can send out a real salvage team."

Alex shrugged. "You know, there could be rotters down there. Preserved somehow, away from the hot and the dryness. It could be bad."

Jarrett suddenly looked pale. Keane popped his neck with a snap of his head and sighed. "I'll take point. We'll sweep every room before we start shopping. Okay? I'm not gonna take any chances with you guys. C'mon."

"What the hell," Alex said. "Might as well make something of this trip."

"Wait!" Jarrett said. He pointed, hand trembling, at something approaching the hill.

It lurched forward, the gaunt, thin-limbed thing, still partially hidden in the shadows of the buildings but beyond all doubt a rotter. Its stilted, insane run, its head thrusting downward with each step—it was alien and horrifying and yet they'd seen it a thousand times before.

But this one was a little different.

It ran like a bird, its arms held behind its back and its gray head making rude pecking gestures. As it came into the light, Alex saw the reason for its bizarre posture: it was handcuffed.

They'd never know why. They'd never know if this man had been some sort of prisoner, or if he'd been placed under restraint due to infection. They'd never know why he, or it, a starving scavenger just like them, was prowling the streets of Old New York alone and in old-style police handcuffs.

"Buzzard," Keane breathed, following the rotter's movements. "I mean, we call 'em that, the lone ones... but never seen one that really was." And with that, he descended the hill and, with a powerhouse swing, decapitated the rotter. Its body ran past him, scrambling halfway up the hill before collapsing and rolling back down to the street.

The head, its few teeth gnashing madly, lay in the grass. Keane stomped it to dust.

"Still want to go poking around?" Alex snapped, heart racing, face flushed. He looked at Jarrett, expecting to see terror in the boy's eyes; but he only saw morbid fascination.

Alex knew he'd been outvoted.

\* \* \*

"You feel that?"

"What?"

"Like a little quake. Just now."

"No."

They had gone into a corporate tower whose windows were long gone and whose floors had been given over to the local flora and fungi. Sunlight streamed in from all four sides—high noon—and Alex watched as rats scrabbled down into their burrows, going under the floor.

"Think they're infected?"

"We can't ask. Just kill 'em if they get too close."

"I feel bad for them," Jarrett said. "They don't know. They're just living, like us."

"It's nature," Alex said in an attempt at a calming tone. "We have to protect ourselves. Nature understands."

"The rats don't."

"Ever hear of a rat king?" Keane muttered. He was using his bat to clear a closet of debris. "It's an Old New York legend. Rats, they live under the city, millions of them. Some of 'em get mashed up together and twisted—tangled, their tails, their legs—and they just go on like that. They become this one thing that just goes around taking care of itself. A rat king."

"You mean like a huge ball of rats?" Jarrett sputtered.

Keane nodded. "It probably happens."

"It probably happens that they get all tangled up and can't separate," Alex said, "but I don't think they become one entity or whatever. They just struggle and die."

"Why not?" Keane asked.

"Because all every rat cares about is taking care of its own self." Alex found a brittle sheaf of papers; they could be moistened and used as bandages or cloths down the line. Maybe he'd even do a little writing. "Each rat for itself. Rat king wouldn't work. It's not nature."

Jarrett looked troubled. Alex gave him an inviting smile, wanted him to speak up; but he didn't.

* * *

The basement was a parking garage, empty. Beyond that was sewer access.

"I say we check it out," Keane said.

"What're we gonna find? Hundred-year-old crap."

"New York sewers aren't just pipes, man! There could be another fucking building down there. Let's just look for fuck's sake."

"Okay. Lay off the 'fucks'?"

"Why? No one's around."

"I'm around."

"It's just a word."

"I'm tired of words that mean things like fuck and shit and all of that. If you're in a good mood then talk like it, okay?"

Keane shrugged at Alex. "Right. All right."

A ladder went down to the sub-basement in place of the long-dead elevator, and from there was a door. An actual door into the sewers.

"Why would they put a door?" Alex asked.

"Because there's more than shit—I mean garbage—down there." Keane rapped the bat on the old metal door. The room was small and dark and there was no echo. "Who knows? A vault or a bomb shelter or a god-please-let-there-be-a-pot-garden."

"What's pot?" Jarrett asked.

"Nothing you need to know about," Alex said, and approached the door. "Take a torch, Keane. You're on point right?"

"Right."

The door sounded like a banshee's dying cry. Jarrett covered his ears while Alex lit a torch and shouldered his axe. "I'll take the rear, Jarr. You go after Keane."

There were stairs; wet stairs, Alex noticed immediately, old carved stone steps that collected tepid little pools of water from some unknown source. Had to be the humidity. It was hot and fucking damp in that narrow stairwell. *Drip-drip-drip* from down below rattled the nerves. Jarrett was breathing hard, looking from side to side at the flat black walls as they descended the winding staircase, Alex and Keane each holding a torch and a weapon. Jarrett was approved for weapons, but all he had was a length of pipe tucked against his calf, down in that one old holey sock he wore on his right leg. He knew to strike them in the eyes and teeth. Blind them, disable them, evade them. Rotters weren't to be messed with. It wasn't Man's cause to seek out and slaughter the living dead. Just stay out of their damn way and let them rot.

"I almost hear a rumbling," Keane said.

"Well, do you or don't you?" Alex whispered.

"I don't know. It's kinda in my feet, you feel that?"

"I don't feel anything. And I don't hear anything. We're down in solid rock here, Keane, I don't think you're really feeling anything moving about."

"Just the earth?"

"I don't know. Your imagination. Your heartbeat."

"So dark," Jarrett breathed. "How far do you think these stairs go?"

"Don't know, son," Alex replied. He was beginning to feel claustrophobic, despite being the rear guard, and he thrust his torch toward the ceiling. "Flame's dancing a little. I think there's some air coming up from below."

Keane nodded. "It's getting a little less damp. We're onto something." He grinned at Jarrett.

The stairs ended. There was a tunnel, and another door, sodden wood bulging with just a few tiny holes letting some cool air push through. Pungent, but cool.

"What do you think the city was like back then? When it was New New York?" Jarrett asked.

Alex stared at a blank wall. "All I know is, it was always the same down here."

"Definitely a sewer behind this door," Keane grunted as he tugged at the old, swollen wood. "But there's gotta be something more. This passage wasn't carved out so some guys could clean shit outta the pipes."

"Language."

"Yeah," Keane mumbled. "I'll bet this was here before the sewers. I'll bet they came later and took this up as part of 'em, but this used to be something else—something—"

The door roared as it fell apart, an icy wind with the smell of rancid waste smacking each man in the face. Then it was gone. A gaping hole remained.

"Blew my torch out," Keane whistled.

"Here's another."

"I can get this one to go again. No problem."

Jarrett approached the opening on trembling legs. There was a black vacuum, a soundless, sightless void.

"Here," Alex said, and tossed his torch through the doorway.

It splashed, and fizzled, but didn't go out. It illuminated the six-foot drop, managed by ladder, and the cavernous sewer tunnel extending from right there to the end of the world in both directions.

"Lookit this," Keane said, perched in the doorway with eyes wide. "It's huge. By Adam, you could drive a truck through this here! Two trucks! What were they flushin'?" he laughed, and it echoed throughout the system, making Alex's skin crawl.

"Keep it quiet."

"You honestly think there's anything down here? We had to kill that door to get through!"

"Don't stir up the rats!" Alex hissed. Keane threw his hands out in mock horror. "God forbid I should have to mash a few rat heads."

"Rat king," Jarrett said, "could fit through there. Big enough for a rat king."

"Rat kings aren't real." Alex shot a stern look at Keane, who just rolled his eyes. "But there are almost certainly rats in there infected with the Plague or something else and I don't want to mess with 'em."

"So we're not going in there?" Keane pouted.

"Are you kidding?"

"What'd we come down here for? What'd I rip apart that door for?"

"It's just a sewer! There isn't any gold down here, man! Do you see anything but a little river of shit water? There aren't any other tunnels or doors or anything. It's just a big-ass sewer, that's all. I'm sorry," Alex sighed. "I wish there was something down here. It would've made this day worthwhile. But there's not."

They all felt the rumble.

"What do you think that was?" Keane asked.

"Maybe..." Alex leaned through the doorway into the tunnel, feeling the slight breeze. "Maybe there's water down here. Maybe there's like some sort of river system that still exists, and it shifts things around. Could be natural caverns underneath all this."

"Wouldn't that be something to see," Keane said, smiling at Jarrett.

"We're not sight-seeing, though, we're—" And then Alex fell.

It was a jarring drop, not lethal, not frightening, just jarring. Painful and shitty and wet. He landed in a fetid slop and knew his ankle had turned. "GOD! FUCK!" It probably was just a sprain. Just a sprain, Keane could haul him up if he could just grab that ladder.

Alex looked at his hands, looked for cuts in the dying light of the thrown torch. He couldn't see shit for shit.

"Keane, gimme a hand. I'm okay."

Jarrett's head shot into the tunnel. "Are you all right?"

"I just said I'm fine," Alex grumbled. He sat up and scooted his butt forward a little, sloshing in the muck. He was going to stink for days. The group hadn't come across fresh water in a week, and it would probably be another damn week before they did. Alex saw the coming days going to hell; saw himself sitting alone in a dirty tent and just when he'd gotten up the nerve to ask Tru if she wanted to lay with him.

"Need more than a hand, looks like," Keane said, clambering down the ladder.

"No, I can get myself up there, I just need—"

"Man, forget it. I've got you." Keane clapped Alex's back and coughed. "You smell like shit."

"Thank you."

There was another rumble.

"I know you felt that."

It didn't stop.

Then the thing came around the bend, filling the tunnel, all of it, claiming every inch of space in its insane locomotion.

Torsos, heads, limbs, all desiccated, all human, all undead, all packed together with mud and blood and everything else and wound tight with threads of bone and flesh and fungus. A gnashing moaning rumbling thing that pawed at the walls with skeletal hands, feeling old grooves, having run this track a thousand times like a polished marble. Broken teeth and watery eyes and bloody gums all searching for the least bit of meat. Plunging through the tunnel, the rumble now a crescendo of wails and grunts and other things going on inside the wet pulsing core of the rat king.

Jarrett's head snapped back as the thing came by, and he saw a split-second flash of faces and feet and skulls and things he never wanted to see, ever, ever again. The thing swept by and rolled up Alex and Keane into it and swallowed them and it continued its terrible progress through the bowels of the city, searching for every last warm morsel to sustain itself.

\* \* \*

Jarrett never explained the rat king to the others, to anyone. He didn't tell them just how the rotters had taken Alex and Keane. He didn't think they would understand. Only nature would. Nature, who, he now knew, was a goddess in Hell.

# TEN / THE POLITICS OF MADNESS

"I'll pick up the tab," Blake said, sipping from a terrible cup of coffee. He motioned across the diner to the waitress.

Voorhees had barely touched his sandwich. It was ice-cold now, two and a half hours after it was dropped in front of him, two and a half hours of trying to wrap his head around what Blake had been telling him.

"There are some elements that can only be contained, not cut out."

Crime was an inevitability, and in today's world, there were greater priorities than the futile pursuit of trying to eliminate wrongdoing.

The answer? Government-sanctioned organized crime. Finn Meyer's boys ran protection rackets, prostitution, smuggled illicit goods like alcohol into the city. But they pledged not to commit acts of violence. No sexual assault, no homicide, noting that violated their "honor code" and nullified their standing with the city administration.

Of course, there was the occasional slip-up. Unavoidable. But wasn't that occasional fall from grace better than a robbery spree or, God forbid, a serial rapist?

So what was the role of the Peace Officer, if not to fight crime?

"We keep an eye on Meyer, sure, but mostly we're just a presence on the street for people's peace of mind," Blake had told him. "Our hands are tied a bit, but so are his. There's a balance maintained and the people of Gaylen are better off for it. Don't get me wrong = every so often a domestic spat or something escalates, or one of Meyers' goons crosses the line, and we get some actual police work. But for the most part, street crime stays within the honor code."

"Honor code," Voorhees growled. "Bullshit."

"I know it sounds wrong, I know it does. But this is a new system, and so far it works."

"How long do you think Meyer can be contained? Are you really so naïve as to think he doesn't already have other rackets going on right under your nose? That prick thinks he owns the cops. Far as I can tell he's right."

"The city can't pour all its resources into a war on petty crime, Voorhees! Meyer may be a bastard but the fact is that the thugs under his umbrella are kept in line. So they take credits from local businesses and use them to buy booze. So they pimp—don't you think a streetwalker is safer with a pimp watching her back? I know it sounds wrong, Voorhees, I know we're supposed to cling to this ideal that says no crime can go unpunished, but for God's sake that's not the reality we live in!"

"We're supposed to try and make it that way!" Voorhees yelled, pounding the table. Neighboring patrons tried not to stare. "So we can't bring crime down to zero. Does that mean we sit on our hands or, worse yet, *help them?* This is fucking depraved."

"But like he said, it works."

A middle-aged woman with light brown hair and a sash around her overcoat slid into the booth beside Blake, flashing her P.O. badge. "Emily Halstead. Hey there, partner."

So now it was going to be two against one. Voorhees threw his hands in the air. "Forget it. I've gotta put in my resignation. This funny farm can find another fake cop."

"Blake, would you mind letting us get acquainted? That is, unless you two are already joined at the hip." Halstead winked at Blake, who sighed and got up.

"Like I said, I'll get the check. Think before you walk, Voorhees."

Halstead took Voorhees' plate and looked the sandwich over. "You gonna eat this?"

"I don't have an appetite."

She nodded and took a bite. "Mustard. Pricey."

"So you want to preach to me, too?" he muttered.

She shook her head, chewing. "The system's been broken from the beginning. Nothing makes sense inside these walls."

So she wasn't nuts. Voorhees leaned forward, taking up his coffee. "Don't drink that," Halstead advised.

"Why do you do the job, then?" he asked.

"In hopes that things will start to change. This is still America, right? You read the history books, you know change is possible. If not here, not anywhere."

"What're we gonna do? Go on strike? Let Finn Meyer put his own cops on the beat? Or do we lobby the Senate to shake up their precious sandbox?"

"How long have you been inside the Wall, Voorhees?"

"About five months."

"You catch on pretty quick, you know that? I'm guessing you tend to resist this whole notion that the world out there no longer exists."

"Of course." He picked a wet French fry off the plate. "I'm thinking about enlisting. I'd rather deal with rotters than this."

"You'd still have to live here," she said. "Why not fight the system from the inside? You may feel helpless right now, but believe me, you're in a position to make a difference."

"You really think so?"

"I do. It just means pissing Casey off now and then. Maybe he'll dock your pay, maybe Meyer's boys won't want to be your buddies anymore. I've been threatened more than once and I'm still here.

"Like Blake said, think before you walk."

* * *

Voorhees made the mistake of visiting Casey's office and trying to be rational.

"If you'd rather live in the badlands, get your shit and go," the S.P.O. snapped. He wheeled himself out from behind his desk and asked, "Did they tell you how I lost my legs yet?"

Voorhees shook his head. Another mistake.

"I came north early on to help with construction. On my way up here—didn't have a military convoy flanking me like the later ones— my friends and I were held up by badlanders. Highwaymen. They shot me. You can't see it, it's above me hairline, but yeah, they shot me and left me for dead.

"Then they came back."

He kneaded the stumps of his knees, sweat running down his brow. "They came back that night and took my body to their camp. They were sure I was dead, you see. And they were hungry."

He narrowed his eyes to fiery slits. "They're just like the rotters, those people—lawless, godless animals. Take society away and that's what you're left with. The human animal.

"It was my screams that alerted a nearby Army patrol. They'd begun sawing off my legs."

He took a deep breath and massaged his temples. "Oh, Voorhees. Don't you see, that's the alternative? If we didn't have Meyer and his honor code, there would be animals running loose in the streets. And we wouldn't have the strength to stop them. Everything would fall apart—the Great Cities are in their infancy and we have to safeguard their development."

"And then what?"

"We'll cross that bridge when we come to it."

*And Meyer will set it ablaze when you're halfway across*, Voorhees thought.

# ELEVEN / BEST-LAID PLANS

Ian Gregory sat in on his first Senate morning meeting, positioned behind and to the left of Gillies as the Senate President spoke to his fellow statesmen.

"I spoke with Britain by radio last night. They're still being difficult, but I think they're beginning to come around, at least as far as the airfield is concerned. I assured them that it would be finished by November."

"Isn't that cutting it a little close?" asked Senator Georgia Manning.

"If you need more manpower, Georgia, then get it. You've got a whole damn city at your disposal."

"Enough people already know about the airfield," she retorted.

"Then *lie*," came the exasperated reply. "Go outside of that construction company for volunteers—I don't trust those people anymore. Tell the volunteers that they're working on the site for a new hospital. They don't have to know anything!"

Gregory had tuned out the conversation and was studying each Senator's face. He tried to separate the loyal ones from the opportunists. It was always visible in the face. As a man of God— and Hand of God's leader—he had honed his ability to sniff out sin.

Maybe that was why Gillies made him just a little uncomfortable.

But everyone had their flaws, their secrets; and, though he fought it, his mind drifted again to Barry.

The final days of the Wall's construction... the burn pits, trenches twenty feet deep and piled with crippled, decapitated and paralyzed rotters. The foul stench of death, so thick and pervasive that all the soldiers standing guard had to wear gas masks. And the moaning. The moaning and gurgling as the undead flailed about in a slurry of leaking fluids and decaying meat. The burn team hadn't come by in days and trucks were bringing in all of the ferals that had been picked off along the Wall's perimeter. They said it would be more efficient this way. It was madness. Weird, otherworldly groans filled the sky day and night.

Finally the burn team arrived. The dead in the pits were liquefying beneath the summer sun, and a fog of putrefaction had settled over the place; seeping into clothing and skin, staining every man and woman on-site.

When the burn team pointed their flamethrowers into the pits, the things erupted like volcanoes. Instead of ash and lava it was gore and thrashing, living limbs that rained down on everyone. Suddenly all was chaos, and the insanity that had been building for a week finally screamed to life. Everyone was in a panic, including Sergeant Ian Gregory. He was frantically searching through the smoke and slaughter for Kendra Barry. He pulled off his mask and screamed her name, then the stench of roasting flesh filled his nose and eyes and throat and he fell to his knees vomiting.

Somewhere in there, in the madness, she had fallen. Perhaps shoved, perhaps tripped, or maybe she'd just run blindly into the flaming pit and been caught in the blackened claws of the undead.

They did manage to recover her body a few days later during the cleanup; official cause of death was smoke inhalation. But Gregory, identifying her body, had seen the marks around her throat where they had choked the life from her.

\* \* \*

"Has Finn Meyer been extorting credits from you?"

Voorhees leaned on the counter and looked Becks hard in the eye. She gave him a what're-you-gonna-do shrug and said, "It keeps people from stealing. He polices the market more often than the cops."

"But he *is* stealing from you, don't you see that?" Voorhees sighed.

"It could be worse," was her reply.

"How, exactly?"

"I have a business here, Officer, and a home. I have a normal life. I was the only one from my hometown to reach the Great Cities. We were being followed by rotters. We had to try to swim across this lake—then suddenly there were rotters all over the shore, on all sides, surrounding u. Fourteen went in. By the time an Army convoy happened by, I was the only one still treading water."

"I'm sorry," Voorhees said. "I'm sorry that happened to you. But how does that make this all right?"

"It makes this tolerable," she said. "I spent two days in that water. I watched as people sank, one by one, around me. I ran out of tears. I couldn't scream anymore. I could only fight to stay afloat. And their eyes—the rotters, every pair of eyes was on me. Those soldiers could have just passed me by but they fought those bastards for hours just to get to me. They brought me here. I'm grateful."

"Don't be grateful to Meyer," Voorhees told her. "His days are numbered."

"What are you trying to do?" she asked softly, sadness in her eyes, pleading eyes. "Life is okay now. Please."

Someone nudged Voorhees' back. Remembering that he was blocking the checkout, he stepped back. A hard-faced woman in a long coat offered her hand. "Pat Morgan."

"P.O. Voorhees." He gave her a firm shake. "Are you another officer?"

"No, air," she said, with the slightest twinkle in her eye. "I work for Mister Meyer. He'd like to buy you lunch."

# TWELVE / CANDY

Meyer had a handful of colorful rock candy, probably homemade, that he munched obnoxiously as he and Pat Morgan walked Voorhees down to the shore of Lake Michigan.

"I thought this was an invitation to lunch," said Voorhees. Meyer shrugged. "Not hungry."

"Crooked *and* cheap. But I'll bet your whores are top dollar."

"Interested in a lay, Officer?" Meyer grinned. "I can get you a special deal. You ever fucked an Asian girl? I do mean *girl*, by the way."

A quiet chill settled in Voorhees' gut. "What do you want? If this is about either bribes or threats you'd best just save your breath. I don't care."

"I have a lot of little girls," Meyer continued, as if Voorhees hadn't spoken. "In basements all over Gaylen. They're quite willing, too—"

Voorhees seized Meyer by the collar of his coat. Morgan whipped out a .45 and stuck it against his temple.

"I didn't think guns were allowed in Gaylen," Voorhees said through gritted teeth. He didn't let Meyer go.

"Oh, they're not," Meyer replied, his breath sickly sweet. "Neither are booze or hash or meth, but there seems to be a steady demand and, well, why send people away empty-handed? I don't believe in that. The government doesn't believe in that."

"You're trash. If this were my city I'd—"

"Yes, I've heard how you did things back in Louisiana. So trusted, so admired that nearly every citizen and all your cops bailed on you when the military withdrew? Leaving you with what, a handful of bums? What else happened down there, Voorhees? I've

59

heard lots of strange talk about weird things in the southern badlands.

"You know what they say?" Meyer asked, delicately extracting Voorhees' hands from the folds of his coat. "People say that there are ghosts and gods roaming about out there. They call these days the Last Days. But I don't subscribe to that, and I'm sure you don't either, being a rational man. Just the same—"

He slugged Voorhees in the stomach, doubling the old man over, and shouted in his ear "In here, *I am God!*"

Morgan clipped Voorhees in the back of the head with the butt of her gun. He fell to his knees, vision swimming, the voice of Finn Meyer fading in and out and then gone altogether.

He looked up to find himself alone. It was starting to snow.

* * *

Upon arriving back at his office—a warehouse basement downtown—Meyer was informed that he had a couple of sellers sitting upstairs. He liked to handle this end of the business personally. He removed his coat, smoothed his suit and headed up.

The couple was sitting in a small windowless room, isolated from the goings-on in the rest of the building. Entering with the lieutenant who had summoned him, Meyer shook their hands warmly and said, "First things first. How much are you asking for?"

The woman looked at the man, who cleared his throat and said, "Ten thousand."

Meyer clapped his hands on his knees and laughed. "Well, this must be quite a filly! Ten thousand? Let's see her. Where is she?"

The lieutenant opened a narrow door into a smaller room, where a few toys—dolls, blocks, crayons—were scattered about on faded carpet.

Lily looked up from her place against the wall, arms and legs crossed, and said "When do I get to go home?"

Meyer licked his lips. He looked back at the couple. "How old is she?"

"Twelve," Jack Calvert said.

"Come on now," Meyer said in scolding tone. "I'll need to see papers on that."

"She might be thirteen or fourteen. We've only had her a few months."

60

Meyer said to Lily, "Just another minute, sweetheart," and closed the door to the smaller room. To the Calverts he asked, "Why ten grand? You must know how steep that is."

"Yes," Jack said, "but we're in debt—we owe people and they want it all now. Or else."

"I see." Meyer crouched in front of them and said, "Maybe you should refinance with me. Wouldn't that be better than selling off the girl?"

Jack and Molly looked anxiously at one another. "You're not really in debt, are you?" Meyer smiled coldly.

Jack stared at his feet, clearing his throat again, trying to find the right words to say. "Just tell me the truth," Meyer said. "What are you into?"

"You must know about the airfield," Jack said. Meyer frowned. "Airfield?"

"They're building an airfield east of the city. The Senate. I think they're going to have planes come from somewhere and take them out of here. We just—I need to buy seats for me and my wife. We have to get out of here. The girl—Lily—we only took her in for the government support check. We can let her go. We just want the money."

Meyer stood in silence, staring at them while he sucked on a piece of candy. The room seemed to grow even smaller to Jack and Molly, pressure building behind their eyes, hands trembling... finally he spoke.

"Seven thousand credits."

Jack nodded immediately. He'd probably expected a lot less than ten. He put his arm around his wife and said, "Yes. Seven. All right."

"Give this man here your account number. Expect the transfer within the hour. It'll be entered in as a tax refund. Understand? You were never here. In fact, you never had the girl—I'll take care of it. All of that clear?"

They both nodded. They looked like they wanted the hell out of there. Meyer decided to suck his candy and let them stew a few more minutes.

What sort of person would sell their child, even a foster child, into sexual slavery? Of course Meyer could make it right on his end, but how did they live with themselves? Heartless people. At least she'd be taken care of now. And she'd be loved... oh, his clients would love little Lily with her budding breasts and long dark hair. S.P.O. Casey would *really* love her.

"All right. Give my guy your account and walk out of here, and then forget all this," he said. They scuttled from the room like spooked roaches.

He opened the door to the smaller room. Lily looked a bit more apprehensive. She hadn't figured it out yet, but she soon would.

"My name's Finnegan," he said. "Want some candy?"

She shook her head.

"That's good. You don't take candy from strangers. But soon I won't be a stranger, and then when I offer you candy you'll take it. Okay?"

He knelt in the doorway like he was talking to a puppy. "Jack and Molly can't take care of you anymore. They want you to stay here for now. There are lots of other girls here. You'll like it."

She drew into a ball and whimpered, "I want to go home."

"You *are* home, sweetheart."

# THIRTEEN / RUNNERS

A light dusting of snow had given the earth a corpse-pallor which was matched by the night sky. A black shape broke the monotony of lingering clouds and headed north.

It had been ages since Dalton had seen a bird in the sky. There was one high above him now, a hawk, circling over a shadowy patch of earth beyond the Wall.

What was the hawk stalking? Based on its behavior it seemed likely that it wasn't infected, that it was after a small mammal. An infected raptor wouldn't look outside its own species for prey. But Dalton had orders, and he sighted the hawk through his rifle's scope and fired.

It was true that people had become infected through contact with animals. If you cornered one, forced it to bite, you'd signed your death warrant; Dalton had seen too many soldiers infect themselves by catching and eating plague-ridden rodents out in the field. There were so many ways that the nightmare could begin—so the military demanded every safeguard enforced. So he fired.

The hawk plummeted to earth, out of view. Dalton needed night vision goggles. The pair he'd owned had been "requisitioned" by a burn team for their evening sweeps. The lights on the Wall just weren't enough, but they'd have to do. He heard generators humming to life as they came on.

No rotters today. Fewer and fewer each week. But wasn't it only a matter of time, some would ask, until the hungry dead clustered in the badlands ventured north in search of food?

No, the scientists said. Field studies indicated that the dead stayed close to the communities from which they originated. They didn't think like people, nor like animals; they didn't think at all. If they sensed meat nearby, they went after it. Otherwise they just stood and rotted.

Dalton knew it was bullshit. He'd seen a newly-dead soldier shoot at human prey. He'd seen rotters that had felled small trees to block a road and then laid in wait for the next Army patrol. Most of them, he believed, retained some scrap of intellect. If you believed the stories about regeneration, maybe it was possible for rotters to get even smarter.

Don't worry, the scientists said. Even if it was true, their food supply was dwindling. They were starving out there in the badlands. Someday, Americans could live outside the Wall again. Maybe even in Dalton's lifetime.

He didn't buy it. Because he knew that the apocalypse wouldn't just fade away. He was a man of God and he'd seen the signs. He'd seen the Reaper.

What did the scientists say when confronted with dozens of accounts of the rider on his pale horse? Post-traumatic stress disorder. Psychotic break. Those who openly spoke of seeing the Angel of Death were flagged and relegated to menial jobs: quarantine watch, processing center clerk, orientation aide. Their personnel files had extra forms with red ink. They were called in periodically to chat with a counselor. And hey were always asked: do you still think you saw Death?

Dalton had seen him riding his white steed in the burning remnants of a Louisiana town called Jefferson Harbor. Like many towns, including the Great Cities, Jefferson Harbor had its own wall. It hadn't made a damn difference.

Bigger walls. More soldiers. More work for the undead, but hardly a deterrent. There was no deterrent. They were zombies.

A runner came into the light. Stumbling toward the Wall, clothed in bloody rags, jaw hanging slack, fingernails black with old gore—the rotter streaked into view and right toward Dalton.

The hawk must have been circling him. It had alerted Dalton to the enemy's presence, and he'd rewarded it with a bullet.

It wouldn't make things right, Dalton knew, but he went ahead and put two rounds through the top of the runner's spine, nearly severing its head from is neck. Then he grabbed his radio.

"Section nineteen. One rotter down."

His dogs were asleep in the guard post. They were probably awake now, even with his gun silenced. Assured there were no other undead coming, he climbed down to see the Rotties.

At least Logan hadn't made any more excuses to come by. He was probably busy in Gaylen, anyway. The night made it easier for him to go about his disgusting business.

* * *

"I'm looking for a date," Logan said to the woman in the doorway of the apartment building. She tossed her dark hair back and looked him over. *Already back?* her expression said.

The transaction was completely under the table. No credits. Just bullets. Two full clips.

She led him down a dark hall. Campbell was well-built, firm and leggy and all, but she was also tough as nails. At least around her clientele. Logan had thought a few times about asking her out, getting the both of them away from this ratty dump of a tenement, but he quietly laughed the idea away. *After what she's seen me do?*

Campbell led him down a well-lit flight of stairs with a murderous-looking black guy watching Logan's every move. It was the walk of shame, that hallway, these stairs. All for a few seconds of pleasure. But his heart was already pounding with anticipation and he felt himself stiffening.

Down one last hallway, one with several doors and a man guarding each one. Sometimes Logan forgot just how dangerous this was. If the P.Os or the brass ever found out, they'd burn the place to the ground. He'd be discharged, maybe sent away to some awful place where the unwanted were sent. But he told himself: *They aren't women. They're things. Like a pinup or something. It's not unnatural.*

Campbell opened the last door in the hall and tapped a scarlet nail against her cheek. "Same girl, right?"

He nodded at the floor as a man patted him down. Campbell pulled on a glove and tugged at his pants. The man who'd searched him shone a lantern's light down there. Logan shut his eyes tight, feeling himself go soft in her hand, resisting the urge to push her away and leave and forget all about it. Finally satisfied, the girl stepped aside and allowed him into the dark room.

There was a candle burning beside the door. Once that door was closed, it was the only light. But it was a soft, small light and it helped with the fantasy. It helped hide some of the sores and the rot, if there was any, which there almost certainly was. The air was thick with a flowery scent. That helped with the odor that occurred once things got going.

And then there was her, splayed out on a mattress with hands heavily bandaged and chained to the wall behind her head. She still had nice legs. They kicked, and the teddy shifted, revealing her in the candlelight.

It was a thin, loose bit of lingerie, easy to pull up over her hips and down past her breasts. Her skin looked clean; she was checked frequently for any signs of blood or open wounds. Occasionally someone would get in with a knife and cut a girl up. Depraved. Guys like that were beaten to a pulp out back and banned from the joint. Perhaps more depraved were those who tried to fuck a girl in the mouth and got it bitten off. They were taken out back, too, but they didn't return to the lights of the city.

Yeah, at least he wasn't one of those guys. He knelt before his girl, holding her legs apart with his knees, and undid his pants. There was a bowl on the floor with wrapped condoms from some other decade. He hated that. He and she had both been checked out, so why not let them both feel it? Yes, he still believed that she could feel it, and that it felt good. He knew she would get wet when he touched her. Part of her wanted him.

But still, not a woman. Not rape. Just a *thing*.

She was heavily made up. He couldn't tell what she really looked like under there. Just as well.

He pulled the teddy down, and her marbled breasts fell free. Her head started to move. She looked at him with yellowed eyes.

Her teeth were gnashing. They left the teeth in to dissuade kissing. She tossed her head, blonde wig falling in front of her eyes, and she ground her teeth and bucked her hips. She wanted him all right, but not in the way he believed. Logan put that out of his mind and entered her.

She made low rasping sounds. Her hips continued thrusting, and he slowed his rhythm to match hers, as if they were making love. He stared into her face and kneaded her breasts, pinching her nipples to harden them. The hair fell out of her eyes, and she glowered at him, mouth wide open, just waiting for him to make the wrong move and come close enough for a bite. He kept himself propped up and rocked against her, whispering: "I love you. You feel so fucking good, I fucking love you."

She tugged at her chains and started shaking her head. He knelt to kiss her breasts, keeping his scalp away from her teeth. Moaning, Logan thrust deep into her, sitting up and spreading her legs wide, and he came staring into her defiant dead eyes.

Pulling the condom off with a wet snap, he tied the end and held it between his fingertips. He'd have to take it out with him. Buckling his pants, he turned away from her, not wanting to see her now as the monster she was. Not wanting to acknowledge that he'd fucked *it*.

Another walk of shame, another night of trudging through the streets and trying to justify it to himself. Eventually he'd smoke some pot and go to sleep, but then the dreams would come, dreams about teeth and tearing and Logan loving it and he'd awaken in the morning in a film of sweat.

* * *

There was something very wrong here.

The other girls had too much makeup on, and they looked miserable. Lily sat in the long room and watched as the children in neighboring beds trembled or rocked or just stared blankly at the ceiling. When the man named Finnegan entered, they all flinched and tried to make themselves invisible. He walked from bed to bed, looking each one over. "Is that a bruise? You're getting too thin. Start eating. I mean it."

He came to Lily and smiled. "I'm going to take you to meet someone."

"Who? A new mom and dad?"

"No, not like that. A new friend."

He reached his hand out, but she ignored it, getting off the bed by herself and pulling on her shoes. "I don't have any of my stuff," she told him.

"You'll get new things," he replied curtly.

He led her out of the warehouse and into a side street, where he stopped to talk to someone. Lily stayed at his side, not wanting to make him angry like the other girls had. They must have made him mad for him to do whatever he'd done.

Glancing up at the sky, she saw s tiny silhouette in an upstairs window. Another girl, about her age, staring down. Lily waved. The girl didn't wave back.

There was something wrong with the way she looked; as Lily stared. She began to make out the girl's features, and the girl turned slightly toward the light in the window and Lily saw that a smile had been carved into her face.

She turned, shaking, to look at Finnegan. His back was towards her, and he was digging candy from his pocket while he snarled at the other man. Lily started to back away.

Finnegan glanced over his shoulder. "Hey, you stay put."

He saw the terror in her eyes.

He knew that she knew.

"Come here," he barked, turning toward her. She broke into a run. "Goddammit!" he yelled, and barreled after her.

She ran into an alley filled with carts, some kind of market, and she bolted behind the carts but kept moving because he would find her if she stopped. She could never stop running, not as long as she heard his puffing and cursing in the distance. She had to keep running.

# FOURTEEN / TRIPPER

Boyish good looks could only get you so far. Tripper had gotten his hands dirty a few times, but he strove to live by the code he'd learned up north: honor the living and fuck the dead.

He pulled his tattered jacket around his thin frame and reclined in a broken couch, seated in a garishly-lit alley in deep downtown. Not even Meyer's boys bothered coming around here. What was there to be gained? This district was a hovel for bums. Strange people. Tripper had known a guy with a CD player once. He had *The Best of the Doors* and that was all he had, played it incessantly. Humming to himself, Tripper fished a lighter from his pocket and patted himself down for a joint.

"People are strange, when you're a stranger..."

Tripper was undocumented. He'd snuck across the Canadian border during Wall construction. As far as Gaylen was concerned, he didn't exist. And he wasn't the only one.

Strange people. Lots of 'em.

It was a lot better to live off the grid, outside the system. Especially one as fucked as this. He wouldn't be tied down when the ship started to sink. *Honor the living...* well, the people around here acted like they were already dead. He supposed they might as well be.

"Over here sweetie."

Campbell led a small girl into the alleyway, closing a chain-link gate behind her. Tripper sat up and asked, "What's the haps?"

"I found her a few blocks over," Campbell said gravely. "I think she's running from Meyer."

"Shit." Tripper beckoned to the girl. "It's okay. We're nice people. What's your name?"

She wouldn't speak. Tripper looked to Campbell, who nodded and knelt beside the child.

"My name's Cam. Will you tell me your name?"

"Lily." The girl looked up slightly, almost meeting Cam's eyes. "I like your voice."

"I'm from Australia," Cam said with a smile. "Do you know where that is?"

Lily shook her head. Tripper got up off the couch and sat on a box beside his girlfriend. "Where are you from, kiddo?"

"Louisiana."

"That's a long ways away. Not as far as Australia, but still pretty far."

"Where did you come from just now?" Cam asked. Lily's eyes fell again.

"It's okay," Cam assured her. "We aren't going to take you back."

"I want to go home," Lily said, lip trembling. "But I don't have one."

"Neither do we," said Tripper. "But do you know what that means? It means bad people can't find us."

Cam put her hand on Lily's back. The girl flinched a little, but quickly relaxed. "Where's Australia?" she asked.

"It's a really big island on the other side of the world," Cam told her. "They've gotten rid of almost all the rotters over there. It's a nice place."

"Then why did you come here?"

Cam winked. "To kick zombie ass."

It wasn't far from the truth. She was a free spirit, to say the least. Working as a dancer in Adelaide, she'd seen the undead presence all but stamped out while reports were pouring in from around the world, all saying one thing: they were dying out there.

What could a twenty-four-year-old stripper do? As much as anyone else, she figured. Other countries were sending radio transmissions bouncing across the atmosphere begging for some kind of support—for anything. Were they simply going to ignore the cries? Was she somehow entitled to live in a world without the plague while everyone else suffered?

Her friends didn't understand. They weren't much for soul-searching. But they hadn't lived her life either. She was a lot tougher than she looked.

The question was not just where to go, but how o get off Australia. It wasn't as if planes and boats were leaving on a daily basis. No, the only people who were crazy enough to go out into no man's land were the scientists.

She'd bought her way onto a ship bound for French Polynesia's plague labs. From there, she caught another ship to the wasteland that was Mexico. And by the time she'd hacked her way to the southern U.S. border, there weren't soldiers guarding it anymore.

She'd never felt more alive than she did among the undead. To live and die in Adelaide without so much as a whimper, that just wasn't her style.

Settling here with Tripper hadn't originally been part of the plan, but he had awakened her to humanity's fatal flaws and the way they were manifest in these Great Cities. And, after he introduced her to a man named Thackeray in the badlands, she understood that, in order to defeat the plague once and for all, they first had to bring this system down.

Thackeray had told her about Cleveland, about how it was no longer part of the safe zone, even though the Senate claimed it was. Undesirables—criminals who wouldn't bow to men like Meyer, or those who challenged the politics of the Great Cities, or those with communicable diseases—they were "relocated" to Cleveland, outside the Wall, and left for dead. And if Cam and Tripper were ever caught, the same would happen to them.

The same would likely happen to this little girl if she were ever recovered.

"We'll take care of you," Cam told Lily. Tripper nodded solemnly. Lily tried to smile, but something in her had broken and she couldn't do it.

# FIFTEEN / INFERIS

Adam lay beneath a pile of refuse, silently observing the inhabitants of the latest town. They were typical rotters, standing in the road and in storefronts and under trees, staring at nothing, asleep for all intents and purposes until something came along to stir their senses.

This was the first time he had experienced the drop in temperature as winter approached. A thin layer of snow lay atop him and in the alley where he rested. It was prickly and bitter cold, permeating his flesh.

The dead began to move.

They were looking down the street, toward a point he couldn't quite see, and they were starting to shuffle in that direction. Adam slowly pulled himself from the garbage and crawled toward the mouth of the alley.

There was a dead man in the road holding torches: two in one hand, one in the other. Attracted by the flames, unafraid, the other undead crowded around him.

He started throwing the torches into the air.

Juggling.

He began to walk backwards. He was leading them out of the town!

Adam leapt to his feet ad strapped the scythe on. He didn't understand what this was, but it had to be stopped—

The hammer caught him in the base of the spine and sent him hurtling into the street.

Dizzy with pain, Adam started to push himself up. The Strongman's massive weapon swung into his side and he was in flight again, sailing away from the Fire Juggler and smashing into the shell of a pickup truck.

The Strongman ran at him like a behemoth straight out of Hell. Adam threw the truck door open and deflected the hammer long enough to get on his feet. He broke for the other side of the street.

What was happening?

*"He talked his performers into turning with him. They were willingly infected—most of them anyway."*

The Strongman, a tableau of inked horrors across his muscular torso, bore down on Adam with the hammer held high over his head. Adam feinted left, bolted right. The Strongman moved with him, graceful for his monstrous size; and Adam was knocked through a window into a general store.

He crashed through a counter and slammed into the wall. Pain erupted in every joint of his body. He saw red. He'd never experienced anything like this before—and he was afraid.

He felt something clamp down on his leg, and he was dragged back through the wreckage of the counter and swung into a metal shelf. Jags of pain like long, thin needles ripped into him. He was picked up and smashed down again. It was almost as if he were going to sleep now, the world darkening and slowing down around him. Was this unconsciousness? If he were knocked out, what would happen to him then?

He knew what would happen. He would be destroyed.

Adam lashed out with the scythe. He struck something hard. The hammer.

The Strongman stumbled back as Adam swung viciously, the blade streaking through clouds of dust scant inches from the rotter's flesh. The Strongman looked around for an exit.

Adam ran at him—

And a cluster of rubbery limbs ensnared him, dragging him back into the shelves. He felt at least three arms tightening around his throat. He tried to swing the scythe backwards—the blade struck a wall and was pulled off his arm.

*NO!*

A smothering weight forced him into the wall. Struggling to free himself, Adam got his first glimpse at his assailant—a four-armed man with gaping, fish-like jaws.

The Geek's arms were malformed, underdeveloped, but still strong enough to hold onto his prey. The elasticity of his flesh meant there was no slipping free. He had Adam wrapped up in his limbs and was gnawing at his face.

Adam forced his hand up through the tangle of arms and drove his fingers into the Geek's eyes. The rotter snapped at him, thrashing his head about, but Adam pushed harder and sunk his fingertips into the sockets of the undead's skull. Now he was the one with a handhold.

The Strongman could be heard heaving shelves aside. He was coming.

The Geek released Adam and pawed at his eyes with all four hands. Adam kicked the rotter into the Strongman's path and ran for the back of the store. He hit a door, plowed right through it, and was outside again. The cold slapped his shredded face.

The scythe was still inside! He didn't stand a chance without it. Before he could think of what to do, he heard footfalls, dozens of them—runners. They were coming around the building.

It was true. The King of the Dead and his traveling circus were real. As Adam fled down the back street, the image of the Fire Juggler flashed through his mind. Drawing the dead in with those spinning torches...

The circus was recruiting.

Something barreled into his legs and he went sprawling. It was a dwarf, with a pinched rotten face and spurs of bone, like horns, growing from its skull.

Adam scrambled down an alley and back toward the main thoroughfare. If he could just make it to that store!

A literal human pincushion staggered across the street toward him, skewers of all lengths stuck through its body. The metal rattled loudly as the thing came at him. From the sidewalk approached a stiff-legged, cadaverous giant, not as wide as the Strongman but taller. Yawning wounds in his flesh had been filled entirely with bone tissue, and outgrowths of bone threaded through the rotter's limbs and ribs, weaving in and out of gray flesh. The aberrant skeletal growth made the Petrified Man look as if he were armored.

Transfixed with horror, Adam almost didn't see the Geek pushing through the dead in the street. The locals were mesmerized by the Juggler; only these sideshow curiosities were pursuing him. They behaved more like animals than rotters. They must have developed a pack mentality, complete with hierarchy... which meant the King himself was nearby.

And he was.

As Adam ran away from the rotters, further into town and away from his scythe—he saw Eviscerato standing alone in the road, cane twirling in his bony hands.

Leaping into Adam's path, he sent the cane crashing into his knee. Adam tried to stay upright and keep running but the rotter jumped onto his back, and then Adam was on his knees and the cane was choking him. There was no risk of suffocation for Adam—but there was the risk of his head being torn off.

Eviscerato bit into Adam's scalp. Adam grabbed the cane and tried to force it away, but Eviscerato was too strong! The world began to go dark again.

He went limp. The very last thing he saw before losing consciousness was the Fire Juggler's approach, and the last thing he felt was searing heat.

# SIXTEEN / SEEDS OF FEAR

Casey brought everyone into the squad room early the next morning. There were a few P.Os Voorhees had never seen before; but then he was barely acquainted with his own partner.

"Senator Manning is going to be giving a public address at the amphitheater in about two hours," Casey told them. "Something about plans for a new hospital. We'll be doing security. This shouldn't pull you away from your regular beat for too long."

Emily Halstead rolled her eyes at Voorhees. Casey caught it. "This might not seem like much of a priority to some of you, but it's the job. Orders are from Gillies himself. Your streets can wait."

*Under Finn Meyer's watchful eye,* Voorhees thought.

He hadn't told anyone about his lakefront exchange with Meyer and Pat Morgan. Probably wouldn't have done him a damn bit of good.

He glanced Halstead's way. Maybe he'd tell her about it. She seemed to have her head on straight.

He and Blake were assigned to stand out on the stage where Manning would speak. They'd be surrounded on three sides by Gaylen's citizens. Their primary responsibility would be to keep people back from the stage. Voorhees hefted his baton in his hand and sighed. It'd be worthless against a shooter, but of course *no one* in Gaylen owned a firearm.

The other cops would be positioned in the backstage area and throughout the audience. "Guess I won't be seeing you out there, partner," Voorhees said to Halstead.

"Let's grab lunch after this is over. Then we'll head into the Red."

"The what?"

"Lake district. It's red on the city map. Keep up, Voorhees."

He smiled at that.

* * *

Backstage at the amphitheater, Georgia Manning looked over her notes, memorizing the lies, affirming them in her mind so that they'd come out of her mouth as gospel truth. She told herself it was necessary; the airfield had to be completed.

*And why should you feel bad for lying to these people? You'll be leaving them behind, won't you?*

She had tried not to think about that. She had hoped not to acknowledge the great betrayal until it was over and done with. Gillies had forced her into this damn speech. Why couldn't he have taken care of this? He was the sociopath who loved playing man of the people. This was his grand plan—

*And you've gone along with it like an obedient dog.*

She closed her eyes, swallowed the doubt and the shame, and composed herself for her public appearance.

Something sharp stuck her in the back. She turned with a loud cry. "What was that?"

"Sorry," came the reply. Manning rubbed her back with a scowl, then returned to her notes. Jesus, that really hurt. She'd have to find out which of the civvies shuffling around behind her had done it. Might have been on purpose. A thankless lot.

Out on the stage, Voorhees looked over the thin crowd. Maybe a hundred fifty people. He'd anticipated a real security issue when Casey pulled every officer off the street for this.

Manning came out from the backstage area to sparse applause. She moved slowly, hands on her lower back, looking more than a little out of sorts. Voorhees tried to catch her eyes, but she looked right through him.

*It hurts. It hurts a lot more than I first thought. Oh God, it hurts...*

Senator Manning stepped to the edge of the stage. The crowd quieted down. Voorhees and Blake exchanged concerned glances.

*I don't feel right... everything seems so far away... it's like I'm not really here.*

Manning's eyes were glazed over and half shut. She let go of her back and slumped forward. She was going to fall. Voorhees moved quickly toward her.

*I don't... I'm not...*

*It doesn't hurt anymore...*
*I don't hurt anymore.*
She fell forward.

Voorhees caught her arm and pulled her back, lying her down on the stage. Blake rushed over, speaking into his radio. "We've got a situation out here. The Senator's down. I repeat—"

The Senator's eyes were closed, her body limp. She felt like a corpse. Voorhees checked her pulse: none.

"Oh my God."

Then she woke up.

She lunged at Voorhees' arm, snapping her teeth, and he stumbled back and fell on his ass and scrambled for either his radio or his baton, he wasn't sure, while the Senator got to her feet and stared out at the crowd with dead eyes.

Murmurs turned to screams.

Manning ran at Blake, who dropped his radio and swung out with his baton, cracking her over the head. She stumbled, but continued headlong into him, and they both collapsed in a tangle of thrashing limbs.

"VOORHEES!" Blake screamed. The other cop looked up, just as he drew his baton... and he saw Manning tear a thick strip of meat from Blake's left forearm.

The amphitheater was in chaos. People threw one another down toward the stage as they fled. Killian and Halstead ran out from backstage and saw Blake running from Manning, blood spurting from his arm.

Tackling Manning, Voorhees drove her face first into the stage. He slammed the baton into the nape of her neck. Why in the *fuck* didn't he have his widowmaker? She struggled beneath him with shocking strength, trying to claw his legs and bite his wrists. He brought the baton down on her over and over. He heard her skull give and felt his weapon sink into gray matter. Still she fought, and hissed, and then she threw him off of her back and off of the stage.

Manning rose with wild, feral eyes—Killian smashed her mouth with her baton. Manning caught it in her claws and wrenched it away from the cop. Halstead shoved Killian aside and met the Senator's broken, gnashing jaws with her own baton. Black blood gushed forth.

Killian recovered her baton from the stage as Voorhees climbed back up. Most of the audience was gone, save for those frozen with terror.

Manning had been a lovely woman, poised and painted and always ready to be presented to her constituents. Now she was a gruesome parody of her former self, racing across the stage like an animal and flying back as she was hit again, and again, and again.

Blake was howling. Manning saw him lying prone at the end of the stage and charged. Voorhees clipped her knee with his baton and she went sprawling. Halstead and Killian fell upon her, smashing her head into a lumpy pulp, sending bits of bone flying and blood spewing from what remained of her face.

Her arms and fingers kept twitching. She was still undead. But she'd been immobilized.

Other P.Os swarmed onto the stage, and Casey came rolling down the center aisle, barking into his radio.

All was madness. Voorhees peeled off his overcoat and shook the gore from it. Blake screamed in agony, seeing Manning's quivering corpse and knowing what he was to become. Emergency services arrived, and the techs recoiled from Blake when they saw his gaping wound.

"Oh God," he wept, grabbing at Voorhees' leg, "I'm dead... Voorhees, I'm dead."

The techs finally got up the nerve to approach the man and set down their equipment, wrapping gauze around his arm while they took his vitals. Blake just rocked back and forth, shaking his head. "Dead. Dead. Deadeadead."

The he saw the scalpel, wrapped in plastic, in the tech's treatment kit.

You can never know until it happens to you. How you would react, what thoughts would race through your mind... and what dark, primal instincts might take hold. Blake saw the scalpel. There was no further thought. He snatched it and pushed the blade through the plastic into his carotid and he dragged the blade through his windpipe with a gurgling scream.

Voorhees watched numbly, his baton slipping from his hand.

Killian shrieked and tried to grab the scalpel, but she was far too late.

Halstead turned away with a shivering grimace, a look that said she had seen it a dozen times before and knew she would see it again.

Casey simply set down his radio and sighed.

Blake hit the stage, and one of the techs stifled the arterial spray with a rag and everyone sat in silence as a man became a memory.

# SEVENTEEN / AUTOPSY

"It shouldn't have happened," Killian said, pale-faced, as she stood with the others in a hospital corridor.

A door marked MORGUE opened, and Casey stuck his head out. "Voorhees?"

"Why me?" Voorhees asked as he followed Casey through the door.

"Because you saw her better than anybody else." *Except Blake* went unsaid.

Manning's headless body was strapped to a table in a brightly-lit room. A thin man with a crooked smile stood over her, pulling on latex gloves. "I'm Doctor Zane," the man said. "Please direct any questions you may have to me, and I'll ask the deceased."

Voorhees let that one go without comment and stood silent while the doctor cut away the twitching subject's garments. Laying them open, Zane began prodding Manning's flesh with his fingertips, looking for the bite.

"Can you tell us how long she'd been infected?" Casey asked. Zane shook his head. "Infection period always varies. Still don't know why. You know what they say, though, about spiritual constitution. 'The flesh is willing if the spirit is weak.'"

"Do you really believe that?" Voorhees asked.

"It'd make perfect sense," Zane replied, "if I believed in the spirit to begin with. But since I don't, no. That's a load of crap."

One at a time, he loosened the restraints of Manning's limbs and lifted them for examination. "The real question is, if she'd been infected for long, why hadn't she told anyone?"

"Simple. She didn't want to be sealed away in quarantine to die."

"Dead is dead," Zane muttered. "I don't understand people."

"She wanted to settle her affairs," Casey suggested. "Or maybe she was just hoping she wouldn't turn. The infected aren't known for their rationality."

"Well I'll be." Zane lifted Manning's hips slightly and called the P.Os over to his side of the table.

"Fresh puncture to the left lower back," he M.E. said. "And look at this..."

He produced a pair of tweezers and carefully removed something from the small wound. "Looks like a bone fragment."

"There were bone fragments all over the place out there," Casey said.

"But that wound was small, and covered," said Voorhees. "How did bone get in there?"

"It was lodged in the meat," Zane said. "My guess is, it's part of whatever made that wound."

The room started to spin. Voorhees slammed his hands down on the autopsy table. "*Wait.*"

He stepped back, taking in the sight of Manning's nude, twitching body. Then he said, "This was a murder."

Casey gaped at him. "How?"

Voorhees pointed to the tweezers in Zane's grip. "That bone is infected. It's from a rotter."

"She was *stabbed with infected bone?*" Casey cried.

"Not bad," Zane whistled.

"You can't be serious," protested Casey. "How would the killer have known that Manning would turn on stage?"

"Maybe that wasn't the plan," said Voorhees, "or at least it wasn't *necessary* that she turn right there at the amphitheater. She could have turned anytime... at a Senate meeting, for example."

"Manning was assassinated," Casey breathed.

"And we were forced to destroy her," Voorhees said grimly.

"Hey, don't do that to yourself." Zane patted Manning's clutching hand. "Remember—they're not us. *Homo inferis*, gentlemen. No longer human."

He dropped the bone fragment into a bottle. "I'll test this for infection to confirm your theory. Good luck finding the sicko who did this."

Voorhees already had a suspect. But he knew that neither Casey nor the Senators would like it.

Maybe this would be their wake-up call. Maybe this would be the end for Meyer.

# EIGHTEEN / FALLEN

Adam awoke in flames.

He saw his charred arms and hands, black fissures brimming with fire, and began rolling frantically back and forth.

He was lying in the same street, only now it was empty. Eviscerato had taken the dead.

It was midday; he must have been smoldering for at least twelve hours. It was upon realizing this that the pain hit him in a blinding wave.

*GOD!* He could feel it throughout his entire being. From the yawning open wounds where the heat had split his skin to his very core. He writhed on the broken asphalt and screamed to wake the dead.

The scythe. The general store.

He forced himself to his knees, new pain knifing through his legs and back. It spiked through him and exploded in his brain. He couldn't see. He could only smell his burning flesh.

He fell and rolled again, rolled over and over until there was no way the flames couldn't have been extinguished; but the heat persisted, gnawing at every nerve in his body, rushing over him in waves that made his fingers splay to their widest point and his toes curl into his feet. He was a brittle, blackened shell of a being. Why hadn't they just torn him apart?

Because they were thorough. Humans always burned the undead to ash. It was the only way to be sure.

He got up again, throwing himself to the sidewalk. He just needed to get inside the store... if, in fact, they had left his scythe there.

But they couldn't touch it. It would kill them. Had they found some other way? Had the huge man pulverized it with his hammer?

Pushing through the door, Adam crawled across the floor, stopping every few feet to scream as renewed pain washed over him. Would the pain ever end? Was he capable of healing? He didn't know! *I wish I were dead!*

No. No! He couldn't think like that. This couldn't be the end, a smoking husk lying on the street in some godforsaken town that would never see life again. He had a mission. He had purpose. And he had will.

He willed himself across the floor, feeling for the blade. His fingers found it. He let out a defiant roar, channeled the pain into his throat and forced it from his lips until the walls seemed to shake.

Adam was able to stand. He limped across the store and stumbled through the door into the sun.

The Omega stood at the end of the street, shovel planted in the asphalt.

Adam pulled the straps over his arm and secured the blade as best he could. The heat still crawled through his nerves, blurring his vision. But he stood and faced his nemesis.

The Omega pulled the shovel free. Adam ran at him.

He was knocked back with a blow to the head that made his ears ring. The world spun and swam around him; he tried to regain his bearings, but-

The Omega slammed the shovel into his back and, as he doubled over, brought it down on his neck like an executioner's blade. He felt it bite into his flesh and moaned.

The rotter grabbed the crisp tatters of Adam's suit and flung him headfirst into the ground. Asphalt buckled. He was wracked with pain, paralyzed. He could only lie there and feel the shovel raining new agony down on him.

Then the Omega rolled him over and stood on his abdomen. He placed the shovel against Adam's throat. He was going to cut his head off. It was the end.

Adam summoned every bit of strength he had. It wasn't enough to move his arm, to move the scythe. The shovel pushed into his clay-like skin. It met resistance in the charred, hardened flesh. The Omega placed both hands on the back of the shovel handle and prepared to shove it through into the street.

Staring into the undead's eyes, Adam saw something. He saw something *inside*, something distinct from the rotter, something old

and hateful and familiar. It terrified him, and that terror gave him the strength he needed.

He swept the shovel away from his throat and shoved the scythe through the Omega's gut.

*It did nothing.*

The rotter pulled the blade from his innards and cast Adam's arm aside. He raised the shovel over his head.

Adam threw his legs out and knocked the Omega off balance. He got to his feet and ran.

Every footfall blinded him; every wisp of wind touching his open wounds nearly crippled him. Still he ran. Greater than the will to continue fighting, there was the will to survive. And fear was flooding his limbs to match every stab of pain.

The shovel struck him between the shoulders. He crashed into the corner of a building and rounded it, fleeing across an overgrown field. The dry grass scratched his burnt flesh and rocks dug into his bare feet. He felt the shovel graze his arm and tried to quicken his pace. Then he was falling.

He tumbled down a steep hillside and landed on a heap of scrap metal. Jagged points tore through him, skewering him there, and then he no longer had the will to do anything.

The Omega stared down at the former Death, an unmoving ruin, and was not satisfied.

*Is he really dead? How can we be sure?*

*If not, we shall take great pleasure in breaking him again. Yes, we will make his death last days; yet still he will not know a fraction of the suffering we have endured!*

*First, we need to feed. We need to find undead.*

*His time will come...*

The Omega took leave of his nemesis. He, rather they, were right—they had all the time in the world to make the Reaper suffer. Even after the world was gone, they would still have precious time.

# TALES FROM THE BADLANDS / THE WOMAN IN WHITE

Many years ago, an Army private named Briggs was separated from his unit. He spent two days wandering in the wrong direction before realizing his mistake. By then he was half-dead from exhaustion and fear.

He finally collapsed in a ravine, under a copse of trees, and lay on his back watching the sky through the leaves and waited for the end to come.

He passed in and out of consciousness, each time thinking that he was finally dying; and then the scene changed.

He was lying in a bed, a comfortable bed in a small bare room. There was a window beside his head, looking out on a well-kept lawn with a garden. He was propped up on several pillows. Glancing down, he saw a bowl of warm broth in a lap, and a spoon in his hand. Had he been eating? How long had he been here? What—

She entered the room with a pleased smile. She was wearing a hooded cloak, white as snow, and she was the most beautiful woman he'd ever seen.

Long dark hair framed delicate, soft features. Her skin was fair, flawless, and she had deep brown eyes that captivated him, rendering him speechless. He sat, frozen, as she filled the spoon, raised it to his lips and told him to swallow.

Briggs realized his tongue was no longer swollen and sore. He didn't ache of thirst or hunger at all. The tightness in his upper body was gone, and feeling had returned to his tired legs. In fact, they weren't tired at all—he felt like he could get up out of bed at that very moment.

The woman in white sensed what he was thinking and placed a hand on his chest. Warmth flowered there, spreading through his body, and he suddenly felt tranquil.

"You need more rest," she said. Her voice was like cool water. He nodded, lying back on the pillows. Not only had he been physically restored, he was also rid of the nagging fear that was a part of every man's life in these Last Days—and so, unafraid, he slept.

It was hours or perhaps days later when he awoke again. She was sitting in a chair beside the bed, prodding gently at his legs with her fingertips. "You have a lot of injuries," she said. "Some old, some new. This will take time."

"What are you doing?" He asked.

Tilting her head slightly and encircling his ankle with her fingers, she said, "Healing you."

"Are you an angel?"

"Maybe I was once."

Maybe once... but no longer, no longer cold and unreachable. Instead he was lying in her bed while she tended to a lifetime of suffering.

"I guess there is a God," he breathed.

"Of course," she answered. "He's not always here, but he's always *there*."

"Heaven?"

"I suppose so."

"What do you mean, suppose so? And *maybe* you *were* an angel?" He sat again, still amazed at his strength, and stared at her until her soulful eyes met his.

"I'm here, you're here," she said, as if it were just that simple. "I know He's there, but I don't know where there is."

He had already accepted that she was possessed of some sort of magic, but it didn't seem that either of them knew its origin. As he sat silent and watched her work on his legs, then his arms, he thought that her ability almost seemed like the antithesis to the corruption of the plague. And so he had to ask.

"Do you know about the virus? Where it came from?"

"It wasn't always a virus," she said. "It's simply an energy. It has many forms. In each, it sows only ruin because it is the very essence of chaos, and impurity—you see, it is not our God who visited this upon us—even His best-laid plans were always vulnerable to chance. A long time ago, before this universe existed, there were other gods, old ones who had never conceived of light and were only darkness. When Creation came into being, these gods fled to places unnamable—in doing so, they cast off dark energy that became ensnared in the developing existence. But even then it was not by design—it was mere chance that the energy settled here, in our world. And what is God to do?"

"What are you saying?" Briggs stammered. "That the plague is just something that happened? How can you say that?"

"We give ourselves purpose and significance, but we are as fleeting as any thought in all the cosmos," she told him. "Existence is existence. A cloud, a pebble, a person. To think that you and I are more than that is arrogance. God's love is only that—love, plain and simple. Where we end up all comes down to chance."

Her eyes glistened. "This is why I became what I am—to love as He does. Thank you for letting me do that."

She pointed out the window. "Your unit is a few miles in that direction. A storm is coming, and they've made camp. You can reach them tonight if you start now."

"But wait," he protested. "There's still so much I don't understand."

"You're not meant to," the woman said. "And neither am I."

She led him out onto the lawn, giving him his equipment and helping him pull on his jacket. "What you know now is enough for you to fulfill the purpose you've given yourself," she said. "Now go."

He turned to her, looked into her endless eyes. "I don't know how to say this..."

"I love you," she said, and kissed him softly on the mouth.

He turned back. There was a small town visible on the horizon. From it, down a long dirt road leading to the woman's cottage, shambled a lone rotter. Briggs went for his knife.

"Don't," the woman in white said. She stepped past him and extended one hand, palm out, toward the creature.

A light bloomed in her hand. Briggs had to turn away, but for one split-second he felt the heat, hotter than all of Hell; and when he looked back the rotter was gone, only a glassy streak in the road to mark its passing.

He made it back to his unit.

He rose swiftly through the ranks, known far and wide for his strength and fearlessness. Few, though, were ever told about the woman in white, and those who heard the story from others dismissed it as a fanciful rumor. Except for those others whom she had loved.

# NINETEEN / NERVES

"There's a panic spreading through the streets," Casey said, hands folded on his desk. "People think there's been an outbreak, that infected are everywhere. Senator Gillies tried to reassure them in his weekly broadcast, but I don't think anyone was even listening."

"What *did* he say?" Halstead asked. "Surely he didn't tell them Manning was assassinated."

"No. There hasn't been an official explanation for her infection. What I've heard is that, about a month ago, Manning went outside the Wall on a fact-finding mission. She could have been bitten there and concealed it."

"And you're all right with that lie being passed off as the truth?" Voorhees asked.

Casey sighed. "Would you rather that the unrest in the streets becomes full-blown pandemonium? Do you want riots? Do you want to see what it's like when crime really gets out of hand?"

"And what about the killer?"

"We're increasing security for the city admins. You'll be pulling double shifts over at the administration building. I might be forced to deputize some new men—"

"Whose men? Meyer's?"

"Don't be a fool," Casey snapped. Voorhees didn't buy it.

"We'll be devoting nearly all of our resources to this investigation," Casey went on. "When the results of that bone fragment test come back, and we've confirmed our weapon, we start there."

"How do you figure?"

"There's no way someone could have smuggled that into Gaylen. It had to have already been here." Turning to the map behind his desk, Casey pointed to the hospital. "There's a lab where they test infected tissue. It's the only source I can think of."

He turned back to Voorhees and Halstead. "You're excused. Send Killian in."

She was a wreck—red-eyed and sallow-faced from lack of sleep, her uniform rumpled. "Are you sure you're fit to work right now?" Casey gave her a sympathetic frown. "Blake was your partner—you can take bereavement leave."

"No," Killian said. "I can work. This is the job."

"Well," said Casey, opening his file cabinet, "I have something for you. You can work this one alone if you like. It's a priority case—it'd be our number one case if it weren't for what happened yesterday."

He spread a file open on his desk. "Missing girl. Here's her description. She was downtown with her parents and they lost her—think maybe someone grabbed her. Name's Lily Calvert."

* * *

Voorhees stood at the edge of the market and watched as a stone-faced Becks worked behind her counter. If only she hadn't been Blake's, if only she weren't grieving—he wanted to ask her about the layout of the amphitheater. Could there have been a passage that the killer used to slip in and out, past security? If there was, who else knew about it?

"Sorry to hear about our friend Blake."

Meyer gnawed on a bit of rock candy, surveying the market. "Poor girl over there. I think they were going to be married."

"I'm sure you're real sorry," Voorhees said in a low growl. "I'm sure you never planned on Blake getting killed. What do you call that? Collateral damage?"

"Are you accusing me of being involved with this tragedy?" Meyer appeared taken aback. "Officer Voorhees, there's a very tenuous balance between my people and your people. Why would I risk upsetting that?"

"Because you think you're untouchable. You think you run this town." Voorhees leaned in close. "Like you said, you're God here."

Meyer winked at him with a sly grin. "I did say that, didn't I? Well, I suppose you've got a point there." Sucking his candy, he continued, "But just because I *could* pull it of doesn't mean I did. I meant what I said about that balance, Voorhees, ever so delicate. And I don't think you'd want to upset it either."

"Meaning... ?"

"Imagine Gaylen without ol' Finn Meyer. Think of what these streets would look like. Think of just how difficult your job would be. My God, what a sad picture."

Meyer had smuggled guns and drugs into Gaylen. He could have gotten his hands on infected bone.

Voorhees' gaze narrowed. "You're nothing new, Meyer. There are men like you everywhere. And if you were taken out, any one of them could replace you—so don't go thinking you're too precious to be locked away and forgotten."

"What do you mean, prison?" Meyer laughed. "There's no *prison* here! They wouldn't even send me to Cleveland. You know why? Because I'd get back in, and then I'd have *all their fucking heads on pikes!*"

He stepped in close to Voorhees and snarled, "Just try to bring me in. Do it now! Slap the cuffs on me and march me out of here. You won't even make it to the street."

Voorhees nodded. "I see. Looks like I've gotten under your skin a bit, Meyer. You know that's not good. That's a sign of weakness— and among your people, that could get you in real trouble. Know what I mean? The slightest sign of weakness and all that loyalty you command is gone. Get a hold of yourself, Meyer."

Voorhees turned away before the man could reply. He strode out into the street with nary a glance over his shoulder.

* * *

Meyer called Casey on his radio.

"Did you get things taken care of with the girl?" he demanded.

"I've got one of my best working on it," Casey responded. "We'll find her."

"Haven't had one run on me in a long while," Meyer muttered. "I'll need to make an example of her."

"But before you do... ?" Casey said, an edge of desperation in his voice. *That slightest sign of weakness.*

"Sure, you can have a go at her," Meyer replied. "You'll really like this one, Casey."

\* \* \*

Dr. Zane sat before a small cage, his expression dark. He watched the rats inside; one was lying on its side, and the other was sniffing it timidly. Little white rats, pink-eyed and trembling, blissfully unaware of their world.

The rat lying down twitched. Its eyes opened. Tiny appendages grasped at the air.

It sat up and tore the other rat's throat out.

Zane had ground up part of the bone and fed it to the rat. Without the benefit of an actual lab and scientific equipment, this was all he could do to test the sample—but it was enough. He shook his head in sadness as tiny carnage unfolded before him.

# TWENTY / STRANGE PEOPLE

Adam was lying in a bed in a small white room. Blankets were tucked in around his arms and legs, and he could feel the soothing moisture of wet wraps around his burns.

The woman entered. She was the most beautiful woman he'd ever seen

Adam had not known the meaning of beauty in his former life, but he had admired (envied) Man's creativity and often was taken by simple architecture. He had spent many long hours wandering the streets of great cities where buildings more than a century old stood beside new works, contrasting the minds of then and now, structures complimenting one another and holding the Reaper in sheer awe. He loved the geometry of it. Masons had once thought geometry to be the language of God. Certain angles and curves seemed to please him more than others, perhaps appealing to his supernatural essence, and he grew to favor specific artists.

In this woman's face he saw a masterwork in flesh. Every angle and shade was exquisite in itself, and when it all came together, smooth angles framing the dark pools of her eyes... it was overwhelming.

"Stay still," she said, moving to adjust the pillows behind his head. "I don't know if I can heal you, but I'll try. It will take time."

"I... I'm not a man," he croaked.

"I know," she replied. "I'm not a woman." And she smiled at him then, and he knew that she had once borne the Reaper's burden.

He knew there had been others before him, but never had the slightest notion of what had become of them when they left their station. He'd wondered what had made them quit. He'd wondered what they looked like, which mortal myths each embraced as their guise—but he'd never imagined that someone like the woman in white could be one of them.

"It's snowing," she said. "You've been here a day and a night. For a time, I thought you were gone. What did this to you? Surely not the undead. Were they living?"

"No, no," he coughed. "It was an undead. A strange one. There's something else driving him."

"Do you have a guess what it was?" she asked.

"No." He studied her face. She just looked too... too human. Too *real*. And yet—"You were a Reaper," he said.

She nodded. "A long, long time ago. You are probably the one that took it on after me. It's been ages since I've met another. Tell me—why did you leave your post? I'm always curious."

"I'm just as curious about you," Adam said.

"Tell me yours," she said, "and I'll tell you mine."

"It was a child," he said. "I couldn't let her die. Not like that. But there was nothing I could do... then it came to me. *Quit*. Just quit. And all I had to do was *do it*, to exercise this will. That was it."

"Did you save her?"

"I think so."

"I'm glad." She pulled over a small hand-carved chair and sat beside him. "Relax your body. I'm going to try to relieve your pain."

"What about your story?"

"Patience," the woman cooed. She gently laid her hands on his belly. He gasped in pain... then it was gone.

"Civilization was young when I fell," the woman said. "And civilization, which I thought would save Man, only led to more reasons for war and greater means by which to shed blood." She massaged his legs as she spoke. "Early men fought for basic needs. Now they fought for status, influence, pride. I wept for humanity as I realized that they would only get better at harming one another."

The way she laid her hands on him was almost sedative. He forced himself to sit up straight and asked, "You said you *fell...*?"

"We are all fallen," she answered. "Those of us who are born into our stations, as we are, never to grow or change—when we *do* change, we fall and become like men. It's not as bad as it sounds.

"There was a time when I thought civilization and faith heralded the dawn of a new peace, but I was so wrong... so inhuman then. I didn't know Man as I do now."

Adam nodded. "The American government actually made the plague... I believe the power existed long before that, in some form, but they willfully created afterdead. That was when I first became aware of them. It's *how* I became aware of them, I suppose."

A small, sad smile crossed the woman's face as she looked at him.

"Adam," he said, unsure what she was searching for.

She laughed. "I didn't know you *had* a name."

"Don't you?"

"I could never settle on one. Sometimes I wish God had named me the way parents name their children. But we're not His children, are we?"

"You speak as if you know Him."

"I do, in my way. There was a time when I had memories of being in His presence—I think—but they've long since faded. Now I can only pray, and imagine, as they do."

Adam clasped her hand. "What of the afterdead?"

She told him. She told him about gods long dead and about humanity's rotten luck.

He didn't take it well.

"Not even God knows what it is or what to do about it? Then how are we to stop it? Do you even try to fight them?"

"When I must," the woman said. "I concentrate on healing. I have a hope, silly as it may seem, that one day I might heal the undead."

"It does sound silly," Adam muttered. "Ridiculous. You were the one who said the plague was without reason. That even Creation is random in nature. So how... ?"

She turned over her left hand and opened her palm. There, right in the center of her soft flesh, a seedling sprouted, green and healthy. Alive. Life from nothing.

"We are *potential*, you and I," she told him. "We're not just clay. There is still power within us, such as what you used to make your scythe... it's just a matter of channeling it.

"Once, we were simply bookkeepers, watching life come and go, observing the random. Now we are part of it."

"Remarkable." Adam touched the seedling. It curled away from his fingers, withering to dust.

"You'll learn," the woman in white said, still smiling. "You have eternity."

* * *

The Omega had returned to the hillside to find Adam gone. He broke north, drawing on all his energy until he was starving once again.

Now he crouched on a snowy ridge, watching a pack of rotters below. More than a pack—an army. Hundreds. Following a dead man who hurled brilliant flames high into the air. The Omega nearly started after him, but the voices interrupted his rapture.

*We need to eat!*

*Yes, eat... then find the Reaper!*

The Omega slipped down from the ridge.

There were several stragglers at the rear of the pack, undead with broken legs or limbs nearly rotted off. The slowest was a female walking on what looked like sticks. Sweeping through the night, the Omega swung the shovel and cleanly decapitated her.

He tore a handful of ragged meat from the stump of her neck and stuffed it in his mouth. A few of the shambling rotters glanced back, then continued on their way.

* * *

"Sleep now," the woman in white said to Adam. "Dream,"

"Of Lily," he whispered, closing his eyes.

The woman paused in the doorway to watch him sleep. It was something she couldn't do. He seemed to find happiness there, though, there in the dark.

She wondered if he'd been replaced yet.

# TWENTY-ONE / THE PACK

Nickel, who had handled the rotters in Eviscerato's circus, stayed close to the pack leader at all times. He had faithfully followed Eviscerato into undeath, and his loyalty was unchanged on the other side. The King of the Dead had no queen, of course, nor any friends among his court; but Nickel was something close to a companion. The beta zombie.

As such, he was sometimes one of the few allowed to feed alongside Eviscerato when the scraps were few. There were long periods roaming the badlands where they didn't encounter any fresh meat—only more rotters to join the ranks and increase the need for food.

Despite that frequent shortage of flesh, the pack continued to grow. Eviscerato was fiercely territorial, and he wanted every undead under his reign; he also wanted enough troops for the Great Feast, when they reached the end of the road and found all the humans in their nest up north.

His sole drive was still self-preservation, as was the case with any undead, but unlike the others, he saw past his next meal. He knew his family would outlast the ferals who survived alone.

It was true that, in the beginning, they had traveled in wagons as the old circus. It was easy so long as he could contain his minions until they had gathered the meat beneath the tent. But word spread quickly from community to community. The living told stories.

So the badlanders grew to dread the sight of Eviscerato's caravan. They would be prepared when he came. The King adapted. The element of deceit was traded for the element of surprise. The pack was growing far too large for even that now. Now they would have to rely on sheer numbers.

Eviscerato thought about these things, in his simple way, and he led his pack accordingly. Nickel always at his side, the Strongman at his back, then the rest of his freaks.

In life the Strongman had been called Jordan. An artist, he had designed all of the elaborate tattoos that adorned his massive bulk. His hammer still served the same purpose it always had—to pulverize flesh into a slick slurry—and sometimes after a meal he would sit and draw strange images in the blood that had pooled at his feet.

Claud and Chevis, the Siamese twins. They had been born into circus life. There wasn't a surgeon that could separate them, not in the badlands, and they didn't want to be apart anyway. In death they found that two mouths for one stomach was a luxury.

Thom, the many-limbed Geek, used to bite the heads off of infected animals. It was a wonder he hadn't been infected himself until Eviscerato turned him. He still liked to pull the heads off things.

Walsh had been the name of the horned Dwarf. The runt of the litter, so to speak, he was able to squeeze himself past the others in a feeding frenzy and get what little he needed. Sometimes he was able to get into a barricaded building when the others couldn't, slipping through a duct or crawlspace to ignite chaos among the living huddled inside.

Lee had juggled the fiery torches. In life, when he could spare it, he'd fill his mouth with grain alcohol and blow fireballs into the air. Now his belly was always saturated with fuel. It bled from all his orifices. He could produce a fireball at any time; it always captivated the crowd, living or dead.

The Petrified Man had been a reluctant performer, forced into the life by poverty and loneliness. A genetic defect caused his connective tissue to ossify when damaged, and the fusion of joints had led to his moniker in life. Undeath's never-ceasing dance of decay and regeneration had now resulted in ossification beyond anything seen in the living world. Murphy had been the given name of this strange man of bone; he, however, had never known it.

The Fakir had never known his name either. He was little more than a cheap imitation of the traditional Sufi mystics, but he had graduated from firewalking to feats of suffering. A human pincushion, aroused by the needles he threaded through his skin, he was also a "blockhead" with a hollow cavity in his skull that allowed him to hammer nails into his head. He'd spent his life in a haze of drugs and pain; he awoke once to find *"Regret cuts deepest"* tattooed into his flesh. Apparently he'd entreated the Strongman to ink the words in his skin. Angry at himself, he'd tried unsuccessfully to carve it out with a razor... only later would he learn the Strongman had used an infected needle. He was to become part of Eviscerato's undead family. And he held on to bitter regret until the very end. The words endured still in gray scar tissue.

This motley crew had progressed from the mindless state of the feral rotter to shrew animal intellect. But even they did not compare to the Omega, who at this moment was mingling with the rear of the pack and selecting his next victim.

Soon he would need to resume his search for the Reaper. This time, he would not walk away until the deed was done; this time he would have the strength necessary to simply tear the ghoul limb from limb. To Hell with prolonging the demon's suffering.

# TWENTY-TWO / OUT OF THE NIGHT

Voorhees was posted at the front entrance of the Gaylen City Administration Building. Halstead was in back. Two of the other officers, Ernie and Gulager, were upstairs with Senator Jeff Cullen.

"Voorhees." Halstead's voice came over the radio. "You asleep yet?"

"Nope, just freezing."

"Just you and me on this channel. Wanna talk dirty?"

He smiled and answered, "If you don't mind my chattering teeth."

"Kinky," Halstead laughed. "You're what, Voorhees, sixty?"

That was a mood killer. "Somewhere up there. I forget," he cracked. "I suppose it's still a crime to ask a woman's age."

"You've got about fifteen years on me, old timer. Be glad—you're that much closer to retirement."

"I plan to die on the job," he said. "Where would I retire to?"

"I used to live in a town called Tucson. A little hot, but beautiful."

"I've seen about enough of this great land of ours, thanks."

"But you're not happy here, are you?"

"Where else is there but here?"

"I'd like to go back to Tucson someday. See if my house is still there. It's not that far-fetched."

"Government's given up. If Tucson wasn't already a wasteland, it will be."

"I thought you had more fire in you, Voorhees. I thought you were gonna shake things up."

"I'm tired," he sighed. It was true. He'd planned to work himself to death, and that didn't seem too far off these days.

"How far back do you remember?" Halstead asked. "What's your earliest memory of the rotters?"

"My dad killed one on the front lawn when I was six. Chopped it up with an ax. Then he brought me out to help him build a fire for it. I cut my teeth early. That's how Dad wanted it, and frankly I'm grateful. That's why I don't understand the people around here— how they can act so nonchalant. Everyone has come face to face with it at some point. Everyone gets it."

"Your dad made you tough," said Halstead.

"Yeah, he did."

"And he's passed away?"

"Long time ago. Infected."

"I'm sorry."

"Don't be. That's life—that's my point."

Voorhees scanned the streets. It had been snowing all evening, and there was nary a footprint to be seen. People were all huddled around ovens or heaters or fires somewhere, huddling together, thinking *at least we're safe.*

"I had to shoot him," he said, into the radio.

"How old were you?"

"Doesn't matter. I don't think being younger or older would've made a difference. He had told me, a long time before, that the way things were going I was going to have to put a bullet in him someday. Kill him before he turned. Burn the remains. Become a man."

"Is that why you never raised a family?"

That was a leap. But she was dead on.

"If someone has to kill me," he said softly, "it'll be a stranger. Not my own son."

Halstead was silent. Voorhees pulled his coat around himself and shook the chill from his body. The radio crackled, then silence again.

"Come again? Halstead?"

No reply.

He switched channels and called, "Ernie? Gulager? Have you—"

A shout blared from the radio. *"Backup! We need back—"*

Silence again. By then Voorhees was running inside.

Down the hall, up a flight of stairs, kicking open a door to find Gulager and Ernie both lying prone in a corridor. Voorhees ran to the door beyond labeled SEN. JEFF CULLEN—CITY ADMINISTRATION. Someone shouted from within. The door was locked.

Voorhees whipped out his baton and smashed the knob to pieces. Rearing back, he kicked the door down and saw Cullen behind his desk, trying to get through another door. After him was a man dressed in black: gloves, coat, hat, even a stocking covering his face. In the killer's hand was a knife carved from bone.

Voorhees' baton spun through the air and clipped the killer's hand, sending the knife flying. The stockinged assassin looked at the cop: surprise? How had he missed the guy standing out front? Must have come through the back, taking out Halstead. Voorhees hoped she was only knocked out.

For this guy's sake, she'd better be.

Cullen scrambled through the door behind his desk. The killer retrieved the knife and sprinted after him. Feeling no pain in his adrenaline-fueled body, Voorhees vaulted over the desk in hot pursuit.

They were heading upstairs. Feet clattered loudly in the narrow stairwell, Cullen's screams bouncing off the walls. Why had he run through the damn door? No way Voorhees could catch up while on the stairs.

They hit another corridor, and Voorhees surged after the killer. Cullen was tugging at locked doors in hysterics. The killer closed in—

Then spun to swing a fist into Voorhees' jaw. He sprawled out across the carpet and shouted "STOP!!"

The killer edged toward Cullen. "You're not gonna get out of here," Voorhees said, sitting up. "Give it up now. Don't get another senator's blood on your hands."

The killer tilted his head slightly, as if considering. Then, in a grand leap, he cleared Voorhees and went for the stairs.

Voorhees snagged the killer's ankle. He went over with a cry

*A female cry*

But recovered and was off down the stairs.

Voorhees gave feeble chase. His mind was spinning. A woman? That it was a female wasn't a shock; it was that it narrowed his field of suspects considerably.

He found Ernie and Gulager sitting up and rubbing their heads. "Cold-cocked us both," Ernie muttered.

Voorhees continued down the hall and located the rear entrance. Steeling himself, he opened the door.

Halstead lay in the snow, almost peaceful, her hair matted with blood. He knelt over her and checked her pulse. She was good.

Her eyelids fluttered. "What are you doing here, Voorhees? Stop him."

"Her," he said. "And she's gone."

But she wouldn't get far.

\* \* \*

Patricia Morgan and Finn Meyer didn't exactly seem surprised to see four cops walking into their office. Feet perched on his desk, Meyer called, "What's the occasion?"

It was Voorhees who saw the bandage on Morgan's right hand. Where he would've hit her with his baton.

"What happened there?" he asked mildly, then grabbed the hand and yanked her to her feet. "I fucking burned it!" she snapped. "Let go!"

"You're under arrest for murder," Voorhees said. "And you, Finn, for conspiracy. And why not treason?"

"What in the hell are you talking about?" Meyer growled.

"We know it was Morgan. I busted her hand with my baton," Voorhees said.

Morgan snarled and ripped the bandages free. She exposed a blistered, pink patch of flesh. "*Burned* it, asshole!"

The air was sucked from the room. Voorhees' stomach dropped into his shoes.

Meyer cocked his head. "You don't look happy, friend."

Voorhees turned and stormed from the loft.

\* \* \*

Around four in the A.M., Senator Gillies was alone in his Chicago office, watching the snow fall. The city looked lovely in white, he thought.

There was a click and hiss from behind him. He turned to see Finn Meyer lighting a cigar. "You don't mind, do ya?"

"What are you doing here?" Gillies snapped.

"I've seen some interesting things the past few days, Senator. Did you know they're building an airfield outside my city?"

Gillies smiled. "Now Meyer, you didn't think we weren't going to tell you, did you? Of course, you would have found out anyway."

"Hmm." Meyer took a puff and held the smoke in his mouth. He spoke through a cloud. "You've got planes coming? Do I get a window seat?"

"Your seats are reserved, Meyer," Gillies assured him. "I have to tell you though, I don't appreciate you coming out here like this."

"I like to handle things face to face."

"Meyer—what do you know about Manning's death?"

"Just that it was a shame. Damn shame."

"I mean it."

"Me too. I hate to see a beautiful woman go rotten like that."

Meyer stepped closer with a grin. "Maybe I know something, maybe I don't. But I'm on your side. Just let me know when those planes are due... Of course, Ill find out anyway."

With that, he disappeared into the shadows, leaving only the spice of his smoke as a reminder.

Ian Gregory stepped out from the darkness. He had been less than a foot from Meyer, ready to take him down if necessary.

Gillies clenched his fists. No matter, he told himself. He had ways of dealing with bottom-feeders.

# TWENTY-THREE / THE STUFF OF BEING

"The pain that I take from others, when I heal them—I've learned to channel it through my body and direct it like a weapon. But only for protection."

The woman in white sat atop the roof of her cottage with Adam, watching a hazy sunrise. She'd given him some men's clothes to wear—not that it really mattered, but for the sake of appearing human. As he gazed at her, he found himself wondering what was under her cloak.

She caught his eye and smiled, a bit slyly. "It takes time for it all to return, but it does."

"What does?"

"The soul."

"But... I don't have a soul. I never have. Like you said, I was made a Reaper."

"Remade, really—reborn, Adam. It's complicated. I'm not trying to be cryptic. I just don't think you can handle it all at once."

"I appreciate your confidence."

"Sarcasm." She beamed at him through the gentle snowfall. "I like that. That's good."

"I dreamt about her again."

"The girl?"

"I see her covered in frost. She's terrified. I have to reach her soon."

"There's some of that power I was talking about," the woman said. "The power that still exists in you. The bond you've forged with her is unique."

"Do you think she dreams of me?"

"I think she might."

"I hope she knows I'm looking for her. She—"

"Damn." The woman in white grimaced.

"What?"

She pointed toward the sun. There were a half dozen rotters standing out in the snow.

"They come from that town, sometimes." Rising, she shook the flakes from her cloak. "This is your forte, Adam, not mine."

"I'll get the scythe."

Wearing a sweater, slacks and winter boots, Adam exited the cottage and stood on the white lawn. Though his pain had been eased considerably, he was still blackened and cracked. The clay of his flesh was hard at the edges of the yawning fissures that covered him from head to toe. He hadn't seen his face yet, but he suspected it was the same: he no longer possessed a pale, benevolent countenance but a patchwork of angry scars.

Because of them.

The rotters were a few hundred yards off. The cold seemed to have slowed them a bit, but it would not stop their hunger, and they did not yet know that they were dealing with something as inhuman as themselves.

Adam readied the scythe and beckoned.

*We're not just clay. There is still power within us... it's just a matter of channeling it.*

What power resided within this broken body of his? She said his dreams were a sign of it. How could that help him against the undead?

The first pair came at him. He sank the scythe into the side of one's head, kicking its companion back before yanking the blade free and positioning himself for another strike.

The first rotter slumped to the ground. The second took a step back. Now it knew.

It lurched at him. He threw his left arm out to knock it back, but it caught the arm and sank its teeth into him.

He shook his head. "No good." Split its face from crown to chin.

Four more and they were coming fast. He could try and take two out with one shot. He crouched, tensed.

The rotters suddenly stopped and looked up. A brilliant light swept over Adam and engulfed the undead. He saw them briefly frozen, as if enclosed in a bubble outside space and time, jaws agape—and then they simply blew away, turning to ash and dissipating before his eyes. Just like that, all four were gone.

He looked up to see the woman in white standing at the edge of the roof. "I couldn't bear to keep watching," she said.

"What do you mean?" he snapped. "You took pity on them?"

"You can't let hatred drive you," she said.

"You don't understand," he retorted. "You didn't have to serve through this nightmare. You didn't have to see all that I saw."

"I've seen all of it and worse," she shot back. "Do you know how old I am? Do you have any idea what I've witnessed? I have walked this globe a thousand times and I know things you may never learn. And I know you aren't going to last through this if it's nothing but anger driving you."

"I'm not just angry!" he roared. "*I'm afraid!*"

They both stood in silence.

"It's her," he whispered. "I don't want them to get her."

"They won't," said the woman. "You won't let them. Because that's who you are now. I'm coming down."

He waited on the lawn for her, staring into the gray sky. She touched his shoulder. "'And you are but a thought.' It's a line written by my favorite storyteller, a man named Mark Twain. And it's true. But we give our own lives meaning. She is your purpose."

She was right.

"You go through so much in these first years after the fall," she said. "But I think love is already overcoming anger."

"Then what?" he asked. "After I've found her?"

"That's up to you."

Her face grew serious. "There is one thing, however, that you must do after falling, and I don't think you have done it. You must decide on a replacement."

"I thought—wouldn't God just... make one?"

"That's not how it works, no. Like I said, you were *reborn* into this form. The stuff of your being was changed, rearranged, and you entered into your role as Reaper with no memory of what came before. But you were once human."

Adam could only stare at the woman in white. *Human?* It wasn't possible. How?

No, not how—why?

"I don't know how to answer your question." The woman just shrugged. "The agents who watch over mankind are culled from humanity itself. We rise—and then, some of us fall back down. Seems to be our nature."

"But I'm not human now. What am I?"

"If you live long enough, Adam, you might come closer to reclaiming your humanity. You've already begun the process."

That was why she was so different from him. So real... so human.

"How long has it taken you?" he asked.

"It doesn't matter. It's different for each of us."

"Is there anything I can do that I haven't done?"

"Decide on your replacement, Adam—and *live*."

He paced in the snow. "How do I know who?"

"You'll know when you know. And they'll bee ready and willing."

He asked quietly, "So it was you, wasn't it... you picked me."

"Yes, I did."

"Why?"

"Because you gave me faith in Man," she said, and went into the house.

# TWENTY-FOUR / BREAK

Voorhees walked into the hotel that served as police department and P.O. housing. He had been thinking of going upstairs and catching a few hours' sleep, but he decided to spend the afternoon in the squadroom.

There hadn't been any leads in the Manning case. They now knew beyond any doubt that someone was targeting senators for assassination, including Jeff Cullen, who had been moved to an undisclosed location. Murder by infection. It was the cruelest M.O. Voorhees had ever heard of. It said something about the killer and her agenda. Her targets may have been political, but there was a personal edge.

He entered the squadroom.

In the aisle between desks, Casey's wheelchair lay on its side.

Voorhees drew his baton and made his way back to the S.P.O.'s office. He peered inside: empty.

Heading out into the hall, Voorhees exited the department and headed for Casey's ground-level living quarters. The building was deathly silent. He wondered if any of his colleagues were upstairs. Dammit, he'd set his radio on his desk before spying the wheelchair. No time to go back for it. For all he knew, Casey was already dead.

It had to be her. He knew it in his gut. First the senators, and now cops. Likely feared they were closing in on her. But the killer had had the opportunity to kill three cops at Cullen's office, and didn't...

The door to Casey's place was barely ajar. Voorhees eased it open and stuck his head through.

The killer's back was to him. She had Casey trussed up in a desk chair and was gagging him with a towel.

Voorhees took one slow step, then another, across the room. The killer remained hunched over Casey, unaware, tightening the ropes that bound him.

The bone knife flashed into view. She raised it over her stockinged head.

Voorhees knocked it from her grip with a sharp blow, then brought the baton down over her head to lock her in a chokehold. She pushed off of Casey's chair and drove Voorhees back into the wall. He held firm, and heard her gasping for breath. "It's over," he grunted in her ear.

She stomped on his foot. The pain knifed through his leg, but he refused to let go. Instead, he tightened his grip. She was going to go to sleep.

Casey toppled over in the chair, trying to turn his head to see what was happening. The killer continued stomping and thrashing, but already she was growing weaker; and finally went limp in his arms.

Voorhees relaxed his grip.

She sprang to life. *Stupid!*

She slammed an elbow into his sternum. Suddenly his baton was in her hand and she cracked him across the face. The world was red. He stumbled wildly, flailing his arms. Another blow to the back of the head.

He caught the baton on the third strike and seized her arms. "Stop! It's over! *Give up!*"

They stumbled across the room together, colliding with the overturned chair, and they went through the window in a strained embrace.

Voorhees heard a noise like the world being torn in half as glass shattered around his head. The curtain whispered over his face. Then he was free falling, the killer sailing away from him.

Still falling. *But we're on the bottom floor.* Then, in a final thought, he remembered.

The road behind the hotel slanted sharply downward, below ground level. Kids often played there. They were safe there, in the shadow of the police department; it was into that shadow that Voorhees fell, and just before he hit, something clicked in his mind. It was a hunch, a half-formed idea. A collage of memories that resolved into something brilliant, and though it was only a hunch, in that split-second before impact Voorhees knew he was right. *It's a cop.*

Then he hit.

* * *

"P.O. Voorhees? Can you hear me?"

It was dark. His head felt thick and heavy. Drugged. But it was Dr. Zane's voice, and that meant he was in the hospital. "I thought you were the medical examiner," he croaked.

"I do a lot of things." Zane's hands prodded his stomach. "Any pain there?"

"No."

"All right, your nurse and I are going to help you sit up. Your right wrist is broken, so don't try to prop yourself up. Let us do the work."

Zane listened to Voorhees' breathing. "What's your birthday, Officer?"

"August seventeenth, twenty fifty-two."

"And what's your full name?"

"Joseph Thomas Voorhees."

"Good. In case you were wondering, by the way, your eyes are bandaged. You busted your head pretty good in that fall."

"Fall?"

"Do you remember the fall, Officer?"

"The last thing I remember is... I was going home. Where did I fall?"

There was low muttering, then Casey's voice spoke up. "Voorhees, you ran across the killer. She was getting ready to stick me when you showed up."

"I don't remember that t all."

"You both went out the window. She got away."

"Now," Zane said, "we don't yet know the extent of the damage. You're all put back together, but it's very possible that there was deeper trauma. Trauma we'd be able to scan for if we had a facility like Chicago's, but around here we've got jack shit."

"Can we send him there?" Casey asked.

"He'd be on a waiting list. Might as well work with him here. Once you're up and about, Officer, we can do some basic tests and make sure you're functioning all right."

"The fact that I can't remember..."

"Oh, I would've expected that. For now the amnesia's not a problem."

It smelled so sterile and dry. He was uncomfortable in this little bed. And he needed painkillers, lots of painkillers. He really just wanted to go to sleep.

"The others will probably stop by later," Casey said. "You get some rest. You're a hero."

He heard Casey leave. Zane was messing with something beside his head. "Think we can increase my morphine?"

"As soon as some gets here," Zane replied. "Right now you're not on anything. I'm giving you something so you can sleep through it. I guess there'll be a guard posted outside, so you can relax."

It hadn't occurred to Voorhees that he might be a target now. Somehow he didn't think so; the killer was... she was...

Off to sleep.

* * *

Tow days later, the bandages came off his eyes.

"They'll likely be very sensitive," Zane told him. "Fuzzy too. Now, I'm not going to release you back to duty, but so long as there aren't any problems getting about we'll probably send you home."

Voorhees felt the cool air reaching his eyes. He blinked. They ached terribly, as did his entire head, but it was tolerable. At least he'd no longer be an invalid.

He waited for the final layers of gauze to come off. Zane paused. "Well?"

"Well what?"

"How's your vision?"

"What do you mean?"

Fear seized Voorhees' heart. He reached up to his face. "Oh my God. Oh dear Christ."

"What is it, Officer?"

"I can't see. I can't see anything.

"I'm blind."

# TWENTY-FIVE / BAD DREAM

"Security's extra tight because of the assassination," Logan told Tripper. "It's all right though, you've got some pretty girls down there already."

The only way to get anything undead into Gaylen was for it to be brought in by the military and delivered to the lab beneath the hospital. Very rarely, a whole rotter was requested. That was Logan fudging his copy of the requisition forms. Then, when his team delivered the materials, Tripper would be waiting, and the rotter would vanish—as if it had never existed.

And so a new girl appeared in the tenement that many knew about but none spoke of.

It was part of Tripper's "honor the living" philosophy. A prostitution racket was very profitable, especially when one dealt directly in bartered goods rather than imaginary credits. But he refused to exploit human women or, worse, children. That was Meyer's game.

"So we're out of luck for a while, eh?" Tripper sighed. "Well, keep me posted. Couple of the girls are starting to look pretty rough. I need some new faces."

As Logan left the warehouse where Tripper ran a soup kitchen, a young woman P.O. could be seen approaching. "Shit," Tripper muttered under his breath.

"My name's Killian," the cop said. She handed him a piece of paper. "Have you seen anyone matching that description?"

Tripper read it over. It was Lily.

"Nope. Sorry." He handed the paper back.

"Who runs this place?" Killian peered over his shoulder, hand on her hip all businesslike. Tripper quickly said, "The church on West Avenue. This place was condemned 'til we fixed it up."

Killian nodded slowly. "Mind if I ask around about the missing girl?"

"Be my guest," he said. As soon as she was out of his face, he trudged out into the snow. It was really starting to pile up alongside the buildings and curbs. The Army wouldn't be bothered to bring a plow truck through until after Christmas.

A few blocks from the soup kitchen he quickened his pace. Ducking into a nondescript office building, he ran up the stairs to his and Cam's place.

* * *

Lily was asleep in the back bedroom, and dreaming...

She found herself in a dark cave, its length seemingly infinite, with small black candles set into recesses in the walls. Though each burned with a brilliant light, their glow did not fill the tunnel; each cast only a small halo about itself. Lily walked in an uncertain blackness.

The tunnel widened, and the walls smoothed, leaving the candles behind; now an eerie phosphorescence emanated from the blue stone surrounding her. The ceiling rose as the tunnel expanded into a great hall lined with pillars. It was freezing; she hugged her arms across her chest and proceeded forward despite a growing sense of dread.

Shadows between the pillars resolved into great bronze statues. She saw a horned, demonic thing with yawning jaws and bat-like wings; an angelic form scarred with deep cuts across its face and chest; a nude figure wrapped in chains, its expression pure malevolence. She saw a bearded man with his hands held out as if to embrace her. And finally, at the end, she saw the last statue: the Reaper.

Robes billowing about his crouched form, he clutched his scythe and peered out from under his hood with blank eyes. Lily reached out to touch his face.

The bronze cracked loudly. She jumped back, looked at her fingers; blood trickled down her palm. The fissure in the Reaper's cheek widened, and smaller cracks webbed out from it, covering his face and spreading over his body and cloak. The statue groaned. Lily stood rooted to the floor and watched.

The Reaper buckled, knees shattering, bronze splinters flying out and making tiny cuts in Lily's cheeks. The scythe cracked and fell apart, crumbling to powder. The Reaper's eyes caved in, and then his head collapsed into his torso and then the entire statue went.

It crashed to the floor with a horrific sound. Lily spun away from the shower of jagged shards. They scored her arms and legs and clattered like bits of glass on the stone floor.

He was gone. Shattered.

Lily stumbled through the remains and stood on the spot where he had been. She picked up a piece of his face. Tears streamed down her cheeks.

A long shadow stretched down the great hall and engulfed her. Lily turned, sobbing, hands trembling, and looked into a hateful, rotting face, a face hauntingly familiar; and then the shovel came down.

She awoke with a scream. Cam grabbed her, saying "It's all right, just a dream," and cradling her, even before Lily started to cry. "My friend..." she wept. "He's in trouble."

"We're all in trouble," Tripper muttered from the doorway. "The cops are looking for you, hon."

"What should we do?" asked Cam.

"I'd say disappear, but we can't. Thackeray needs us here."

"How do we know that his plan is even being carried out?"

"You herd about Manning. It's happening, babe, as we speak."

And Tripper was fulfilling his role. He had storehouses full of goods, ammunition, supplies. They'd be ready when it all came down.

Cam got up and rummaged through a dresser beside the bed. Glancing over, Lily saw something tattooed on the outside of Cam's thigh. "What's that?"

"Oh, that?" Cam tugged up the hem of her shorts, revealing the image of a skeletal green face, with one bulging eye and strange hair that stood straight up in the middle of its head. "It's from a talking picture," Cam explained, "called *Return of the Dead* or something."

"What's a talking picture?" Lily asked.

Cam smiled. "Poor kid."

"Cam's real serious about her zombie shit," Tripper said, grinning.

"Language," Cam scolded.

"Sorry, sorry." Tripper sat on the edge of Lily's bed. "I've seen this girl kill more rotters than I can count. That's why I hang out with her."

"Yeah, that's why." Cam wiggled her ass at him, then pulled a blanket from the dresser drawer. "Here sweetie. It's getting extra cold in here."

"Thanks." Lily let Cam bundle her up, then sighed. "I hope my friend is okay."

"What's his name?" Cam asked.

"Death."

The two adults glanced at one another. Then Tripper shrugged. "Fair enough."

"I guess we're all pretty well acquainted with death these days," Cam mused.

"Yeah," Lily said. "He let me ride his horse."

# TWENTY-SIX / AWAKENING

"Too bad about your eyes, friend," came Finn Meyer's voice.

Voorhees sat bolt upright in his hospital bed. He heard Meyer sauntering across the room. "I hear they don't expect you to recover. Shame."

"Get the fuck out of here," Voorhees snarled.

Meyer laughed. "You won't presume to tell me what to do anymore, Voorhees. You're finished. If you're lucky they'll set you up in one of my slums and you can rot away there. If you're not lucky... well, there's always room in Cleveland.

"Do you know about Cleveland?" Meyer asked. He was standing right beside Voorhees. If the cop wanted to, he could grab the bastard and wring his neck right now.

"Cleveland's where we send all the rubbish," said Meyer. "It's outside the Wall. Not many people know that. Casey does. Cullen does.

"See, we're on the same side, myself and those fellows. The system works. And those who threaten it... well, we have ways of dealing with them. Discreetly."

Voorhees took a swing. Meyer must have seen it coming, stepped back. "You want to be stupid?" the thug snapped. "Fine. You'll see, Voorhees. You're done!"

Meyer stomped out of the room. Voorhees threw the sheets off himself and stumbled out of bed, fumbling to the door and out into the hall. "Nurse!" he barked. "Nurse!" He was getting the hell out of here.

A hand grabbed his elbow. "What are you doing?" Halstead exclaimed.

"Leaving," he said. "I need my clothes."

"They're in your room," Halstead said, pulling him down the hall. "C'mon, I'll help you."

Once back in the room, she said, "Look, Casey's putting you on paid leave until this is all sorted our."

"You mean, until they take my job from me? Until I'm thrown to the wolves? Forget it. Meyer is behind these attempted killings and I'm bringing him down."

"How? Voorhees..."

"Yeah, I know. I'm a cripple. Well, I'll be goddamned if that stops me. Seems like I'm the only one who gives a shit about what's wrong with this town."

"You're not." She touched his hand. "But you can't just storm in there and arrest everyone. They're protected. Even if you could prove it... it's going to take something else."

"I do things by the book," Voorhees said. "Give me my damn clothes."

He quickly dressed himself, no regard for her presence, and felt his way back out into the hall. "Where do you think you're going?" Halstead yelled.

"I'm going to work," he shouted over his shoulder. "You can help me or you can stay out of my way!"

He pressed against the wall and moved forward. Couldn't tell if there was a damn thing in front of him. All that talk about the other senses compensating for loss of sight was bullshit. He *was* a cripple.

She took his arm. "This way to the stairs."

She led him through a door and held onto him as they slowly descended. "Thank you," he said quietly."

"Don't thank me," she replied. "I don't deserve a partner like you, you know that?"

He patted her hand. "Yeah, I'm a pain in the ass."

\* \* \*

When they entered the squadroom, he heard voices fall silent. Halstead led him to his desk, and he sat down.

"Well, I'm back," he announced. Still no one said anything.

Casey's wheelchair, crossing the room. The S.P.O. cleared his throat and said, "I think Halstead told you you're on leave. Why don't you go home? Were you even supposed to leave the hospital?"

"Your breath smells like candy," Voorhees said.

"What?"

"Officer Voorhees really wants to work this case," Halstead said. "Even if it's only from his desk—"

"Not your call," Casey interrupted. "Voorhees, Halstead will take you up to your quarters."

"What's your game?" Voorhees asked. "Are you part of it, Casey? Is that why the killer came for you? Taking care of loose ends?"

"What in God's name are you talking about? Halstead, get him out of here!"

"You want me out, Casey, you take me out."

"Don't make me suspend your pay!"

"You think I care about—"

Two desks behind Voorhees, unseen to him, but horrifyingly clear to everyone else—Killian rose from her chair with a guttural moan. Her dead eyes locked onto Gulager, and she ran at him.

Gulager fell backwards over his desk, swinging his baton wildly. Ernie threw a chair into Killian's path. She jumped it and headed in his direction. "Oh God!" he cried.

"What the hell?" Voorhees yelled, standing. Had a fight broken out?

"Killian's turned!" Halstead said, drawing her baton and catching Killian in the mouth. The undead went down hard, smacking her head against the floor, but rose unfazed and grabbed Halstead's arms. They staggered back into Voorhees. He fell to the floor.

"*Help me!*" Halstead screamed. Voorhees heard her baton clatter on the floor. Everyone was shouting now, in a panic, unable to act. He yanked open the top drawer of his desk and grabbed something from under a pile of papers.

"Where is she, Halstead?" he yelled.

They had fallen onto his desk. Killian had Halstead pinned and was trying to bite her wrists. "She's right above me! Your twelve!" Halstead screamed.

Voorhees reached out with his left hand. He touched Halstead's hair, her arm. He followed it up to Killian and seized her by the hair.

"I'm sorry," he muttered, and swung the widowmaker.

It cleaved Killian's face in two. Halstead swung her head to the right as gore spilled from the yawning wound.

Killian stumbled off of the desk and stood in the aisle, the two halves of her skull slowly pulling away from one another, her gibbering silenced. She swayed, then dropped with a thud.

"What the FUCK?" Ernie yelped.

Voorhees set the widowmaker on his desk and swallowed a deep breath. Adrenaline coursed through him. Casey grabbed his trembling arm and said, not without a bit of awe, "You killed her."

"That's what widowmakers do," Voorhees said.

""Look at this," Halstead gasped.

"What is it?" Voorhees asked.

"In Killian's desk... it's a knife, made from bone."

"It was Killian?" Casey exclaimed.

"She must have accidentally cut herself," Voorhees said.

"Maybe it wasn't an accident," said Halstead.

"God," Casey sighed. "Assassins. Terrorists. There must be more to this."

"We'll find out if there is," Voorhees said.

"All right," Casey said. "You can have your desk after it's cleaned up."

Halstead picked the brains from her coat. "I'd better get to the hospital."

"You'll have to be quarantined."

Voorhees caught Halstead's hand as she passed him. "You'll be okay."

"I know," she said. He heard the smile in her voice.

# TWENTY-SEVEN / THE BLOOD OF ANGELS

"Who was I?" Adam asked the woman in white.

"In all honesty, I don't remember," she said. "But does it matter? You're still you."

"So I'll never know?"

"What would it affect if you did?"

Adam was silent for a moment. They were seated in the front room of the cottage, before a crackling fireplace. Outside, snow was coming down in torrents.

"I dreamt of her again," he said. "She was frozen... she looked pale as a corpse. I don't think these things have come to pass, not yet—but I feel powerless."

"Adam, that *is* your power," the woman in white said. "Precognition. You can till save her.

"You should go," she said, standing up. "I don't want to keep you any longer. Just trust your instincts. You'll find her."

He nodded and rose to stand beside her. "Thank you for everything."

A window shattered somewhere in the house.

Adam snatched up the scythe and strapped it onto his forearm. A terrible feeling permeated his being; he felt weighed down, weak, and suddenly he knew it was the Omega's presence. For the first time he sensed the ties that bound them, the ties that had allowed the rotter to stalk him across the badlands for months.

This time with the woman in white had awakened his mind, brought dormant abilities to life. He wondered if she was clairvoyant too; had she known where to find him? Had she seen all this in her mind's eye?

"It's the one who attacked me," Adam whispered to the woman in white. "You have to get out of here."

"You said something else was driving him," she breathed. "What did you mean?"

"I mean he's not like the others." Adam edged toward the door leading to the hall. "There's something inside him, controlling him."

"Adam." She caught his shoulder and turned him to face her. "Sometimes the dead are angry. Sometimes they don't understand why it was their time. They blame God, or they blame themselves... sometimes they blame Death."

Just as he began to realize what she was saying, the Omega leapt through the front window with a horrendous crash, landing right behind them. Icy air blasted their faces as they whirled to face him. The woman spun, fire blooming in her open hand; the Omega swung his shovel down and hacked it off at the wrist.

The woman screamed. Adam swung the scythe into the Omega's leg. The rotter responded by slamming his shovel into Adam's gut. He kicked his legs in agony as he was lifted off the floor. Pulling the scythe free, he slashed the rotter across the throat. Black blood sprayed from the ragged wound.

With her remaining hand, the woman grabbed the Omega's head and sunk her fingers into his left eye. He shook his head frantically, losing his grip on the shovel. Adam fell, prying himself off of its blade.

The rotter turned on the woman in white. Raising the shovel over his head, he drove it like a spear into her breast. She sagged, eyelids fluttering. He was *killing* her.

The scythe exploded through the Omega's ribs. Adam turned the blade sharply to the right and raked it through the rotter's black guts. Ichor spewed from the undead's mouth. Throwing the Omega into the wall, Adam fell upon him, hacking flesh away from bone, the rumble in his throat building to a roar that blurred his vision. All he saw was his blade coming down again, and again, and dark chunks of meat spattering the walls.

Adam collapsed in a heap, exhausted by his rage. The Omega was a ruin. The rotter gnashed his teeth, staring at the ceiling as he tried to gather his spilled guts. As Adam watched, the thing's trembling hands fell motionless.

He crawled over to the woman in white, lying on her back, eyes barely open.

"I'm sorry," he whispered, touching her face, her beautiful face, looking into her glistening dark eyes. He felt something welling up in him, and choked; his vision blurred again, this time from grief, and he felt wetness spreading beneath his eyes.

His tears fell on her cheek. She blinked and looked up at him. "Adam?"

"I'm so sorry," he wept.

"Don't be." She took his hand, his ugly, charred hand, and said, "I love you."

He buried his face in her neck. She sighed, and then he was alone. Snowflakes swirled around their prone forms.

Adam staggered to his feet and crossed the room to where the Omega lay. He knew it was still in there; the blue spark of undeath still resided in those rotten bones. He was still in there, while she was gone.

Adam drove the scythe through the rotter's face and into the floor. He fell to his knees and screamed, "*WHY HER?*" He forced the blade deeper. "*WHY? TELL ME WHY?*"

There was no answer from the Omega. It was just a rotter, after all, dead and dumb. Just a rotter that had killed a woman.

He pulled the scythe out and sat back on the floor.

*Lily.*

Something about the woman in white had reminded him of Lily. He couldn't place his finger on it. He only knew that he wouldn't— couldn't—let the same fate befall the child.

# TWENTY-EIGHT / MEMORY

There was a knock on Voorhees' door. He dragged himself out of bed and limped across his quarters.

He'd already started to get used to the blindness, at least as far as mobility was concerned. He knew the layout of his place and could move about with confidence. He'd tried counting his steps at first, but it was easier just to trust his gut.

How much longer would he be a cop? Casey was being supportive now, but Voorhees suspected the man didn't have a strong sense of loyalty. He was part of the problem. No, Voorhees would be out on the streets soon enough—Meyer's streets—and what prospects did he have then? He'd been a cop as long as he could remember. A damn good cop, even blind, but they wouldn't see it that way.

*Goddamn you, Killian.*

He leaned against the door. "Who is it?"

"Halstead."

He opened the door, and she took his arm. "I need you to come see this."

*See.* "What is it?"

"Stir-fry and rice."

She led him to her place and sat him down at a table in the front room. The smell was mouth-watering. He heard her pouring something, and she placed a wine glass in his hand. "Two thousand California merlot. Just uncorked it a few hours ago."

"This is illegal, isn't it?"

"Hence why it's in police custody. Try it."

She guided his hand to his fork and napkin. "I figured stir-fry would be easy for you to eat. Might be a little messy, I guess. Don't sweat it."

125

"I didn't know you cooked, Halstead." Voorhees carefully lifted a mouthful to his lips.

"My dad taught me to cook," she said. "He made sure I could take care of myself. That was life in the badlands."

"Tucson."

"Right. I had a big family. My folks and I lived with two uncles and aunts and three cousins. We actually used to play outside. Can you believe that? Huge fenced-in yard with a clear view of all the roads. If any rotters appeared on the horizon, one of my uncles would be sitting on the roof and blow their heads clean off. He'd call down to us whenever he spotted one. 'Two o'clock!'" She laughed softly. "Those were the best years of my life."

"What finally brought you north?"

"Same reason as everybody else," she said. "I lost everything."

"I'm sorry."

"You don't have to say that. I know."

They ate in silence for a few minutes. He heard her refilling her glass. "We were attacked one night," she said. "From a distance, they looked like badlanders—they even carried torches. They had a caravan drawn by dead horses. They surrounded the house, lining the fence. By the time we realized they were undead they'd already thrown the torches. The house was on fire.

"They just waited. They could have brought the fence down and stormed the house, but they smoked us out. Then they came for us."

She sighed, long and loud; trying to hold back tears. "My cousin and I were the only ones who got away. My cousin Will. We managed to survive for a few weeks in the desert before the infection took him."

She drained her glass again. "He was the first rotter I killed."

"Sor—" Voorhees stopped himself. Instead he asked, "It was a caravan. You mean like the old King of the Dead legend?"

"It's no legend," she said quietly.

Another moment of silence. Voorhees scraped his plate to make sure it was clear. "Well, I can't eat any more."

"Neither can I. But I could use another drink. You?"

"Sure."

She topped off his glass. "Here's to looking forward instead of back." And she clinked her glass against his.

Suddenly he remembered going out the window; shards of glass tinkling in mid-air, Killian flying away from him. He remembered thinking *it's a cop* before he hit the street.

He remembered he hadn't thought it was Killian.

Killian, like Casey, like Blake, like all the others, believed in the system. No, he had only one sympathetic ear when he complained about the state of things.

He reached his left hand across the table. She touched it gently. He seized her fingers, and she gasped in pain.

"Did I break any of them? When I hit you with the baton?" he asked.

She rose from her seat and he rose with her, snatching her other arm and pulling her to him. He wrapped her in a cruel embrace. "And you must have hurt your back when you fell. Did you?" He shook her roughly.

She cried out. "Stop!"

"Was it worth it?" he shouted. "Was it worth killing Blake and framing Killian? Was it worth *blinding me?* Did you get what you wanted? Huh?"

She tried to break free, but he held her like a vise. "I didn't want to hurt anyone else!" she said. "I tried not to hurt any cops—you know that!"

"I know you fucking failed! Miserably!" He threw her to the floor and swept the dishes from the table. "What's it all about? Destabilizing the government? Throwing the people into a panic? Destroying Gaylen? Is that how you're going to fix things? You goddamn fool!"

"You don't understand!" she cried. "There are people all over the city preparing for this! People in *every* city! We're going to bring down the Wall and give America back its resources—it's about saving the rest of the country, Voorhees!"

"You're out of your mind!"

"Undead like the King are going to flourish out there if we just seal ourselves up in here and pretend the badlands don't exist! They'll come for us! They'll be the ones to bring it all down—do you want that?"

*"I WANT MY FUCKING SIGHT BACK!"*

She was backpedaling across the room, toward the door. He broke into a run. She screamed and swung a fist into his jaw. He didn't feel it. He didn't feel any of his aches or bruises. He was on fire. He grabbed her, and she tore at the bandages on his head. He slammed her against the door like a rag doll. Finally, they both fell, entangled in one another.

"You don't understand! I can show you!" she was wheezing.

"You *will* show me," he growled. "You're under arrest. And you're taking me to the others."

He pulled the handcuffs from his belt and snapped them tight on her wrists. "Do you have a gun?" he asked.

"W-what?" she stammered.

"Don't give me any bullshit. Do you own a gun?"

"Yes."

"I want it. And I want your radio."

\* \* \*

Adam pulled the woman in white's cloak over his shoulders, the hood over his head. He stood in the shattered front window of the cottage and stared into the snowy wasteland that awaited him.

With her cloak and his blackened flesh, he looked like a negative image of his former self. He felt just as different. With his growing sense of identity came confidence.

He looked back at the woman's body, covered by a blanket, cold and still. *I'll honor you.*

Then he climbed outside.

# TWENTY-NINE / THE GOOD NEWS

The British were coming.

They had agreed only to send one plane, carrying an assessment team, but it was enough. Gillies only hoped that the weather wouldn't get any more severe.

The airfield was close enough to completion. The workers had been sent home, and the plane would be touching down at dawn. The senator already had his affairs in order, and was ready to bid farewell to the Great Cities.

He'd always known that collapse was inevitable, with the military having lost the war in the badlands and the undead multiplying every day. They had maintained the cities long enough to get the airfield done and get the British on their side. And Britain was the Promised Land.

In their radio communications, the Brits reported that "the others" were all but extinct, and though the casualties had been steep, they'd won their war. So they would send their team across the Atlantic to see the so-called Great Cities, and the senators would return with them to Britain, under the premise of studying their strategies against the undead.

Then they would seek asylum. Forget about America. Leave it to the rotters.

He loved his country, he did, and by God he had tried to save it—but that was just it, wasn't it? By God, by His will, a nation of sin and excess had been condemned and there was nothing any man could do about it. On to greener pastures.

"We'll be leaving on the plane tomorrow," he told Ian Gregory as they rode to the airfield in an armored Humvee. "I should like you to accompany me. You'll be the only member of my detail to do so."

Gregory stared at him in confusion. "Leaving... ?"

"It's over here, Ian. You and I are men of God. We understand. You do *get it*, don't you Ian? He's already left. Anyone in their right mind would. Our work, yours and mine, isn't done."

"We're going to England? We're staying there?"

"That's right."

"What about the cities? The people?"

"A day won't go by that I don't mourn them," Gillies intoned, hands clasped. "But I'm not going to sacrifice myself for a failed cause."

Gregory sat back, a frown creasing his brow. This didn't make sense, not at all. To run from the battle... it went against every instinct in his body. He couldn't do this. Yet he felt he had no choice; he was already hurtling down the course, hurtling towards a dark end.

* * *

Halstead knocked on Tripper's door. Voorhees pressed the muzzle of her .45 into her back.

Tripper opened the door. "What are you doing here?" Then he saw the balled scarf gagging her mouth.

"Inside," Voorhees said, revealing the gun, and pushed his way in.

He slammed the door shut, holding onto Halstead's arm, then positioned himself behind her and pressed the barrel of the gun into her throat. "Don't try anything. Either of you." He'd heard a chair scrape when they entered, meaning there was a second person in the room; and as Tripper said, "Okay, okay. Stay there Cam," Voorhees knew his bluff had worked. They didn't know he couldn't see. He'd be goddamned if he couldn't still do his job.

"Calm down, man," Tripper said. "You a cop?"

"That's right. And who are you?"

"I'm nobody," Tripper said.

Voorhees scowled. "Are you the one behind this? Or are you just another hired killer? Answer me!"

Halstead struggled against him. He pressed the gun hard into her neck. "TALK!"

"Mister Voorhees?"

The girl. Lily. What... ?

He was distracted for only a second, but it was all Halstead needed. She slammed her elbow into his ribs and spun away from him. Grabbing the gun with one hand, she tore the scarf from her mouth with the other and spat "He's blind!"

They fought for the gun. She slugged him in the head. He groaned, crashed against the wall; then the gun slipped from his grip. He threw his hands out and yelled, "No!"

Halstead clipped his temple with the butt of the pistol. He slumped to the floor.

"No! Don't hurt him!" Lily again. It was the last thing Voorhees heard before fading out.

\* \* \*

The Humvee stopped at the fence surrounding the airfield. A plainclothes guard nodded to Gillies and waved them through.

A cadre of vehicles was already gathered at the edge of the landing strip: the other senators, all having abandoned their posts to await escape.

As Gillies got out of the Hummer, he saw a young man and woman walking across the tarmac. He didn't recognize either of them. Security? No. Trouble.

"Senator?" The man extended his hand. "Jack Calvert."

"How did you get in here?" Gillies snapped.

"I was part of the construction crew," Calvert said. He hugged the woman against him. "This is Molly."

"What are you doing here?"

"Well Senator, see, the thing is—I know why you're here. I know there are planes coming. And we'd like to go too. We have credits—ninety-five hundred credits. Our savings."

The Calverts looked hopefully at the Senator; a young couple trying to make it in a brutal world, willing to surrender all they had for a second chance.

Gillies laughed.

"You must be joking. Credits don't mean a thing where we're going."

Jack Calvert's face went white. "But..."

"Have you told anyone else about the airfield?" Gillies asked.

"No, no!" Jack insisted. "It's just me and Molly."

Gillies nodded and turned to Gregory. "Kill them."

"What?" Gregory held out his hands. "Senator—"

"Somebody kill these trespassers!" Gillies shouted. The other senators and their people looked over. Jack and Molly Calvert began to back away, sputtering. "We'll go. We'll just leave. We won't tell anybody." Jack shook his head frantically. Molly was clinging to him, wide-eyed.

One of Senator Cullen's bodyguards drew a gun.

"Run, Molly!" Jack screamed.

They took off across the tarmac, hundreds of yards from the fence, nowhere to hide, just running and screaming, still begging for their lives even as the first bullet punched through Jack's leg. He kept running, told Molly to keep running, saw her head jerk forward and blood arc through the air.

He broke down in sobs as he limped past her, straining every muscle in his body, and still hundreds and hundreds of yards from the fence.

Jack turned. He started back toward Molly. He cried her name, though he knew she was dead. He just wanted to pick her up and take her away from this. He wanted to undo it all. He'd take poor Lily back, he'd go home. He was willing to take it all back—couldn't he take it all back?

The guard shot him in the throat. He slumped to the ground and crawled toward Molly. He could no longer speak her name. His strength was leaving him in gouts. If only he could touch her again, her face, her hair. If only he could tell her he was sorry.

He almost made it.

# THIRTY / DEAD TO RIGHTS

It was nightfall and the snow was still coming down. Dalton was climbing down from his post on the wall, rifle slung over his shoulder. The dogs had started baying inside the guard post. They'd been in there for a few hours and were probably going mad from the confinement. But he didn't want them running around in this weather at night. They'd just have to put up with it; but at least he could give them some chow and calm them down for a while.

When he opened the door, the dogs ran past him to the gate and began pacing in front of it, making high-pitched whimpers.

They sensed something. Dalton dropped the rifle into his hands and approached the gate. "Back. Get back."

What could they possibly be on to? Maybe they did just want out after all. But his instincts were sharp, too, and their behavior told him something was wrong. Dalton unlocked and unbolted the gate, muttering into his radio. "Section nineteen, going out for a quick look around."

He peered through a pair of binoculars and scanned the horizon. Nothing but falling snow on a flat plain. All the trees and foliage had been cut away to provide a clear view. Not a damn thing.

He turned and saw the dogs backing away from the gate. Kneeling, he patted his knee and called, "C'mere! What is it? You're gonna have to show me."

He looked back toward the badlands. Hard to be sure whether or not there was anything out there. He took another look with the binoculars. Nope, not a thing.

Wait. A tiny black shape moving on the horizon. Then another, and another. Then dozens.

Dalton backed through the gate and slammed it shut. He barked into the radio, "Section nineteen! I need backup here... got either badlanders or rotters rushing the gate!"

The dogs already knew which it was. They leapt about him in a panic. He could see nothing but wild terror in their eyes.

"Go," he said, waving them off. "Get the hell out of here!" They didn't have to be told twice.

His radio crackled. "Nineteen, do you have a visual?"

"Hold on." He climbed the ladder and stood atop the Wall. He saw a storm of ragged figures surging toward him. He heard their moans on the wind. There were hundreds, hundreds! Their numbers stretched as far as he could see.

Then a huge rotter broke through the ranks, swinging a hammer over his head, and the gate was blown off its hinges.

Dalton dropped onto his stomach, gasping

"Rotters!" into his radio. He started crawling along the Wall, but grim dread weighed his limbs down and he knew there was no point. He was alone in a sea of undead. And they'd already seen him.

Something was clambering up the ladder. He sat up, shaking, and took aim.

\* \* \*

*Devour her!*

*Get up, now—consume her flesh! We need her power!*

*GET UP!*

The Omega could barely move his fingers, let alone move across the room—but the voices screaming in his head urged him on, and slowly, painstakingly, he began tugging his mutilated corpse across the floor.

It was the consumption of the Reaper's flesh that had thrown open the gates of Hell, had let them into this simple creature's mind—they, the dead, the damned, untold millions who had passed on under Adam's watch and who blamed him for their ultimate fate. Murderers, rapists, the architects of atrocities that had shaken entire nations. Masters of terrorism and genocide, they had found themselves cast into a dark abyss where there was no peace, no rest, only bitter suffering. And it was because of him—Death!

So, although there was nothing in this world or the next that could free them from the abyss, they would at least have their revenge against Adam. They would tear him apart.

The Omega pulled the blanket from the woman in white's nude form and began clawing at her pale flesh. She was strange—half human, half something else entirely—but there was still power lying dormant in her being and they would have it. They pushed the Omega on, as he filled his hands with bloodless flesh and lifted them to his broken mouth.

He swallowed her. She filled him. He stiffened and began to shake.

His body thrashed on the floor and fresh blood, rich red blood, began pouring from the many wounds Adam had given him. And then the wounds, like mouths, began to close.

He threw his head back and vomited into the air. Maggots and bile splattered on the floor around him. All of the corruption was leaving him. The meat of the undead had only a fraction of this effect! New life was surging through the Omega, regenerating him in a matter of moments—and then he collapsed.

*VENGEANCE SHALL BE OURS!*

*Our Legion is now unstoppable—never again will he leave us in ruins—this time we shall destroy him!*

Their cries echoed through the Omega's mind. He struggled to his feet. Newfound strength bore him out into the night.

*Long live the new flesh!*

\* \* \*

"It's all right. I won't hurt you."

Adam faced a young white horse. It had been standing alone in this field, grazing, probably separated from an infected family. It eyed him cautiously as he approached.

He stroked its head and whispered, "You're safe with me." The horse stood still as he pulled himself onto its back.

To the Great Cities. To Lily.

# TALES FROM THE BADLANDS / CLEVELAND JOE AND THE GHOSTS OF THE OLD GODS

P.O. Billy Rhodes was charged with removing the undesirables from Gaylen. He knew the truth about Cleveland, that it was a hellhole situated outside the Wall, populated only with the worst of the worst. He didn't much care. Made his day job a lot easier getting the trash off Gaylen's streets. Kept the hookers cleaner too.

The guy in the cage, handcuffed in the back of Rhodes' SUV, looked like a filthy mother. Name was Jarrett Willows. Apparently the guy had seen some bad shit go down back East and had lost his marbles. He'd been picked up in downtown Gaylen, preaching from a street corner about some gibberish that Rhodes couldn't understand.

The perp was doing it now—muttering "*Ia, Ia,*" under his breath and rocking in his seat. It was creeping Rhodes the fuck out. He slammed his fist against the cage separating them. "Shut up, Willows!"

The long-haired transient stopped rocking and looked at Rhodes in the rearview mirror. His eyes were wide and bloodshot. Crazy. Smoothing his mustache in the mirror, Rhodes tried to make like he was ignoring the kid—Willows was only in his mid-to-late twenties—but he couldn't break eye contact.

"The old gods left the plague here," Willows rasped. "This world's nothin' more than a toilet. They shat their voodoo all through the aether and disappeared from this place, never to return. We're just insects crawling around in a toilet, you get it? Some of 'em are fat flies but they still eat shit!"

Willows dragged his long nails through his hair and glared at Rhodes. The P.O. focused on the road ahead. "I thought I told you to shut the fuck up."

"You don't *get* it." Hooking his yellow nails in the wire of the cage, Willows leaned forward and said, "Their magic is still here. It still responds to the old words. Words long forgotten, but I found 'em—in the books in the forgotten places, I found the words."

God, his breath stank of sour mash and rotting teeth. Rhodes pounded the cage again. "Get back!"

"The new god calls it blasphemy. He just don't want anyone to learn the words, you see, to be able to call on the magic. He calls it evil. Ain't no such thing. Good and evil are social constructs! Feh! Feh!"

Damn fool had almost started to sound lucid for a moment. Rhodes had seen worse, though. Yep, Cleveland was full of nasty motherfuckers. Jarrett Willows was going to have his hands full once he arrived in his new home.

"*Ia! Ia!*" Willows laughed. "I found the books in a library in old Massachusetts. I knew, soon as I laid my eyes upon 'em, what I had. Something strange and wonderful—feh! Evil? Feh! Fuck"

He lowered his head began speaking softly, almost reverently. Well, at least he wasn't talking to Rhodes anymore.

They were on the outskirts of the city. It was twilight; smoke rose into the sky above dark buildings. The fires had probably drawn some rotters into town. Things weren't going to be very pleasant. Rhodes figured he'd drop Willows off at the first intersection.

"Your people knew the old words," the man whispered.

"What do you mean, my people?" Rhodes snapped.

"The niggers, I mean."

Rhodes spun and smashed his fist into the cage. Willows jumped in his seat and threw his hands in front of his face, shrieking, "Blacks! Blacks!"

"I am blacker than black, motherfucker," Rhodes snarled, "I'm fucking Billy Rhodes and I will tear your fucking throat out if I hear one more word out of you. Got me? Huh?"

Willows nodded, cowering. He lowered his head again. Before long, he was whispering his gibberish, but Rhodes didn't feel like bothering with him anymore.

"*Ia! Ia!*"

Rhodes pulled over to the shoulder and killed the engine. "All right. I'm done with this shit. You're home, psycho."

Getting out of the car, he scanned the city ahead for any signs of trouble. Bastards sometimes tried to sneak up on him, to get the car. He'd popped more than a few highwaymen in his time—far more than he ever listed in his incident reports.

They called him Cleveland Joe, those who knew what he did, and he had a no-bullshit reputation that the people around here unfortunately didn't seem to be aware of.

Drawing his Glock, he opened the back door. "Out, Willows."

The loon just sat there, head bowed, unmoving. Was he trying to pull some kind of trick? Rhodes stepped back and pointed the gun at the prisoner. "I said *out*."

Jarrett Willows looked up. A cluster of tentacles unfurled where his face had been, pushing his filthy hair aside and stretching toward the cop.

Rhodes screamed and emptied his clip into the figure, stumbling backwards as he did so. Willows jerked violently in the car and fell over on his side.

"Shit! SHIT!" Rhodes dumped the empty clip and reloaded. What in the blue fuck had that been about?

He looked up to see Willows standing outside the car, his hair again covering his face.

He let out a hideous squeal, and his chest split down the middle—his sternum coming apart in an eruption of blood, ripping open his shirt and turning it crimson.

His arms shot straight out and his fingers clawed at the air. His yawning torso gurgled, then spread wide—and *it* emitted the nightmarish squeal Rhodes had heard. A dozen black tentacles lashed out, and something hit Rhodes in the chest with a wet splat.

He looked down to see a heart beating its last beat on the ground.

Rhodes broke into a run. He wasn't stupid. If a full clip hadn't done the job, there was no sense in sticking around. He'd have to hope that he was able to lead the monster away from the SUV—and then that he could make it back to the vehicle in one piece.

Passing a burnt-out warehouse, Rhodes stayed in the shadows, running across an intersection and toward an alley.

"Hey, copper!" An old man in rags flipped him off.

"Get the fuck outta here!" Rhodes barked. The man dismissed him with a wave of his hand.

Entering the alleyway, Rhodes realized he'd boxed himself in. Shit! He wasn't going to make this his last stand. Had to turn back.

Then the old man's screams reached his ears.

He moved along the wall, slowly, toward the mouth of the alley. The geezer's cries were choked off, and it grew deathly quiet.

Maybe the monster would be too busy to go after Rhodes. He could make a break for it.

He stepped out to see a desiccated rotter tearing into the old man's neck. It was too late for the poor bastard. Rhodes decided to head down the street, away from the intersection.

Before he could, something snapped through the air and wrapped around the zombie's head—jerking the rotter away from the old man and hurling it into the side of the warehouse.

It was Willows—or it had been, once. His torso was now closed—threaded with tentacles like stitches sewing him up. More tentacles were coiled around his legs, walking his forward. And his face—

He had no face. The thing inside him had turned his head inside out. His exposed brain pulsated in a nest of tentacles.

Rhodes took aim at the brain and fired three rounds. Chunks of gray matter flew away from the fiend's head, but it showed no reaction. Then... it stumbled. Staggered. It was losing it!

It fell to its knees beside the old man's body and clawed at his head. Rhodes realized what was happening and shot the fucker's hands, but they kept working at the geezer's scalp, peeling it away, then cracking his head open like a walnut—

And ripping his brain out to plant it in place of Willows'!

"All right motherfucker!" Rhodes reloaded. Last clip. Had to make this count. There weren't any other brains around except his. As long as he could cripple the bastard he was home free. He hoped.

The monster lumbered toward him, arms outstretched. The tentacles in its head flowered, waving lazily in the air. Rhodes stood his ground. Had to let it get close. Had to be sure.

The thing made an excited squeal. That was close enough.

Rhodes dumped all every last round into its stolen brain, pulverizing it, sending the creature reeling. The tentacles in its chest pulled free and swung around, as if in desperate search of something with which to repair itself. The straining appendages found no purchase. Billy Rhodes was already hauling ass down the street.

Old words. Old magic. Old gods.

In a world where the dead walked, anything was possible. Perhaps even something worse than what Willows had become.

From that day forward Billy Rhodes slept with one eye open and his Glock under his pillow.

# THIRTY-ONE / SOLDIERS

Three burn teams arrived in refurbished Jeeps to find hundreds of rotters clambering through the destroyed gate at Section Nineteen. All was chaos; they ran in every direction, the slavering undead, running for the cities just a few miles away.

*Kill. Then eat.*

The driver of the first Jeep was skewered by a pike, its point exploding through the fiberglass shield of his helmet. The Fakir pulled another pike from his thigh and rammed it through the driver's chest.

The other men spilled out of their vehicles, pulling fuel tanks on over their orange jumpsuits and igniting flamethrowers.

Several undead came at them. They unleashed jets of liquid fire, bathing the rotters in scorching heat and sending them to their knees, blind and flailing.

The flames caught the attention of a dozen others. They ran into streams of fire and collapsed. But there were more behind them, and some made it through the fire and tackled the team members to the ground, clawing at their helmets, knocking the flamethrowers aside. One man managed to break free and, in his panic, fired point-blank into the horde. The flames swelled high and surrounded him; the flame-retardant suit could only do so much. Covered in thrashing, burning undead, he was broiled alive.

Shots rang out across the battlefield. It was Dalton, standing atop the Wall and picking off as many as he could before they could reach the burn teams.

The Strongman looked in the direction of the gunfire and spied Dalton. He ran for the ladder.

Dalton aimed straight down at the behemoth's face and shot him between the eyes. Spoiled brain matter slopped out of the gaping exit wound, and the Strongman stumbled off the ladder, staggering into his brethren, his faculties scrambled by the injury to his head; and finally, with a weak swing of his hammer, he went down.

The remaining members of the burn teams had fallen back and once again had the upper hand. They'd brought down a few dozen rotters already. But the others were keeping their distance from the flamethrowers now, instead heading for the cities.

"Get to the Jeeps!" barked a team leader. "Chase them down!"

He turned to find the Fire Juggler standing right behind him.

The rotter crouched and, holding a torch before his lips, blew a fireball into the leader's face.

The man was engulfed in flames. The Juggler had spewed some sort of flammable liquid all over him. It was adhering to the suit, the fuel tanks; the man fell to the ground and tried to roll. The tanks were too goddamn heavy, and searing hot, burning his back; then they exploded.

The rest of the burn teams were caught in the explosion. The force ruptured their tanks. Fire ripped across the open plain, lighting up the night sky.

Dalton watched in horror through the falling snow. One of the Jeeps was on fire. It went up next. It was deafening. And the rotters kept pouring through the gate. Hell had come to the Great Cities.

\* \* \*

The dying screams of the burn teams had been transmitted via radio to a military post just outside of Chicago. There, Major Briggs and his subordinates listened grimly.

When all was static, the major rose from his chair. "Pull everyone you can off the Wall and send them to section nineteen. Then get on the public channel and tell everyone else to meet up with their units—here—and head out there. Tell them we're dealing with a pack... an enormous pack."

"The public will hear—they'll panic—" one of his men began.

"We can't worry about that right now!" Briggs snapped. "Panic in the streets is the least of our problems. The damn P.Os can handle it. We have to stop the rotters from reaching the cities. Clear?"

Briggs turned to another officer. "Open the bunker. I'm requisitioning everything, including the rockets. We'll worry about the paperwork later."

He'd always known this day would come. They'd spoken about it in whispers while the Senate sang their platitudes about the safety of the Cities. Those who had been out there in the field knew what the undead were capable of—and, perhaps more important, they understood the rotters' hunger, a hunger that could never be satiated. Yes, they would come, and they would beat down the great Wall and they would head for the cities.

Following the withdrawal, the Army's remaining weaponry had been stored in the massive bunker beneath Chicago. With God's grace, they'd have enough to stamp out this pack. And then...

No, first things first. Briggs had to keep a cool head. He had to lead his men. Until his last breath, he was their commanding officer and nothing else.

"Someone radio Gillies," he said. Closing his eyes, he thought back to the early days of the war—for this *was* a war—and of the angel in white who had restored him. It had been for this purpose, this very day, that she had done so. He might not be able to count on God tonight, but he'd do right by her.

* * *

Dalton descended the ladder and, drawing his .45, cut a path through the milling undead with surgical precision. A kneecap shattered here, a spinal cord severed there. One after another they fell until he'd reached one of the remaining Jeeps—and then the Strongman brought his hammer down through the windshield.

Dalton spit glass from his mouth and started the engine. The Strongman clambered onto the hood. Dalton stomped on the gas.

They sped into ever-increasing torrents of snow. Rotters struck by the bumper sailed past Dalton and were lost in waves of white. There was only the Strongman, clinging to the hood with one meaty hand and raising his great hammer with the other.

Dalton jerked the wheel to the right. The Strongman nearly rolled off, but righted himself. Dalton emptied the .45 into his face. The undead shook his head as if bothered by gnats; the pulp of his eyes slopped down his face. He let the hammer go and grabbed Dalton by the throat.

A hard left. The Strongman held firm. Already Dalton was seeing red, hearing only the thudding of his heart in his ears. Through a crimson haze he saw the Strongman's head lowering, his bloody jaw falling open.

Dalton's foot found the brake, and he pressed down with all he had left.

The Strongman dropped hard onto the hood, losing his grip on both the Jeep and the soldier, then flew off, landing twenty yards away in a puff of snow. Dalton fell out of the vehicle and pulled his rifle off his shoulder. Fighting to keep his balance, he came up on one knee and took aim at the zombie.

The Strongman's head exploded in a scarlet supernova. His body sagged, hands grasping at the red mist in the air. Then he was done.

Dalton lowered the rifle. He hadn't fired a shot.

A fleet of headlights appeared on the horizon. There were more gunshots. A headless rotter fell beside Dalton.

The cavalry had come. The tide was about to turn.

# THIRTY-TWO / YOU JUST CAN'T WIN

"No plane's going to land in this shit," Gillies muttered, frowning through the window of the Hummer. Beside him, Gregory was silent.

Someone emerged from the storm, rapping on Gregory's door. He pushed it open. "Call for the Senator!" the man said, forcing a radio into the bodyguard's hand.

He passed it to Gillies, who grumbled, "Thrill me."

"Senator, this is a message on behalf of Major Briggs. Rotters have breached the outer Wall. They're all over the dead zone outside Gaylen."

"Where's Briggs? Why isn't he telling me this?"

"He's on his way to the front, sir."

"Jesus." Gillies lowered the radio and tapped his driver on the shoulder. "Get out there and have them close all the gates. I want you posted out there. Tell the other Senators I want their men out there too! Shoot anything that comes near us."

"Me too?" Gregory asked. *Dammit. I should be out with the troops.*

"No, you stay put." Gillies rubbed his eyes with a groan. "I have a headache."

"Want me to go fetch you an aspirin?"

"Don't give me any shit, Ian. You've already let me down tonight."

Gillies' door was yanked open. Senator Cullen stood in the snow. "What the hell are we gonna do, Sam, just sit here and wait for them to surround us?"

"We'll be fine," Gillies sighed. "The entire army's out there. What you should be worrying about is that plane turning back in this weather."

"Do you think that'll happen?"

"I don't know. I'm staying regardless."

Cullen frowned. "Do what you want," Gillies said, and slammed the door shut.

* * *

The other Army vehicles, Jeeps and Humvees, had pulled up beside Dalton and stopped. A hundred men trained their weapons on the horde in the distance.

"Visibility's shit," Briggs said, handing off a pair of binoculars. "All right," he said into his radio, "we're going to try and keep them back with small-arms fire. Use your heat scopes. Reinforcements are on the way to help. With any luck we can get the rotters bunched up close together—then we bring out the heavy artillery."

Silhouettes, barely visible through the storm, were peppered with gunfire. They couldn't see well enough to cripple the rotters; they were wasting ammo. "Let 'em come closer! Put 'em down!" Briggs yelled into his radio.

The shadow figures were scattered sparsely across the dead zone. Dalton knew immediately that something was wrong. He'd seen far, far more than this at the Wall. Where were they? Hanging back, wary of the gunfire? Or plotting?

*Rotters plotting? Undead with a strategy?*

The silhouettes weren't coming closer. They were spreading further out and fading into the storm.

"Heat scopes aren't doing any good!" a captain shouted. Briggs, standing in the front of his Jeep, clenched his fists and sat down. "All right, roll out! Let's find the sons of bitches!"

"They're *behind us!*"

Cries erupted throughout the ranks as a surge of undead came from the back, flying out of the white winds and landing on the troops. Sheer panic overtook the men. Briggs could only watch in terrible wonder as the dead claimed their swift and brutal victory.

* * *

Voorhees was lying, bound, on the floor of Tripper's bedroom. Halstead and Lily sat beside him.

"I'm sorry we hurt him," Halstead was saying. "But you see, he doesn't understand that we're the good guys. Tripper and Campbell have taken good care of you, haven't they?"

Lily nodded slowly. "But why would good guys hurt a policeman?"

"That's what I'd like to know," Voorhees muttered. "You can preach to me all you want, Halstead, but you're not going to sway a child with your bullshit logic."

"You just... if you'd only met Thackeray." Halstead sighed. "He's the architect. He's the revolutionary. He sent us here with a plan, and no, it's not to burn the Great Cities to the ground. This is about liberating this country from the undead. It's about not giving up, not living in denial. And I *know* you understand that logic."

Voorhees rolled onto his back, staring at nothing, and spoke not a word.

He had to get Halstead out of here and be alone with the girl. Halstead wasn't stupid, though. She wouldn't give Voorhees the opportunity to talk Lily into untying his wrists.

But he didn't need that kind of time. He needed only a few seconds—enough time for Lily to help him loose his widowmaker from the sheath beneath his shirt...

Cam poked her head into the room. "It's almost dawn."

"Happy Halloween," Halstead said.

* * *

Eviscerato led his minions over Gaylen's city wall. The few soldiers posted there were slaughtered before they could even reach their radios.

It had taken only a few hours to make it from the outer Wall. The pack had suffered minimal casualties. And even now, some of the dead soldiers they'd left in their wake were rising to join them.

The King of the Dead paid no mind to the solitary Jeep that sped past him into the city. Gaylen was asleep. They didn't stand a chance.

* * *

"I see the plane," one of Gillies' men cried, pointing east. "Look!"

Gillies ran from the Hummer and across the airfield, his heart pounding. The plane was still coming, even through the storm! The British had come through! There *was* a God.

"Will they land?" Senator Cullen cried.

"Of course they will!" Gillies practically screamed. "Light the torches! Guide them in!"

The plane streaked over the airfield and began a sloping turn. Men thrust flames into the air and waved desperately at it.

The plane was coming in. Cheers broke out among the Senators and their entourages.

Gillies clapped his hands and, turning to see Ian Gregory standing behind him, said, "Is your faith still waning, my friend?"

"I can't do this," Gregory said.

"What?"

"I can't get on that plane. I belong back there with the troops. I'm not abandoning all these people. The woman I loved," he said softly, "she died here." He glanced away from the runway, toward the gates. "She died." And he began to walk away.

"Ian! *Ian!*"

To hell with him then. Gillies watched the plane touch down. He jogged back to the Hummer and retrieved his briefcase. Hopefully it wouldn't take long to negotiate his way on board. Maybe he'd just tell them that the rotters had breached the Wall and that all was lost. The truth wouldn't hurt for once.

The plane taxied toward the fleet of parked cars and came to a stop, engines whining. Stairs descended as the side hatch opened.

"All right!" Gillies snapped. "Let me talk to them. Just let me do all the talking."

He started up the stairs, calming himself as he did and putting on a formal air. One last diplomatic dance. He'd have to hit every mark perfectly this time.

As he stepped onto the plane, he was assaulted by a four odor that made him gag: confined, concentrated putrescence, the stench of death. It smelled like they'd come straight from the battlefield. Didn't anyone observe basic hygiene anymore?

The cockpit was sealed. Parting a damp curtain, he stepped into the passenger cabin.

Every seat was occupied. That was a—

*They were all undead*

Gillies staggered back, tearing down the curtain as he fell to the floor. "My—my God! Christ Jesus! Oh no! Oh, no!"

The cockpit opened. Two uniformed zombies shuffled out, starving hunger in their eyes.

So, the war in Britain had been won, after all.

"Oh no," Gillies stammered. He tried to get up. The pilots' hands came down on his shoulders. Passengers were rising from their seats, hands outstretched, eager for the taste of American flesh. :Oh no," the Senator wept. "No, no, NO!"

They fell upon him. "*Nooooooooooooooooo!*" he wailed, choked with sobs, and then with the blood welling in his throat. "*NOOOOOOOOOOOOO! Noooooo...*"

While the pilots licked his bones clean, the rest of the British began to deplane.

# THIRTY-THREE / THE HEAVY ARTILLERY

"Halstead! What's your twenty? Is Voorhees with you?"

It was Casey. Halstead answered into her radio, "I'm downtown. Don't know about Voorhees."

"Gulager just called in from the east city limits. He was checking out reports of gunfire... there are rotters inside the walls. They're on the streets, hundreds of them."

Halstead looked up, her face pale. Tripper and Cam shook their heads in disbelief. "It wasn't supposed to happen this way," she breathed. "This wasn't supposed to happen."

"All right, relax." Tripper pressed his fingers to his temples. "Think. Think. We gotta get to the storehouse, get the guns. Between us and the Army we can mow these fuckers down, right? Cam?"

She nodded, already heading for the door. "We'll have to leave the blind guy here."

"And Lily?"

"She comes with us," Cam replied. To Halstead she said, "Find out what your S.P.O. wants."

"What do you want me to do, sir?" Halstead said into the radio.

"This is the military's problem. What we need to do is clear the streets of civilians... it's all we *can* do. Make a quick sweep of downtown and then report back here. Watch yourself."

"Yeah." She clipped the radio to her belt and turned to the others. "Where's the storehouse?"

"The basement of the soup kitchen," said Tripper. All of the weapons and ammo he'd bartered for were down there, just waiting. He could tell Cam was itching to get her hands on some.

"Let's go."

\* \* \*

"Cullen!" the radio squawked. "This is Briggs!"

The Senators were speeding down the road away from the airfield. Cullen's aide passed him the radio, and he responded, "Major?"

"They're pouring into Gaylen. City's barricades crumbled like they were nothing I've lost maybe a third of my men. Where the hell is Gillies? I can't raise him."

"He's dead," Cullen said numbly.

"Dead?"

"Don't ask."

"Who's the acting President?"

"I am." Cullen fidgeted with his tie. Fuck Gillies for doing this to him! "We need to contain the threat, Major. Agreed?"

"Of course. I'm preparing to move my boys into the city."

"No," Cullen said. "Just raze it. Burn it to the ground."

"What?"

"It's the only way to prevent the spread of infection. No one enters, no one leaves. Just burn it all."

"Cullen! You can't be serious!"

"I'm dead fucking serious!" the Senator yelled. "I refuse to die like this! I may be stuck in this fucking hellhole but I'm not going to die like this. You burn Gaylen down! You shoot to kill if anyone tries to escape! Do you hear me, Major?"

There was no reply.

"He won't do it," Cullen grumbled. "Brian, radio the Chicago outpost. I'll give them my orders. Tell them Major Briggs is no longer running this operation. I am."

"Yes sir," his aide said. Cullen settled back in his seat. He actually wasn't too bad at this.

\* \* \*

The rotters hadn't reached downtown yet. Tripper, Cam and Halstead—Lily on her back—ran through the empty streets. It was seven in the morning.

A man exited one of the apartment buildings. "Get inside!" Tripper yelled. "Rotters!" The man shook his head at them and continued on his way.

Tripper fumbled for the keys to the soup kitchen. Bursting inside, he ran to the basement door, affixed with three locks. "There are others who can help us," he was saying. "We've got to track them down."

"How much time do you think we have?" Halstead said.

"We'll make time," said Cam.

They descended a dark flight of stairs into a musty cellar. Tripper lit a lantern and opened its shutters on the room.

High-powered rifles, automatics, and hand cannons were stacked along the back wall. Boxes and boxes of ammo were spread out by caliber. "We want to travel light," Tripper said.

Cam grabbed a machine gun and started gathering magazines. "This'll work. Ooh, and this." She snatched a Colt Python from a rack and tucked it into her waistband.

"I can't believe this is really happening," Halstead said. She stood in the middle of the room and watched as the other two stocked up. "Believe it,' Tripper said. "Get over here and arm yourself."

Lily had been silent this whole time. She sat on the stairs with a weary look. "It's gonna be okay," Cam said.

"I don't know," Lily replied. "I wish my friend was here. Then we'd be okay."

A distant scream caught everyone's attention. It was a woman. Her screams drew nearer—then they stopped abruptly.

"They're here," Halstead gasped.

"Then we go it alone," Cam muttered. "Ready?"

"We could stay down here, couldn't we?" Halstead asked.

Cam scowled at her. "What happened to the fucking plan, Em? We've got to take these bastards out! Letting everyone die isn't the plan! Now c'mon!" She took off up the stairs.

Halstead held her arms out to Lily. "C'mon. I want you to get back onto my back and hold on tight. Okay?"

Cam walked out into the street to find a trio of rotters ripping the slain woman's skin off. The snow was stained red; steam rose from the corpse's spurting guts.

"Hey mates," Cam called. The fiends looked up.

She unleashed the machine gun. The rotters flew back as bullets ripped through their throats and faces. Skulls opened and vomited out foul matter. They landed on their backs, twitching but essentially immobilized.

"On your six!" Tripper cried.

Cam turned around and cut a rotter in half. It dropped, legless, into the snow and clawed toward her. Gunfire scissored it into half from crown to crotch.

"Where are we going?" Lily cried, clinging to Halstead's neck.

"East!" Tripper said. He stepped into the middle of the street, an Uzi in each hand, and grinned at the oncoming dozens of undead. "Behind me, Halstead. Now watch this."

He unloaded into the horde. Zombies spun and tumbled over one another. Heads exploded, leaving bodies to stagger aimlessly and finally sink into the snow.

"We'll burn 'em later."

It was a different picture to the east. The rotters were running into tenements and knocking down door after door, falling upon helpless families.

Some of the living ran into the street and tried to make a break for it. They were brought down in seconds.

A lone rotter crouched over a dead child and pulled out handfuls of entrails, raising them to its lips.

Eviscerato brought his cane down on the rotter's head, sending it sprawling.

*Kill them all. Then eat.*

P.O. Gulager huddled behind a dumpster in an alley and watched the carnage unfold. All he had was a fucking baton. How was he supposed to do anything?

But he had to do something. He was a cop.

So, with his heart in his throat, running on legs of rubber, he went into the street. A rotter leapt at him. He smashed its teeth in and threw it to the ground. "Fuck you!" he screamed. Another grabbed his shoulder from behind. He whirled and bashed its skull in. "Fuck you!"

A shadow fell across his vision. He turned. "Fuck—"

The lanky giant, with vines of bone that wove in and out of its gray flesh, reached out with stiff arms and hooked its fingers into Gulager's clothing. He was lifted off the ground, toward the thing's gaping maw.

The Petrified Man sank his teeth into Gulager's face, slicing through his eyeball, splitting his cheek, and biting right through bone into his brain.

The rotter cast Gulager to the ground and left in search of its next victim.

# THIRTY-FOUR / HOSPITAL

Dalton kicked open the ER doors and helped Briggs into the admitting room. "Rotters! They're in the city!"

The nurses froze in place, transfixed with horror. Dalton set Briggs in a chair. "His ankle's broken. Look, can somebody help him?"

"I'm fine," Briggs said through gritted teeth. "This place is going to be packed in a few minutes." He pulled out his radio. "Briggs to Fetters. Come in Lieutenant."

"Fetters here sir,"

"Are the men in place?"

"Sir... you've been removed from command. We're taking orders from Senator Cullen. He's instructed us to secure the perimeter and—"

"I know." Briggs dropped the radio into his lap. "Fuck me."

And moments later, just as he'd predicted, people began stumbling into the hospital, most covered in blood, all hysterical.

Dalton knelt by Briggs. "We've got infected pouring in here."

The nurses were refusing to help the wounded. They locked themselves in the triage station. People began beating on the doors and walls.

"Calm down! Calm the fuck down!" yelled a block cop. "Listen to me dammit!" He saw the two soldiers and ran over. "We gotta get the fuck outta here."

"Got any ideas?" Dalton asked. The cop nodded and pointed through a pair of doors to the emergency room itself.

Dalton helped Briggs to his feet. They walked slowly past the others—far too panicked to notice, anyway—and through the doors.

"All right." The cop slammed the doors and threw the bolt, then grabbed a gurney from against the wall and dragged it over. "Those poor bastards are already dead. We gotta start building a barricade."

"What's your name, son?" Briggs asked.

"Rhodes," the cop replied, pulling a Glock from his jacket.

"I thought you didn't carry," said Briggs.

"*I* do." Rhodes motioned to Dalton. "Help me out here!"

They started stacking chairs and medical equipment in front of the doors. They heard cries from the other side.

"Let us in!"

"We need help!"

"I'm not infected!"

"Poor bastards," Rhodes said again.

They were throwing themselves against the doors now. Then someone screamed.

"ROTTERS!"

Briggs, Dalton and Rhodes listened silently to the sounds of death and mayhem. The assault on the doors ended as people tried to escape admitting. It didn't sound like anyone got out.

"Hey," someone said softly. Dalton and Rhodes both spun, guns at the ready.

It was a doctor. Hands raised, he said, "I'm clean. I've been in here the whole time."

He extended a hand. "Name's Zane. So it's finally happening."

"It's happening," Briggs sighed, sweating from the pain in his ankle.

"Listen Doctor," Dalton asked, shaking his hand, "you got any morphine?"

"I don't need it," Briggs said. "I've gotta stay straight."

"You're in agony. You're no good like this."

Zane walked over to the orderlies' station and rummaged around until he found a key. "I'll be right back with something for you."

"We need to barricade any other exits in here," Rhodes said. He ran down the hall.

"We just let those people die," Dalton mumbled.

"Rhodes was right—they were already dead. It's my fault. I couldn't keep them out of the city."

"There were too many," Dalton said.

"We knew this was coming." Briggs clenched his lower leg and moaned. "We tried to tell them, but they wouldn't listen. They really believed they'd be safe forever."

There was renewed pounding on the doors. The undead. Briggs hunched over in pain.

"Sir," Dalton whispered.

"What is it?"

Dalton pried back the collar of Briggs' shirt. He lowered his head and sighed.

"You're bit."

Briggs touched his hand to the wound and looked at the blood on his fingers. He didn't move or speak for several moments. Then he sat up. "I didn't even feel it."

Zane returned with a syringe. "It's not morphine, but you'll be floating. You want it?"

Briggs shook his head with a bitter laugh. "No, that's not what I need." He looked at Dalton, who nodded and drew his sidearm.

"I'm infected," said the major. "I'm sorry. I'm sorry for all of it."

Dalton helped him to his feet and into an observation room. He quietly shut the door.

Rhodes was on his way back when he heard the gunshot. "What the hell was that?"

Zane cocked his head to one side, as if listening, and replied, "That's the Devil laughing."

* * *

Finn Meyer stood back as Pat Morgan and another lieutenant nailed boards across the door to the warehouse where they'd been trapped. "Hurry up!" Meyer barked.

"Help us, Finn!" Morgan shot back.

"Fuck." He didn't want to go anywhere near the doors or windows. But the pounding was getting worse. He grabbed a two-by-four off the floor. "Got another fucking hammer?"

"On the table by the nails!" Morgan snapped.

Finn headed over to a window facing the alley. There weren't any rotters out that way. He'd dick around over here while the others finished up, then collect their guns. If they weren't willing to give them up, he'd take them.

A hand smashed through the window and seized his throat. "Help!" he croaked. "Fucking help me!"

Morgan rushed to him and buried a hammerclaw in the rotter's hand. It held on. She dug into the hand until bone snapped. It finally withdrew.

Meyer stumbled back, coughing. "God! I thought that was it, Patti. God."

"Finn..." she frowned. "You're bleeding."

"What?"

"It must have cut you with its fingernails." She was stepping back from him.

"What?" he shouted. "You can't get infected that way!"

"If it had blood on its hands..."

They stared at each other. For a second, time stood still.

Meyer was faster.

Morgan slumped to the floor, blood trickling from a hole between her eyes. Meyer's other lieutenant looked over in shock. "What in the bloody hell?"

Meyer shot him in the heart. Then he wiped his neck clean with a handkerchief while the man gasped his last breaths.

Then he collected their guns.

# THIRTY-FIVE / SEVERANCE

Ernie ran into the squadroom and locked the door behind him, then grabbed hold of the nearest desk and started building a barricade.

"Officer!"

He nearly jumped out of his skin. Casey came rolling out of his office, a shotgun resting across his lap, and said, "What do you think you're doing?"

"They're everywhere! There's nothing we can do!" Ernie panted as he dragged desks. "It's all coming apart out there. It's already over, man!"

"Those don't sound like the words of a peace officer—" Casey began.

"That's easy for you to say!" Ernie yelled. "You're holed up in here! You haven't seen it! They're pulling women and children into the streets and ripping them to pieces! And they're almost here!"

"I expected better from you," Casey said. Wheeling himself over to the nearest window, he pulled the blinds down without looking outside.

"Help me over here, Ernie."

"Forget the windows, man! We've gotta secure the door!"

"I am still your superior!"

A window on the other end of the room shattered. Casey saw a dark blur fall into the room, between two desks.

"What the hell was that?" Ernie cried.

"Shhh." Casey picked up the shotgun and waited for the rotter to show itself. But none did; there was only the faint sound of dead skin rustling.

The dark shape flew across the aisle and disappeared among the desks again. What was it, a child? "Ernie," Casey whispered, and nodded toward the place where the thing had gone.

Ernie shook his head.

"Ernie!" Casey hissed.

"You've got the gun! You go!"

Tiny feet padded across the floor. The thing was weaving in and out of the desks, drawing ever closer. Casey took aim at the end of the aisle and waited.

The scampering stopped. Ernie crouched behind his barricade.

Silently cursing, Casey began to move forward. *Just a child*, he told himself. *A child already dead. I won't hesitate.*

The Dwarf leapt onto the nearest desk. Casey's jaw dropped at the sight. Then the rotter jumped into his lap and sank its claws into his face.

Ernie shot across the squadroom like a fucking bolt, faster than he'd ever moved in his career, and dove into Casey's office, slamming the door shut.

Casey rolled backwards with the tiny rotter thrashing atop him. The shotgun clattered on the floor. He screamed and pummeled the Dwarf with his fists, trying to knock it loose, but it had its fingers beneath his skin and blood was pouring down the front of his shirt as his face began to come off.

The wheelchair hit the wall. The Dwarf closed its fingers around Casey's left eyeball and ripped it free of the socket. Casey's vision was skewed wildly as the eye came loose. The optic nerve was still connected when the Dwarf popped the organ into its mouth; its teeth finally severed Casey's sight. He wailed.

The Dwarf hopped down and surveyed the room. It heard Ernie pushing Casey's desk against the office door. It charged at the door, seizing the knob and scratching and kicking at the wood. Ernie screamed from within.

Casey sat and watched numbly as blood pooled in his lap, streaming in dark rivers from his ragged face. Why had it left him to go after Ernie? Why wasn't he dead?

No matter. He soon would be.

* * *

Gregory sped down the road from the airfield in Gillies' Hummer. He had plenty of guns and ammunition in the back. He was going to drive straight into Gaylen and bring Armageddon back to those godless monsters.

The British had filed out of the plane and begun shambling across the tarmac. They were too slow and too decayed to catch any of the other Senators before they and their men fled. No one had questioned Senator Gillies' fate. It was every man for himself now—as it always had been, but now without the democratic posturing.

"For you, Barry," he muttered, jostling as he left the road and headed directly for the city.

\* \* \*

The streets downtown were flooding with people.

Some were trying to fight the undead. Though they had the rotters beaten in sheer numbers, stark panic and lack of weapons made it a losing battle for the living. Spilled blood ate at the growing snowdrifts. Soon the humans began retreating west. Those who stayed behind slipped in the guts of their neighbors and were torn apart.

There was little biting. The pack knew that if they bit their prey, they'd be losing meat. And the meat was all they cared about.

"We're chewing through ammo pretty quick here!" Tripper called as people streaked past him.

Cam nodded. "Fall back to the storehouse!"

They ran for the soup kitchen, Halstead in the lead with Lily clinging to her back. "I'm scared," the girl whimpered.

"I'm fucking terrified," the cop replied.

"Thanks."

"Door's locked!" Halstead cried. Tripper stuck his key in the lock and turned the knob. He was met with firm resistance. Someone was inside, and they'd blocked the door.

"Hey! Whoever's in there, let us in!" he yelled. "You've got to let us in! We can help you!"

"We left the cellar open," muttered Cam. "They're set. They're not going to listen to us."

"All right." Tripper glanced down the street and saw a wave of undead sweeping over the civvies. He sighed. "Cathouse."

High overhead, an apartment exploded; ruptured generator. They fled through a shower of burning debris.

\* \* \*

When they entered the dark front hall of the cathouse, Cam caught Tripper's shoulder and whispered, "Listen."

There was a metallic whine coming from elsewhere in the building. Then a long, mournful scream.

Cam took point with machine gun in hand. Tripper locked the door they'd come through. It wouldn't hold long.

Cam descended the stairs to the basement corridor where the girls' rooms were. The whine was much louder now, and more distinct: a gas-powered saw. It was coming from the last room. Cam slowly made her way to the door. There were more screams, a man's screams. She reared back and kicked the door in.

Logan stood over a dismembered rotter, chainsaw held high over his head. He wailed and plunged it into the chest of the spasming corpse.

"What the fuck!" Cam snapped. Logan turned and stumbled, dropping the saw on the floor. Cam kicked it over to the wall and trained her gun on the soldier's head. "You've lost it."

"No!" He held trembling hands out in protest. The others joined Cam in the doorway.

"Don't look," Halstead told Lily.

"Too late," Lily said.

"I just didn't want her to burn." Logan stroked the fake hair on the rotter's decapitated head. "She never did anything wrong. She shouldn't have to suffer."

"What do you mean, burn?" Tripper asked.

"The Army's going to torch the entire city," Logan said. "Orders from Cullen. They're lighting up the perimeter right now."

Halstead's face fell. "So it's over."

"Maybe for Gaylen, but not the other cities." Walking over to Logan, Tripper nudged him aside and felt along the wall until he found a crack gummed with blood. He knocked, and they all heard the hollow sound.

Tripper pulled the panel away to reveal a dark passage. "Cam," he called. She resumed leading the group, now including Logan and his saw.

Tripper replaced the panel behind them. "This used to be part of the sewer system," he said. They stood in a tunnel with no light source. Tripper felt along the floor until he found the torch he'd placed there. Igniting it with his lighter, he passed it to Halstead. "Mind the kid."

"Meyer uses some of these tunnels to run drugs," Tripper said as they walked, "but he doesn't come this far downtown."

"Speaking of which," Cam said, "we should probably find a tunnel going back east. We'll avoid more rotters that way."

"Good idea baby."

The couple led the way through winding, fetid sewers. It was so quiet beneath the city. It almost seemed like the world wasn't coming down right over their heads.

They entered a tunnel lit by lanterns, with several crates stacked along the walls. "Booze," Tripper said. "We're on Meyer's turf now. Gotta keep an eye out for his goons."

Cam stopped at a ladder. She took the torch from Halstead and held it up to the shaft from which the ladder descended. "Looks like a trapdoor up there."

"Let's not bother with it," Tripper said.

"Might be ammo up there."

"You're right." He grabbed the rung above the one she was holding. "But I'm taking point this time."

Halstead let Lily down. "You go ahead of me, okay?"

They ascended into the dark shaft. Tripper nudged the trapdoor with the barrel of an Uzi. "It's open."

He rose swiftly, throwing the door back. Three men with pistols gawked at him.

Lily cringed as she heard gunfire being sprayed up above. People dying left and right. Would any of them be alive in the end?

"Clear!" Tripper called down, and they each in turn climbed up through the trapdoor.

It was a long room lit by firelight and filled with tables and chairs. A long counter ran along one wall, behind which were stocked bottle of liquor.

"Speakeasy," Cam said.

Lily stepped over the bullet-riddled arm of one of the goons. "Is it safe?"

"I don't know," Cam replied. "We shouldn't stay long. Em, grab their guns will you?"

Logan pulled a chair out and sat down, slouching like a man who'd given up.

Tripper hopped up on the bar. "Cullen... why did Cullen give the order to burn the city? What about Gillies?"

"Dead," Logan said.

"Karma's a bitch." Tripper shrugged.

"And what'll you call it when *you* die?" Logan muttered.

# THIRTY-SIX / MAN'S CHARITY

Becks crouched behind a vegetable bin as the Geek crept into her market stall.

She'd heard the cries, seen the carnage unfolding blocks away, and come straight here. She was about to do herself, knife pressed to her jugular, when she heard the rotter and lost her nerve. She didn't want to be food for these things. Even without Blake, she couldn't bear to go through with it.

The rotter had three or four arms, all misshapen and swaying as it walked among the bins. Becks crawled toward the back. There was an exit there. She could race down the alley and to the amphitheater. There were places to hide there.

The Geek overturned the bin right behind her and roared.

She sprinted toward the exit, slamming into the door with teeth-rattling force—and burst through, stumbling headlong into the alley but never slowing down, running for dear life.

At the mouth of the alley, she made a hard right, and hands caught her by both arms in a vise-like grip. She screamed.

"It's me, girl!" Finn Meyer hissed. "They're all over. Where the hell do you think you're going?"

"Amphitheater," she gasped. He nodded and tugged her along.

They stumbled down the bleachers and onto the stage where Becks had performed so many roles—most poorly written by that hack Cullen, but she had always loved the stage no matter what. Still... she couldn't make this her last stand.

The Geek clambered over the gate and onto the bleachers. "Jesus!" Meyer breathed.

He pulled Becks against him. "Sorry," he whispered, then she heard the gunshot. Then she felt the wetness spreading over her abdomen.

165

She fell on her back, sobbing in horror and disbelief, looking up at Meyer, who regarded her coolly before making his exit. He'd left her behind to stall the rotter.

She rolled over and dragged herself across the stage, pain spreading like a wildfire through her stomach and chest. She pulled herself to her feet and glanced back. The Geek was halfway down the bleachers. She had time. And she knew where she was going.

She ran with strength she didn't know she had, strength that should have been ebbing from the wound in her belly, where she had once thought she would carry Blake's child. She ran to the shore of Lake Michigan and dove into the icy water.

She swam out a hundred yards and stopped. The rotter wasn't on the shore. Perhaps it had found new quarry.

She could tread water for a while, until the cold overtook her, and then she'd just drift downward, into blackness. It would be painless.

The Geek erupted from behind her and threw its malformed limbs around her.

* * *

Voorhees pushed himself across the floor on his back. He'd gotten out of the bedroom, and was now in search of something with which to cut the ropes binding him. The widowmaker was right there, pressing into the flesh of his back, but he just couldn't work it free.

Dammit, he wasn't going to find anything feeling around on the floor. He'd have to get up and start knocking into things. There had to be at least a sharp corner where he could start working on the ropes.

Getting up onto his knees, he shuffled along until he struck the door. He knew they'd locked it when they left. At least they did that much for him. He could hardly imagine what must be unfolding outside.

He heard someone running down the hall, trying doorknobs. Pounding. It was someone living. "Hey!" he shouted. "You out there! Over here!"

The doorknob jiggled. "Wait a second," Voorhees grunted. He pressed his face to the door and grabbed the lock in his teeth. If he could just turn it ninety degrees, he'd have someone to cut him loose...

He did it! "It's unlocked!"

The door opened. There was a laugh, and it was the most awful sound he'd ever heard in his life.

"Morning, Officer Voorhees. Looks like your luck just keeps getting worse."

Meyer kicked Voorhees over and entered the apartment, quietly closing the door behind him.

The cop sat up and swung his head, the only way he could defend himself. Meyer laughed again, softly; then it grew silent. Where was he? Voorhees listened intently.

"*Over here,*" came a whisper. He turned to catch a fist in the face. Voorhees collapsed once more.

Meyer grabbed his hair and dragged him over to a chair. "I've had a real bastard of a day too, friend. But I get to take it out on you."

* * *

Ernie lay under Casey's desk with his hands over his mouth and listened. The Dwarf's scrabbling had stopped. How long would he have to wait this out before the Army came through? Would he have any way of knowing when it was over? His radio didn't pick up military frequencies. *Stupid,* he thought.

He heard the door being unlocked, then the creak as it swung open.

How... ? He remained under the desk, which still blocked the doorway, and listened.

Keys jingled. He heard a sound like someone shifting about. Then something thumped on top of the desk. Something heavy.

Dear God, was Casey *still alive?*

Ernie stuck his head out from under the desk. He could see nothing from his vantage point. "Sir?" he whispered.

Four bloody fingers crept over the edge of the desk and curled to grip it.

Casey's face slid into view. Or rather, the absence of it—a black, dripping void.

His other hand came over the desk's edge, holding the keys, and he dropped them on the floor beside Ernie's head.

Casey rolled off the desk and onto the floor. Blood splattered on the walls. He pulled his crippled body toward Ernie, one eye rolling

167

crazily in his crimson skull; and finally Ernie found his voice and screamed, but only for a second before Casey was upon him, and they rolled beneath the desk in their struggle and then a sea of blood washed across the floor.

# THIRTY-SEVEN / IN EVERY MAN

"That barricade isn't gonna hold," Zane said.

"Where do we go? Upstairs?" Dalton shook his head.

"How about into the damn street then?" snapped Rhodes.

"Calm down. I know another way." Zane started down the hall. "Follow me."

The doctor led them down a stairwell and through a pair of doors labeled PATHOLOGY. Producing a set of keys, he unlocked an unmarked door. "More stairs."

This stairwell was pitch dark and smelled of disinfectant. Feeling his way down, Dalton silently chastised himself for coming into the city. Either way, there was nothing he could have done to save Briggs, but at least he could've stayed out in the field and been of some use.

Zane pushed open a heavy steel door and flipped a light switch. The three men entered a long room lined with counters, upon which sat clipboards and vats of preserving fluid. Dalton was sure of what the liquid was, because inside the greenish soup twitched severed hands and feet.

"Shit," Rhodes whispered. He approached a tank containing a coiled spinal cord and brain. The eyeballs were still attached; they drifted over towards him, and the pupils shrank. "Fuck!" Rhodes jumped away.

"This is where they were studying the plague," Zane said. "I guess none of the docs have gotten here yet this morning—guess they won't be coming in at all, will they? Anyway, the Senate allotted a bit of pocket change to let these guys poke and prod. Pointless, really."

Dalton picked up a clipboard and read the notes scribbled there. "Were they trying to find a cure?"

"Doubt it," said Zane. "The last generation of scientists gave up on that. I don't know what exactly they hoped to understand by playing with these body parts. I think they just didn't know what else to do with themselves."

"'Spiritual constitution,'" Rhodes read from a clipboard. "'Quantifying the temporal bond.' What is this shit?"

"Let me see that." Zane took the clipboard. "Oh dear. Looks like they bought into the ol' spiritual strength versus rate of infection nonsense. They really were scraping the bottom of the barrel."

A dull thud resonated through the room. Dalton and Rhodes drew their weapons. "It came from down here," Dalton said softly.

Another thump. At the far end of the room, Dalton noticed a tiny porthole set into the wall. Creeping towards it, he reached out the counter beneath the glass and found that it pulled away from the wall. The porthole was set in a door. He pressed his face to it. "Lord."

A priest lay on the floor of a dimly-lit eight-by-eight cell. He looked to be in his seventies, perhaps older. It was hard to tell because of his gaunt, sickly expression. He had to be infected.

Zane joined Dalton at the porthole. "You've gotta be fucking kidding me."

"What in God's name are they doing to this man?" Dalton breathed.

"Don't you see? He's a man of God. They're testing the virus on him to see how long it takes. They're testing his spirit."

"This is insane!" Dalton cried. He pounded on the glass. "Sir! Father!"

The priest stirred a bit. He looked up through slits and opened his mouth. Saliva ran from his lips to the floor.

"We've got to get in there." Dalton felt along the wall. There had to be a way to open the damn door. They couldn't have just sealed him in there... could they?

"Forget it," Zane said. "He's a lost cause."

"But he doesn't deserve to die like this!"

"Don't waste another bullet!" Zane retorted. "It's still a long way out of the city."

"So you know of a way out? Down here?"

"Maybe. It's been so long since I snooped around down here, I don't know if it's still here. But I'm betting it is."

Dalton looked at the priest. The old man reached a pale hand toward him. Dalton threw himself against the door. "C'mon!"

"Let it go, man!" Rhodes pulled Dalton back. "We've gotta save the uninfected! That means us!"

Zane knelt and crawled beneath the counter. "Here it is." He pried at a grate in the wall. "Help me out."

Rhodes ducked down and kicked the grate with a loud BANG! It fell away.

"Thanks." Zane crawled through the hole. "Follow me."

Dalton shook his head sadly at the priest, mouthing "I'm sorry."

The old man shook his head in response, as if to dismiss the matter, and gave him a small smile.

* * *

They made their way through a cramped passage and rose in an enormous tunnel. Zane produced a penlight and illuminated a set of metal tracks. "Old subway system. They closed it off years back. I just knew they meant to use it as an escape route. Tricky bastards."

"Did you hear that?" Rhodes pointed his Glock down the tunnel. From around a sharp bend they saw moving lights. Electric torches.

Dalton took point, peering through his scope. He saw the silhouette of a man in uniform. "Army," he whispered, and quickened his pace.

"Hey!" he called as others came into view. They trained their weapons on him. "I'm one of you!" he yelled.

A sergeant approached him. "Where did you come from?"

"They hospital. I have two civilians with me. Can I get them out through here?"

"We're not letting anyone out," the sergeant replied gruffly. He turned to his men, and for the first time Dalton saw what they were doing, hunched along the walls—laying charges.

"What?" Dalton gasped. "You're going to blow it? You can't! There are tens of thousands of people still in the city!"

"It's a hot zone," the sergeant said. "No one gets out. I'm afraid that includes you, soldier."

"Are you fuckin' with me?" Rhodes pushed past Dalton and grabbed the sergeant by his shirt. "You'd better—"

A pistol was pressed against his temple. "Back off," a private stammered. "Let him go."

"Better do what he says," the sergeant muttered.

"You can't just sentence all those people to die!" Rhodes cried. "You're supposed to protect people!"

"We are! We're protecting the other cities!"

"Let him go, Rhodes," Dalton said.

The cop released the sergeant and threw his arms in the air. "This is bullshit!"

"Sergeant," Dalton pleaded, "you've got to let us evacuate civilians. They can be placed under quarantine as soon as they get out! Just let them out for God's sake!"

"That's directly defying the Senate's orders," the sergeant said.

"To Hell with them! They've never been part of this war! We're all the same to them—one of these days it's gonna be your ass on the line, Sergeant!"

"My ass is *already* on the line, son!"

"Those people up there aren't dead," Zane said. "Even if the Senate's written them off, they're not dead. Not unless you do this."

"I don't take orders from—" the sergeant snapped, then stopped.

"From who? Civilians? Is that what you were gonna say?" Dalton stood toe-to-toe with the sergeant. "For the love of God, just give us a little time. We can get people out through here. You don't have to help. Just don't blow the tunnels yet."

"I... I can't."

"Yes you can." Dalton looked at the other soldiers, who were all watching the confrontation. "Is this what you want to do? Is this how we win?"

"Sergeant," said Zane. "Women. Children."

"Shit." The sergeant turned from them. He looked into the faces of his men and said, "Shit!"

He stabbed his finger into Dalton's face. "I'll give you a few hours. That's it. I can't give you any more than that. Understand?"

"All right." Dalton gave the man a crisp salute. "Thank you."

"I can't stop the others in the other tunnels. I can only give you this."

"It's enough," Dalton said.

# THIRTY-EIGHT / LITTLE THINGS

Logan was wasted. He'd drained a bottle of Scotch and was slumped, bleary-eyed, against the bar.

"Dead weight," Tripper muttered under his breath.

"Is Officer Voorhees going to be safe at your place?" Lily asked him. Tripper shrugged.

Shoving an elbow into his ribs, Cam stepped forward and said, "He'll be fine. New locks."

"But that man said they're setting the city on fire." Lily pointed to Logan.

"Lily," said Halstead, kneeling beside the girl, "I'm sure he'll be okay. We wouldn't just leave him helpless like that..." Her voice trailed off. Even she couldn't say it with a straight face.

Lily turned from the others and stalked across the room. Tripper walked over to the dead goons and collected their pistols. "We're gonna have to get moving here. No time to waste."

"We need a plan," Halstead protested.

"Stay alive," Tripper replied. "That's the plan."

"Like I said, we continue east. Using the tunnels," Cam said. "If we run out of tunnels we'll take to the streets. I'm not worried about the rotters—it's the soldiers that have got me nervous."

"They won't let us out," Logan said. "They'll shoot us dead. I heard their orders. Have to stay underground."

"Do you know of a way out of the city, Private?" Halstead asked.

"I don't know." Logan took a swig from a bottle of vodka.

Tripper swept it from his hand. It smashed into the mirror behind the bar. "We need you to stay sharp, asshole, or else you're not coming with us!"

Logan laughed bitterly. "You're not listening to me. We're already dead! All of us! You, me, the kid—dead!"

Lily pushed open a door at the rear of the room. "Hey, I know this place."

"Close that," Halstead called.

"Wait," said Cam. "Lily, how do you know this place?"

"I've been here. Upstairs is where the girls sleep."

"Oh, God," Tripper said.

"What girls?" said Halstead.

"Meyer's prostitutes," Cam answered.

"Fuck 'em," Logan slurred.

"They're kids," Cam snapped. Logan looked up at her. "Kids?"

"We ought to go up there," Tripper said. "We have to. Try to get them out."

"You want to add another dozen children to our group?" Halstead shook her head. "Tripper, I feel for them just as much as you do. But we've got to think logically. Safety in numbers doesn't apply here. We'd only make ourselves more vulnerable."

"I don't know who you are," Cam said to her. "Listen. Why did Thackeray send us here?"

"They're burning Gaylen to the ground!" Halstead yelled. "We need to get out of here! Do you think Thackeray would rather that we stay and die trying to save people instead of relocating?"

"All you care about anymore is saving your own ass," Cam said coldly. She walked over to Lily. "Will you show me where the girls are?"

"I'm going too," Tripper said. Logan pulled his chainsaw off the bar and said, "What the hell."

"I guess that's it, then." Halstead sighed and followed them through the door.

Lily led them upstairs to a set of doors. "All the beds were in here," she said.

"Okay. Stand back." Cam leaned against the door and cupped her hand to her ear. "I don't hear anything."

"They might not even be here," Halstead said.

"Let's make sure." Cam took hold of the doorknob and turned it ever so slowly. Then she pushed the door open, just enough to stick her head through and have a look.

The room was very dark. She could barely make out the outlines of the beds. There wasn't a soul to be seen. She pushed the door the rest of the way open. "Nothing?" Tripper whispered. She nodded.

Then a small shadow rose from behind one of the beds.

"Little girl?" Cam beckoned. "It's okay. Come here."

Another girl rose on the other side of the room. Then another, and another. They stood stock-still.

"Come here! We won't hurt you." Cam stepped into the room.

One of the girls walked out into the aisle. Behind her, like a doll, she dragged a severed arm.

"Oh *fuck*—"

Another half dozen girls rose and stalked into the aisle. Low, raspy growls escaped their throats. Then they ran at Cam.

She swung the machine gun up and cut into them, the muzzle flare lighting up their dead faces before they were kicked back into the darkness. They each hit the floor and struggled back up in turn, charging forward again.

Tripper knocked the other door open and sprayed them with Uzi fire. They kept coming—even those whose legs were sawed off by bullets simply pulled themselves along the floor, screaming ravenously.

Halstead grabbed Lily. "Downstairs! C'mon!"

Logan pushed past her and into the room. The chainsaw roared to life over his head. "Get back!" he yelled.

The girls surged at him. He tore into them at head level, cleaving through their little skulls with a metallic snarl. Brain matter gushed into the air. Their tiny hands clawed at his legs. He plunged the saw straight down into their chests, splitting them open and knocking their bodies back.

One girl leapt onto his arm, jaws snapping. He hurled her to the floor and cast the saw blade through her face. Logan turned away to avoid the rain of infected blood.

Downstairs, Halstead pushed Lily toward the bar entrance. "We've gotta get back into the tunnels!"

She threw open the trapdoor. "Go Lily!"

The girl looked toward the door through which they'd just come. The saw's whine and Logan's mad screaming could still be heard. "I want to wait!" she insisted.

Halstead started down the ladder. "Lily, I want you to come with me—"

Her foot slipped on a greasy rung and she toppled out of sight.

Lily looked down the hole and saw Halstead lying prone on the tunnel floor. She backed away, fear overtaking her. Gunfire erupted upstairs. Lily ran for the door on the other side of the room—the door leading out to the street—and started pulling chairs and tables away from it.

She had to get out. The children were going to kill Cam and Tripper and the soldier and then come spilling downstairs and into the tunnel. She had to get out of there. She jerked on the door handle in a panic. "Open! *Open!*"

It did.

She plunged into the snow.

Wading through the drift that had piled up against the building, Lily stumbled into the street and surveyed her surroundings. Distant booms could be heard; distant screams too.

A man ran toward her. She shrieked, thinking him undead, but he cried, "No! No! I'm not one of them!"

He reached out for her. Then something dropped onto his back from a ledge overhead and he fell, and Lily saw it was a hideous four-armed rotter, flaying the man's back open with its black claws, making a terrible rattling sound like corpse-laughter and then the Geek's eyes settled on her.

She ran down the middle of the street. Her fingers and toes were already numb. The wind drove tiny needles into her face, and as she turned her head away from it she tripped over a dead woman's leg. Slamming into the asphalt, Lily rolled over to see the Geek lumbering after her. It was slow, relaxed, confident. Its arms swayed from side to side and it licked its lips with half a tongue.

Lily rose to her knees, her face covered in a thin layer of frost, expression blank, and waited for the end to come. It had always been coming, always right on her heels, a cold shadow nipping at her soul; and now it had her. It hadn't mattered that she'd fled the dead girls. No escape, ever.

The Geek threw its arms open and howled.

The horse's hooves kicked up a violent flurry of snow as Adam drove it down the street, the street from his dreams, slapping the side of the scythe against the ribs of his steed and hollering "*EYAH! EYAH!*"

She saw him. His skin was black and his cloak was white but it was him, her Reaper, and he was hurtling toward the Geek like a locomotive.

The rotter turned. It saw what was bearing down on it and crossed its arms before its face in mortal terror.

Adam swung down, clinging to the side of the horse with his legs, and drove the blade into the Geek's stomach, lifting the undead off the ground and sending its dead body spinning through the air before it landed headfirst with a spine-shattering impact.

Adam swung to the other side of the horse and snatched Lily with his left hand, depositing her in front of him. He wrapped him arm securely around her waist.

"You came," she said breathlessly.

"You knew I would," he said.

"I know."

She glanced over her shoulder. "You look different."

"I am."

"What do we do now?"

"First, I'm going to get you to safety," Adam said, eyes on the road ahead. "Then I'm going to kill them."

# THIRTY-NINE / TORTURE PORN

Meyer had found the rest of Tripper's rope, and Voorhees was now secured to the chair in the living room, blind eyes looking out on a smoky sky through open windows.

"Smell that?" Meyer called, rummaging through the kitchen. "They're never gonna find you. You'll be ash... they'll never know what happened today. But we will."

He walked into the living room with a stack of ragged towels bearing various pieces of cutlery. Setting them on a small table beside Voorhees, he knelt and slapped the cop across the face. "You haven't gone deaf now, have you?"

"You're going to die," Voorhees snarled.

"Strong words for a cripple." Meyer picked through the selection of knives he'd brought out. "Quick story. When I was a lad up north, my father used to take me to a place where you could pay to carve up rotters. They'd have 'em strapped down to a table or lashed to a post, and you could put your name on a snapping undead's forehead or carve a heart into his backside. They had old buggers tied down with years of abuse cut into their flesh—it was a way to let off steam, you see, to turn the tables for a change."

"Sounds like your father was as sick as you," Voorhees said.

Meyer smiled and, holding his hand out, flicked his wrist. A long gash appeared in Voorhees' cheek. The cop gasped in pain.

"Back when they still printed books," Meyer continued, "a lot of folks predicted this sort of thing. Using zombies for torture and sex—entertainment. Some said it could never go that far, that we were better than that. Boy, we showed them. Mankind hit rock bottom pretty damn quick.

"But, as I was saying, we used to go down to this place and we'd buy a few hours with one of the fresh rotters. My dad used to carve

178

limericks into their backs. It was fun, sure, but there just wasn't anything satisfying about parting that bloodless flesh. It split under the slightest pressure and nothing came of it. You could plunge a knife right through a rotter's adam's apple and it would keep grunting and fighting and trying to get at you with its teeth. They didn't feel what we were doing.

"I guess that's why I started cutting myself. I wanted to see blood, you see. I'd slash up my arms and suck on 'em. Sometimes I'd cut my tongue just so I could taste the blood without anyone noticing. I had to hide it, because the old man would never have understood. I started cutting my toes—he wouldn't spot that—and I'd fill my shoes with blood as I walked to market with him. I loved him, I did, but he just didn't get it. Man lived every day of his life in the same miserable shithole, doing the same old thing. Downing a few pints and slicing up rotters didn't cut it for me, pardon the pun. After a while, bleeding myself didn't do it either. I wanted more. And I got it, didn't I?"

He pressed a paring knife against Voorhees' neck. "I won't go back to the existence of my childhood. I'll get out of here, get to Chicago. But first, I want to watch you bleed."

He drew the tip of the blade straight down, spilling only a tiny amount of blood. Voorhees gritted his teeth and fought the urge to scream.

"Hmm." Meyer dug the blade into the flesh beneath Voorhees' left eyebrow. He started peeling the eyebrow away. Voorhees couldn't hold it in any longer, and he howled and thrashed in the chair. Meyer straddled him and held his head still until the job was finished.

"Got a lot left to go," Meyer breathed. "Lots of blood left in you." He stabbed the knife into Voorhees' forehead, grinding it against his skull. "*Bleed!*"

He tossed the paring knife aside and selected a serrated blade. "Here we go."

He began sawing into the bridge of Voorhees' nose. The cop screamed loud and long, his voice becoming a nasally rasp as Meyer sliced down through his nostrils and peeled the nose away, leaving a gaping red cavity. Voorhees choked as blood poured down his throat. He spit up on Meyer's chest. The gangster laughed.

Getting off of Voorhees, Meyer wiped himself off and contemplated the severed nose in his palm.

Voorhees leaned forward to let the blood run down his face. *"FUUUUUUCK YOOOOUUUU!"*

"You really are tough as nails, Officer," Meyer said. "Gonna take a lot more work to break you." Cutting a small strip away from one of the towels, he wadded it up and stuffed it into Voorhees' nasal cavity. Voorhees swooned from the pain. "Stay with me," Meyer cooed.

"Hmm." Without so much as a flinch, he slashed the top of his own wrist. He pressed the wound to Voorhees' lips. "Taste it. Go on."

Voorhees bit into Meyer's flesh and wrenched his head to the side. A chunk of skin was torn away. Meyer yelped. Then a grin spread across his face from ear to ear.

Voorhees spit the flesh from his mouth and screamed again. Meyer held his bleeding arm up to the light. He watched the blood run for several minutes, as Voorhees' sounds of agony became more subdued. Then he went back to work.

He stuck the knife through Voorhees' upper lip and pinned the cop's head to the back of the chair. "No struggling now. I want this to be a clean cut." He pressed his full weight down on Voorhees and sliced the pink flesh away.

"Now for the bottom one."

Voorhees swung his head violently, and the chair rocked beneath himself and Meyer. He growled like an animal, even as Meyer's knife found purchase and dug through his lip into his gumline.

Meyer tossed both lips aside with a triumphant yell. He threw the knife across the room and staggered back. *"Oh! God!"* He ran over to the table and looked over his remaining knives. "We're having fun now, aren't we?"

The cleaver was small for what it was, not too unwieldy. He pressed the razor-sharp blade against the lower knuckles of Voorhees' left hand. "What do you think? All of 'em? Just the first two? Maybe just the whole hand."

He raised the cleaver high and whooped as it came down. CRACK! As the blade bit into the wood of the chair's arm. Voorhees' four fingers flew into the air.

The cop's head sagged. Meyer slapped him hard. "Stay awake! It's no good if we can't both feel it!"

He licked the wound on his wrist and chopped playfully at the remainder of Voorhees' hand. Blood speckled both their faces and rained on the floor. Voorhees' head came up, and he moaned; then it dropped again.

"No!" Meyer grabbed him by the chin. "You stay awake, you hear me? I'll fucking wait for you if you pass out on me! Fuck!" Meyer wrapped a towel around the ruin of Voorhees' hand. "You've hardly lost any blood, you pussy. I thought you were harder than this, Officer!"

Meyer stalked back and forth across the room, muttering to himself. Then he ran at the cop and slammed the cleaver into his leg, just above the knee.

Voorhees sat bolt upright with a shriek. The fabric shot out from his nasal cavity, followed by a shower of blood. He spat and gagged and gnashed his teeth within a lipless mouth. Meyer withdrew the cleaver. He started cutting the ropes.

"This'll make things interesting, yes?" The ropes fell to the floor. Meyer pulled Voorhees from the chair and cast him onto the floor. "Now GET UP! You've still got fight left in you! Get on your feet!"

Voorhees just lay there, panting. Blood pooled around his face and leg.

Meyer hacked into the meat of his buttock. "UP!"

Voorhees barely made a sound. Meyer was losing him.

"Fuck it then." Meyer threw the cleaver at the chair and sighed. "Guess I was wrong about you."

His teeth clenched. He swung his foot into Voorhees' stomach, again and again and again, causing the cop to cough up more blood before falling still.

"Fuck you, man." Meyer opened the apartment door. "I'll just leave you for the rotters."

He left. Voorhees lay utterly still, in silence, the only sound a whistle as blood bubbles formed in the hollow of his face.

*Please let me die. Take me. Please, God.*

But that just wasn't God's style, it seemed, nor Voorhees'. He knew that.

He pushed himself to his knees. With his good hand, he reached under the back of his coat and pulled the widowmaker free.

Meyer hadn't overestimated him at all. In fact, he'd made a grave mistake.

Now it was time to pay.

If it was the last thing Voorhees ever did—and he knew it would be—Meyer was going to pay.

# FORTY / LOSSES AND GAINS

"Where's Lily?" Cam demanded.

Halstead got to her feet in the tunnel and looked around haplessly. "I don't know. She was right beside me, and then I fell..."

"She must have taken off down the tunnel," Tripper muttered. "Lily!"

Taking Meyer's lanterns from the floor, they began the search. There wasn't a sign of the girl anywhere. She didn't return their cries. And she didn't have any reason to fear them—did she?

"Wait." Logan pointed up ahead with his gib-covered chainsaw. "Movement."

He motioned for everyone to move over against the wall. Logan crouched and squinted, fighting to keep his balance, still drunk.

"We're human!" came a call. Three figures appeared in the lantern light.

"Dalton!" Logan yelled.

A soldier, a cop and what looked like a doctor. *Could've been worse,* Halstead thought to herself. *Could've been saddled with three lame geriatrics.*

That, of course, made her think of Voorhees. She'd been trying not to think of him this entire time; indeed, as Cam had so succinctly put it, she had concerned herself solely with saving her own ass. Now the girl was missing because Halstead had gone down the ladder first. And her partner, a good man, an honest man, was lying bound and blind in a building that would soon be in flames.

*I'm shit. I couldn't even finish the job Thackeray entrusted me with... and now Gaylen burns. Somehow it's all my fault. It must be. I've let everyone down.*

"Logan," Dalton said, "we've got an evac route through an old rail system. Do you have any other survivors down here?"

"Maybe." Logan burped. "Trying to find the kid."

"Are you drunk?" Zane asked in disbelief.

"I wish I was," Rhodes grumbled.

Logan pointed down the tunnel behind himself. "There's a bar up there—"

"Shut up," Tripper snapped. "We've gotta find Lily. We can't leave until we find her."

Dalton eyed Tripper's guns with suspicion. "Where'd you get your hands on those?"

"Soldiers traded them," Tripper answered.

"What for? Why would anyone trade away arms? That's a crime."

"Ask him." Tripper angled his thumb toward Logan.

Dalton grimaced. "Logan. You didn't."

"I'm a man. I have needs."

"All right," Cam shouted, "back to Lily. She's about thirteen with long brown hair. She couldn't have gone far."

"Then let's find her," said Dalton. He turned to lead the way.

* * *

The search was fruitless.

They backtracked half a dozen times, screaming Lily's name until they were all hoarse—no response.

"What if she didn't even come down here?" Halstead gasped.

"Then we left her up there with what was left of those kids," Logan said. "Sorry. I really am."

"We can't just write her off like that!" Cam cried. Tripper put his arms around her.

"I hear something." Dropping into a crouch, Dalton crept toward the next corner. He heard the snapping of bone. A grunt. Blood splattering.

Dalton leapt around the bend and trained his rifle on the figure hunched there.

It was a man—a living man. He looked elderly, but based on the rotter at his feet, he still had some strength in him. The man had torn the undead's head clean off.

"Are you okay?" Dalton asked. *Bit?* he thought.

The man held up his hands and said softly, "Okay."

"We can get you out of here. Are you with anyone else?"

"No, alone." The man looked down at the rotter's twitching remains.

"Don't worry about that," Dalton said, taking the man by his elbow. "It's not going anywhere. Nice work."

The man nodded absently. Dalton led him back around the corner, checking him for any bites or scrapes in the lantern light. "Survivor!" he called to the others.

"What's your name, pops?" Tripper asked.

"Eugene."

"Well Eugene, we're getting the hell out of here. You with us?"

The old man nodded. Halstead frowned at him.

What was he chewing?

* * *

Like a shadow on the wall, Adam stole into the West Avenue Church of Christ and, kneeling behind the pulpit, set Lily on the floor.

"I want you to stay right here until I return." As he spoke, Adam surveyed the enormous room with its rows of pews and ornate stained-glass windows, newly restored since the establishment of the Great Cities. It was filled with dark places—but also silence. He didn't sense a threat. Maybe God's presence still had some potency after all.

"Where are you going?" Lily asked.

"To take care of the undead," he replied. "I'll be as quick as I can. Just stay here—don't make a sound, and wait for my return."

He stood up. "Reaper!" she cried.

He knelt back down. "What is it?"

Leaning forward, Lily tenderly kissed his fire-scarred face.

"Thank you," he whispered.

"And my name is Adam."

* * *

A mob of rotters looked up to see a pale horse standing in the middle of the road. Astride it was a dark man with a gigantic blade made from bone, joined to his arm like an extra appendage.

Before they had the time to blink, he was bearing down on them.

The scythe plunged into zombie after zombie, slicing clean through them, splitting decaying bodies in half and sending gouts of gray entrails into the air. The horse tore through the snow at a frenzied pace, driven by the kicks of its rider, and the scythe cut trough air and flesh alike without resistance.

Adam turned at the end of the road and started back. The remaining undead were scattering, flailing their arms and moaning at the futility of their last moments. He skewered heads, severed arms, sent torsos flying. Adam rounded a corner and streaked down a side street to meet a new pack.

The Siamese was at the head of it. Scuttling forward, it roared in twin tongues and made to tackle the horse. Adam pulled back, causing his steed to rear up—and he swung around its body to meet the Siamese mid-charge and split the twins from sternum to waist. The thrashing halves of the Siamese tumbled into the snow and lay still.

A torch struck Adam's head. He fell from the horse and rolled quickly to his feet. It was the Fire Juggler; the rotter hurled another pair of torches at Adam. He spun aside, avoiding both, and leapt to engage the monster.

A pike spread his abdomen. He snarled and turned to see the Fakir drawing long needles from its throat. "Try this," Adam said, and slammed the scythe through the rotter's heart.

The Juggler caught Adam by the arms and hurled him to the ground. More rotters crowded at the Juggler's back. Adam tried to lift the blade, but the undead pressed all his weight down on Adam's arm.

He made not a sound in his struggle; it was eerily silent as the undead closed in and fell upon him.

Then they exploded outward in a wave of fractured bodies, Adam rising up like a phoenix and sending the scythe screaming through the horde. He caught the Juggler on the tip and sent him crashing into a brick wall. Slumping down on one of his own torches, the Juggler groaned. Fire spread across its torso, and its pickled meat ignited like the wick of a candle.

There was an animal cry from the far end of the street. Looking up, Adam saw the King of the Dead standing there, clutching his cane and howling like a banshee.

*You underestimate me, beast,* Adam thought. Never again. He was more than a man, a force of nature, and he would cleave the unnatural into pieces until there was none left.

Eviscerato vanished from sight. Another two dozen rotters took his place.

"Come to me," Adam growled, and climbed atop his horse.

Then he went to them.

The battle raged on beneath an ever-darkening sky, with flames rising over the tops of buildings and the smell of burning death no longer just a grim omen.

# FORTY-ONE / FEAST

The buildings around Gaylen's perimeter had united in a single inferno, a new wall made from fire that struck defiantly upward into the snowy sky. The storm had not relented, yet Jeff Cullen didn't feel the cold; bathed in the warmth of the city, he watched without emotion as those who managed to make it through the fire were gunned down.

As the shots rang out and bodies pitched forward, other survivors were forced to turn back, to turn inward, where the city's festering core was clotted with undead; throngs dragging the bodies of slain citizens to the amphitheater. There, the corpses were being piled twenty deep in anticipation of the great feast. The rotters could scarcely contain themselves as they looked over the sea of flesh; but the King's guidance had brought them this far, and they would wait.

Those survivors still barricaded in buildings were either smoked out or pulled from safety, necks broken, limbs torn off, and their remains joined the rest. There was no shelter to be found from the undead.

Those with guns began committing suicide.

Dozens of gunshots rang out in the city center. Others, families trapped atop apartment buildings, leapt to their deaths, plummeting into the waiting arms of the predators.

Adam was working outward as he hunted down the undead. He missed the amphitheater entirely.

At dusk, the feast began.

Eviscerato stood atop the mountain of corpses and roared. His cry was picked up by ravenous followers, and one by one they threw themselves into the meat.

Nickel dragged a warm child to the stage where Eviscerato was perched. Taking the body in his arms, Eviscerato closed his lipless jaws over the child's blue lips.

Outside the amphitheater, the Petrified Man looked up to see a new group approaching. Thin, desiccated rotters with a peculiar gait, exposed bones coated with frost, joints cracking as they shuffled through the snow.

The undead at the head of the pack nodded to the Petrified Man. "Good evening. Or morning, as the case may be," it rasped in a hollow monotone. Reciting the speech that it had practiced for radio—for Senator Gillies—the Brit said, "On behalf of Prince George and the Prime Minister—"

The Brit paused and leaned forward, scrutinizing the Petrified Man. It lifted a monocle to its shriveled eyeball and, realizing it was addressing a zombie, said, "Hmm. Right."

The Petrified Man knocked the Brit's head off with an annoyed grunt. Then it set upon the other intruders.

* * *

Huddled in the church pulpit, Lily listened intently for any sign of her friend's arrival. All she heard were faint booms, and the occasional scream.

*Please let him be all right.*

A window shattered.

Lily pulled her knees to her chest and froze, refusing even to breathe as glass tinkled gently on carpet, and tiny footsteps pattered across the floor.

The Dwarf leapt into view and splayed its little claws with a venomous hiss.

Lily shrieked and drove both feet into its chest, sending the rotter tumbling head over heels down the steps into the pews.

Lily threw herself at the back wall, searching frantically for a door. She didn't want to run away where Adam couldn't find her—as she had with Cam and the others—but she had to get out of here! There had to be a room where she could hide. She found only locked doors.

The Dwarf hobbled toward her, shaking its head vigorously. Eviscerato preferred the young meat, the soft virgin flesh—but this was all for the Dwarf, its own little feast.

Stumbling back from the rotter, Lily ran for the pews. She dove into the second row and began pulling herself along the floor, under the seats. She'd have to throw the monster off her trail, moving from row to row as it searched for her, and then double back to hide in the first row. Then it would give up, leave in search of easier prey... she hoped.

*Adam!* she silently screamed.

Broken fingernails scrabbled over carpet. She heard a soft grunting at her back, and chanced a glance: the Dwarf was crawling after her beneath the pews. Its horns scraped the undersides of the seats as it strained to reach her feet.

Lily kicked its hands away and got to her feet. She climbed atop the nearest pew and leapt to the next. She was going to have to leave. She had to get to the doors. *I'm sorry Adam!*

She leapt to the next pew—and the Dwarf rose up right in front of her, colliding with her and sending both of them kicking to the floor.

Lily screamed and thrashed about in the darkness. She felt its hands on her legs. Teeth snapped. She flailed her arms and caught one of its horns in her hand. The Dwarf squealed. Lily slammed its head into the seat of the pew, over and over again until she heard a wet squelch with each impact. Then she let go and ran for her life.

The Dwarf was right on her tail. It shook blood from its eyes and jumped at her, swiping at her ankles, making horrible little noises as it pursued her down the center aisle and finally snagged one of her feet. She crashed into the doors and fell still.

The Dwarf turned her over and straddled her, wrapping its tiny fingers around her throat. Lily murmured softly, eyelids fluttering. The Dwarf waited for her to look up into its pinched face.

She seized its ears in her hands and threw the Dwarf aside, rolling over and climbing onto it and smashing its head into the floor with a nightmarish scream. The Dwarf's neck snapped, skull cracking, blood and pus spewing from its splitting skin as its head came apart and spat curdled brains across the carpet. Lily Stood up and leapt into the ruin of the Dwarf's face with both feet, stomping it into oblivion. Its arms and legs continued to wiggle; she stamped on its wrists, shattering them, then twisted its ankles until they broke with a satisfying snap.

The Dwarf's torso spasmed quietly. Lily wiped sweat from her brow and walked back to the pulpit. Her heart pounding in her ears, she didn't hear the footsteps at her back; and, settling down in the shadows, her back was left to the approaching figure as it reached out.

"*NO!*"

"It's me, Lily!"

Adam scooped her up into his arms. "Let's go."

"Did you kill them all already?"

"I can't find the rest. It doesn't matter—the city's on fire. Let's get you out of here."

"What about my other friends?" she asked.

"Who?"

"Cam and Tripper and Officer Voorhees. We can't leave them."

"All right." He helped Lily onto his shoulders, and headed for the doors. "But time is short."

As they exited the church and mounted the horse, Nickel watched from an alleyway. He watched the way that the young one clung to the aberration's neck and the gentle way he bore her onto his steed.

Rusty gears began turning in the zombie's head.

# FORTY-TWO / THE CONDEMNED

With Dalton leading the way, the survivors headed into the subway system.

Lily was simply nowhere to be found and, as Dalton had kept reminding them, they had only a brief window until their only means of escape was cut off.

He prayed that he could count on the sergeant. He didn't count on the undead.

Dalton dropped to one knee and raised a fist in the air. The others fell silent behind him. He peered through his scope and saw a couple dozen rotters ambling through the tunnel.

"We can take them," Tripper whispered.

"I don't even have a gun," Zane complained. Cam handed him the Colt Python. "It's got a kick to it."

"Stay behind me, Eugene," Halstead said to the old man. He nodded.

Dalton opened fire on the rotters.

Their heads jerked up at the sound of gunfire, only to be sent snapping back as his lead found its mark. With skulls blistered and yawning wide, the undead kept coming.

Tripper emptied his Uzis and drew a pistol. He could barely see down here! He only hoped the others were faring better. They didn't have to take every rotter down, just enough for them to get past.

Halstead's gun clicked: empty. She pushed Eugene against the wall and flattened herself beside him. Terror seized her as the undead drew closer.

CRACK! CRACK! CRACK! Dalton shot his targets through the spine. He only hoped the sergeant hadn't seen any rotters crawling around. He might blow the tunnel—

Reality's bottom seemed to drop out for a moment, everything blurring, a low roar building in the air. Then the light from the explosion around the bend lit up the tunnel for a split second—before being squelched by the collapsing ceiling.

"*Goddammit!*" Dalton screamed. They'd sealed the tunnel! There was no way out!

"No!" Rhodes ran at the undead and was swallowed in a cloud of dust. Blinded, he spun in a wild panic. Undead brushed against him. He fired into the cloud. "No! No! Dammit no!"

Jaws closed over his shoulder. He wrenched himself free and turned to fire. Another rotter caught him in an icy embrace and ripped into his neck.

"Stop shooting!" Dalton was yelling. "We've got zero visibility!" The dust had enveloped them all.

Logan's chainsaw came to life. "I've got it!"

Rhodes fell at his feet. He gaped at the dead man, watching numbly as a slavering rotter pulled the man's intestines from his belly and stuffed them into its maw.

Cam slammed the butt of her machine gun into the rotter's skull. "We've gotta get the fuck out of here!"

"Goddamn you!" Dalton screamed into the darkness. Had the sergeant hesitated at all before giving the order? Had it even been his call? They'd never know. They'd never know who had doomed them all.

A zombie grabbed the barrel of his rifle and jerked it from his grip. Another went for his face. Dalton fell back and yanked a combat knife from a sheath on his thigh, slicing into the undead's throat.

"Where is everyone?" Zane cried. He turned in the dust and wiped grime from his eyes. "Talk to me!" The Python was heavy in his hands. He didn't dare use it for fear of killing one of the others. Maybe it would be better to use it on himself—

A teenage rotter lurched into view, grabbing his forearm and tearing a chunk of flesh away. Zane screamed in anguish.

He shoved the rotter back and placed the Python's mouth beneath his chin. "I regret nothing."

The shot tore through the tunnel like a peal of thunder. Shaking off a decapitated corpse, Dalton fumbled through the dark. Someone grabbed his hand.

"It's okay!" It was Cam. She and Tripper hauled Dalton to his feet. "Where the hell do we go now?"

"I don't know," he gasped. "We're dead. We're all dead."

"That's what I've been saying all along." Logan lowered the idling saw and, through the dissipating clouds, pointed to his right. "I think the passage we came through is off that way."

"Halstead!" Tripper yelled.

"Yeah!" She headed toward his voice with Eugene in tow.

They found the entrance to the smaller passageway and left the subway tunnel. Visibility was still pitiful. Dalton glanced over his shoulder and asked, "Who did we lose?"

"The two guys who were with you," Cam muttered.

"At least we've got old Eugene," Logan offered.

"Shut the fuck up."

Making their way back to Meyer's bootlegging tunnels, the group looked for another way out. They couldn't just go up into the street. If anything, the fire was probably concentrating the undead in the center of the city. And, of course, the soldiers would be waiting beyond that point to gun down anyone in sight.

"Ladder." Dalton hustled forward and found himself peering up a narrow shaft. "Must go into some building."

"Inside, outside, what's the difference?" said Logan.

"If you don't give a damn about your safety, you can take point," Dalton snapped.

Logan shrugged and started up the ladder.

All was clear. The building was small, filled with crates and miscellaneous junk. Shelves upon shelves of tattered yellow books rested against the walls. Dalton thumbed through them: mostly Bibles. "I think this was a library, once," he said.

The walls were lined with windows, but the glass was frosted over. So no one could see in, either; just the same, Dalton started moving shelves to block the windows. "Give me a hand here!"

Eugene tugged on Halstead's arm. "What is it?" she asked.

"Have you seen him? The Reaper?"

She wasn't quite sure how to respond to that. She just patted his back and said, "You sit here and rest. I'm going to help the others."

There was thumping at the main entrance. "Fuck. They heard us," said Cam.

Dalton and Tripper lugged a shelf over to the locked double doors and leaned it against them. "Get those crates," Tripper called to the others. "Hurry!"

More pounding. More fists.

A window in the back shattered, and undead hands scrabbled at books.

"Cam, take care of that!" Tripper yelled.

"Let me," Logan said. "Save your bullets for yourselves." Walking leisurely to the back of the room, he fired up the saw and plunged it into the grasping fingers.

Suddenly, from outside the front of the library came a squeal of tires; something crashed against the wall, shaking the entire building. Then they heard shotgun blasts.

"Somebody's got wheels!" Halstead cried. "Oh, thank God!"

One of the front windows shattered, and a man pulled himself in. Dalton and Tripper quickly moved a shelf to block the hole.

The man rose. "I'll be damned," Dalton said.

"Soldier." Ian Gregory nodded curtly to him, a twelve-gauge in each hand. "Need a lift?"

"How did you know?" Halstead exclaimed.

"I saw them congregating around this building," Gregory told her. "Sure sign of fresh meat."

"How about that?" Logan wandered over. "It's a Hand of God reunion. Hey boss."

"Logan." Gregory turned toward the sound of pounding. "I ran a few down but you've got another thirty or so out there. It's gonna be tough clearing a path to the Hummer, especially with more on the way."

"Tough or not, we're doing it," Tripper said. "Like we have a choice."

# FORTY-THREE / ABATTOIR

A series of ear-splitting booms shook the library. For a second, Tripper thought it was all going to come down on them. "What the fuck is that?"

"Rockets," said Logan. "They're using the rockets. Jesus, this is really it. The end."

The doors groaned as the undead continued their assault. Then there was a clattering on the roof. Falling debris? Running to the center of the room, Tripper peered at a boarded-up skylight and listened to the rhythmic sound: *clop-clop-clop...*

The skylight exploded. Wood and glass rained down on him.

A man, shrouded in white but blackened and burned underneath, dropped into the room. He held a child in his arms—Lily!

"You're all right!" Halstead cried. She took a step forward, then narrowed her eyes at the man holding the girl. "Who are—*what* are—"

"His name is Adam," Lily said, climbing out of the man's arms. "He's my friend."

The old man, Eugene, cowered in the shadows and stared at the hooded figure.

Ian Gregory approached Adam with a curious expression. "You look different," he said.

"We saw you come in here," Adam replied. He'd walked his steed up a crumbling wall onto the roof, not wanting to further stir up the dead with his presence. At Lily's request, really... that he save the other survivors, all of them, without incident. As if he were the old elf from winter legend who could grant a child's any wish.

Dalton was silent. He remembered that night, in the badlands, when Hand of God had seen Death in the flesh. He didn't know

195

what to make of the apparition—did this mean salvation or certain death?

Logan backed up against the shelf blocking the window through which Gregory had made his entrance. "Well, I'm about ready to call it a night."

Dead hands tore through the books and seized his head. He fumbled with the chainsaw's starter cord and bellowed, "A little fucking help!"

Cam pried at the gray hands, but others reached through to grab at her wrists. The flesh was peeled from the backs of her hands. She fell to the floor in hysterics.

The saw started up. Logan, his head pulled into the shelf, unable to see, raised the weapon toward his head. "STOP!" Gregory yelled. "You're gonna—"

The blade touched Logan's throat and it blossomed like a flower of gore. His cries turned to a gurgling sputter as crimson showered down the front of his uniform. The saw fell idle at his feet. The dead hands in his hair and eyes tore his head from his shoulders and retreated with their prize.

Tripper cradled Cam, who was staring in horror at her hands. "God—I'm infected!"

"You don't know that!"

"Yes I do! I feel it! Oh God!"

A window burst behind Eugene. He whirled to struggle with half a dozen rotting arms. Halstead ran to him. "I need a gun—NOW!"

One undead hand wavered uncertainly in the air, a shard of glass embedded in its palm. Then it swung down into Halstead's eye.

She wailed as the glass tore a canyon through her cheek and into her jaw. The rotter's fingers slipped into her flesh and tugged her forward. The hands holding Eugene left him and found her.

Lily grabbed Halstead's legs. She screamed in protest as Adam pulled her away. Together, they watched the cop's body slide out the window into the night.

Gregory shook Adam by the shoulder. "Can you help us get to the vehicle outside?"

Adam nodded. He pulled the scythe from under his cloak and strapped it on to his arm. "Where is it?"

"Out front."

"Of course," Adam sighed. He walked over to the barricaded doors and started pulling crates away.

Dalton pulled Cam to her feet. "We need you. C'mon."

As Adam took down the barricade, he sensed something, something vague and threatening that gnawed at the back of his mind. What was it? The horde waiting outside? No, it was something worse.

As he pulled the last shelf away, the doors fell in beneath the weight of the undead. Zombies spilled into the room.

"Open fire!" Gregory shouted.

Adam sliced a pair of rotters in half and kicked their spurting remains away. He turned to grab Lily, pulling her onto his shoulders. He turned back just in time to be tackled to the floor. Lily tumbled away from him.

She scrambled past Gregory, who was busy shearing the heads off of rotters with his shotguns. He knelt to reload—cold hands clamped down on his shoulders. He batted them away and retreated further into the room.

The undead were still pouring in—far more than thirty now. It was a full-scale assault. Adam stood at the threshold and pared them down, but again and again he was overwhelmed by their numbers, and they broke through in waves. Such a wave swept over Ian Gregory. He discharged the shotguns as he fell, taking a couple more with him. He was fading fast beneath an onslaught of teeth, and fumbled through his uniform for the grenade there—released the pin—his last act of defiance.

The muffled explosion threw the dead straight up in a smoking geyser. They came down in pieces, only to be replaced by others. Every blast, every bullet—it meant nothing, the rotters were swarming in at an exponential rate.

Tripper and Cam were backed into the far corner of the room. They turned a shelf on its side and used it for cover until their guns were empty.

Tripper lit a joint, took a long drag and passed it to his lover. "I don't know what to say," he muttered, barely audible above the groans of the encroaching dead.

"There's nothing to say." Cam gently kissed his neck, then wrapped her arms around him.

The rotters pulled the shelf aside. Tripper glared at them over Cam's shoulder. "Fuckers." Then the pair was swallowed.

Lily cowered between a shelf and the rear wall. She screamed as a shadow swooped down to collect her. "It's all right!" Dalton yelled. "We're getting out of here!"

"Reaper!" he shouted. On the other side of the room, Adam turned to see the soldier and child surrounded by undead. He hurled himself into their midst like a torpedo, raking his scythe through flesh and bone and cutting a path to Lily. Dalton handed her over. "The car!"

He stayed glued to Adam's back as the former Death made his way to the entrance. They ran out into the freezing cold, into the night—only to find the sky lit by flames as every building around them burned. Adam glanced up at the library's roof and saw his horse's head hanging over the edge, dead. It must have been struck by shrapnel. So, then, on to a new steed—Adam yanked open the Hummer's passenger door and put Lily inside. Dalton was already behind the wheel. Gregory had left the keys inside. Knew he might not make it back. Good man to the end.

"*WAIT!*" a voice snarled. Adam turned—and was blown away by a volley of bullets.

Finn Meyer staggered toward the Hummer. "*Get out!*" he screamed at Dalton.

Dalton raised his hands and scooted out of the driver's seat. "I have a child here!"

Meyer grimaced. "I don't care!"

Then he heard a sound at his back—a ragged scream, but not that of the undead. No, it was a cry fraught with rage and grief and desperation, and Meyer managed to put his finger on the voice just before the widowmaker separated his head from his neck.

He fell into the snow; blinked a few times, in disbelief, at Voorhees, and at his own decapitated body; then his mind faded.

A zombie bit into Voorhees' shoulder. He hacked into its skull and shoved it aside. Didn't matter now. He'd followed Meyer's gunshots and footfalls until he heard his voice and was sure. Now it was over.

"Voorhees!" Lily cried.

He held his hand out, clutching at the air. "Lily?"

Dalton put his arm around the half-dead man and dragged him to the Hummer. "Here. Get in."

Adam got to his feet and grimaced as he felt the bullets searing his insides. He saw Voorhees, and that Lily was safe, and he left out a sigh of relief. At least it was finally done.

Then Eugene stepped around the front of the vehicle. Adam saw him for the first time, and that feeling of strange dread gripped him again.

"Who are you?" he called.

The old man opened his mouth. He did not speak, yet a voice— *voices*—poured forth like flies boiling from his lips. "*We have many names.*"

*It was the Omega.*

*He'd fully regenerated.*

And, with a strength unlike any man Adam had ever seen, the Omega surged forward and knocked him off his feet, driving him through a burning wall and into the mouth of Hell.

# FORTY-FOUR / THE BEAST

*"WE ARE ONE THOUSAND MILLION STRONG! WE HAVE WAITED AN ETERNITY IN THE ABYSS FOR THIS MOMENT—WE ARE THE END, REAPER, YOUR END, AND NOW WE SHALL REAP YOU!"*

Adam was half-conscious, barely aware of the scorching heat enveloping him as he was carried through a burning room. All was white around him, a swimming storm of flames, a maelstrom without end. Then he was slammed down on a table of glowing steel and the fissures of his burnt flesh opened to receive the pain.

The Omega smashed Adam's head into the table in a mad frenzy. All the while his jaw hung open, hateful words spouting forth: *"DEMON! FUCKING DEMON—NOW YOU JOIN US IN HELL! NOW YOU'LL KNOW WHAT IT'S LIKE!"* Hundreds of voices or more were fighting to be heard, screaming over one another in various languages, all of which Adam could understand—and all of which were saying the same things. They were wrong, he was no demon, he had once been a man himself. He pushed the Omega's hands away from his throat and tried to speak.

*"WE DON'T WANT YOUR LIES! WE WILL HAVE OUR VENGEANCE!"*

The Omega tore the scythe from Adam's arm; wouldn't have done him any good anyway. He tried to look around and figure out just where they were. All he saw were flames.

The Omega overturned the table and sent Adam sprawling. He splashed down in a hot, coppery liquid. Blood. The floor was covered in blood.

Adam stood up. He was standing on the killing floor of a slaughterhouse.

A white-hot chain was slung around his neck. The Omega lifted him off the floor, its own hands blackening as it pulled the chain taut. The façade of a healthy man was being scorched away. It shook Adam violently, throttling him, and he felt his flesh becoming brittle ash and falling away in flakes. *Can't take much more of this.*

The Omega hurled him over a fiery conveyor belt and into a steel wall. Adam landed on his hands and knees and crawled toward an enormous block of machinery. He had to get out of here. He could feel the heat searing the lenses of his eyes. His body was falling apart. Had to keep moving.

The chain snapped against the side of his head and sent him sliding through coagulated gore. He heard the distant braying of livestock as the flames consumed them. Was he to join them, just another servant-animal gutted and cast aside?

The Omega straddled Adam's back. *"We'll burn here together, Reaper—back to the abyss!"* A cacophony of insane laughter tore through the air. The old man's meat was cooking. His skin blistered and split open. *"We're starting to look alike, Reaper! Can you feel it—the burning? The terrible burning? Do you feel it eating you alive? ANSWER US!"* Rising, the Omega turned Adam over and kicked him in the chest. *"SPEAK!"*

Adam coughed up ashy spittle and rasped, "Enough talk." He grabbed the chain hanging from the Omega's hand and yanked as hard as he could.

The Omega stumbled over him and into the conveyor belt. It spun around, but not fast enough, not even close—Adam leapt across the room and drove his knees into the rotter's ribs. Both flew over the belt and into the fire.

Adam sent his fist crashing through the Omega's teeth. Its head snapped back, bone tearing through flesh. It laughed. Adam grabbed it by the wrist and swung it into the wall. Its arm cracked loudly. Still the fiend cackled. *"We're already dead, demon!"*

Its hand found a meathook on the floor and closed over the wooden handle. Adam saw it coming and caught the Omega's wrist. With a grim smile, he crushed it to powder inside his fist.

He swung at its jaw again. This time, it caught *his* fist in its broken teeth. Driving his thumb into the underside of its jaw, he gritted his teeth and twisted... *twisted.* The Omega yelped. It struggled feebly with his grip, and then it grunted and its jaw was ripped free with a wet sound, its black tongue spilling down its chest.

The rotter's eyes were wide with shock. It clawed at Adam's face, and still the voices poured out from the hollow of its throat. *"No! You can't do this! You have no right!"*

"YOU have no right!" Adam snatched the chain from the Omega's hand, coiling it around his fist as the rotter staggered away. "You're already dead!" He charged after it.

"*YOU HAVE NO RIGHT!*" he thundered again. His fist sailed through tongues of flame and shattered the Omega's cheekbone. The voices inside screamed in horror—the killers, the rapists, the corruptors of humanity were all wracked with despair as Adam's fist rained down on their shared limbs, breaking kneecaps in two, driving splinters of ribs into bursting organs, pulverizing joints and crushing tissue until there was a pulpy, sagging bag of bones left dangling in Adam's grip.

"*You can't...*" the Omega pleaded. Ichor ran from its punctured eyeballs and into the creases of its smashed face. It raised broken fingers before itself and hissed, "*YOU CAN'T!!*"

"I am," Adam spat. He threw the crippled corpse into the fire.

* * *

"No!, Adam!" Lily was crying. Dalton did his best to ignore her as he sped down the street. She grabbed at the wheel.

"Stop it!" Dalton barked. "He'll be all right! He's not like us!"

"No, they'll hurt him!" Lily protested.

Dalton was trying to think of a response when a towering beast stepped into the road ahead. He swerved to the left, felt himself losing control, the tires losing the road. Then the impact.

Dalton fell out his door and onto the sidewalk. Where was his gun? Drawing his combat knife, he crept around the rear of the Hummer to see just what had run them off the road.

The Petrified Man seized Dalton's hand, crushing the bones of his fingers within their tubes of flesh, and lifted him to eye level.

"Run!" he shouted, praying Lily could hear him. "Run!"

The Petrified Man glanced downward. Lily started screaming. Dalton craned his neck to see her in the arms of another rotter. "NO—"

The Petrified Man rammed his fist into Dalton's ribs. He was able to see his sternum buckle and split, erupting through his tattered uniform. He was able to watch the rotter pull his spine out through his chest, and lift it overhead to suck the fluid from it. Then, and only then, did he die.

# FORTY-FIVE / FINAL THINGS

Voorhees heard another commotion outside the Hummer. The door beside his head was torn open, and freeing cold washed over him.

"Where is she?" cried Adam.

"I don't know what happen," Voorhees breathed, enunciating as best he could. His strength was failing. He'd held onto this fragile, broken body long enough to finish Meyer; now, just when he thought he could finally lay his head to rest, another crisis. *It never ends.*

"I heard the driver yell at her to run," he told Adam. "Then I heard him die."

Adam strapped the scythe on and turned to face the empty street. Gaylen was an inferno. Somehow, the icy winter winds were still cutting through this concrete canyon, but its walls were all ablaze and flakes of snow were eroding away before they touched the asphalt.

And, at the end of the street, a hunchbacked rotter was dancing. Arms spread wide, head titled, a crazed grin on its face, it writhed in dark celebration. It beckoned to him.

Adam broke into a run. Nickel stopped dancing and lumbered into a mass of flames: a huge building that had been a train station a century prior. Adam followed without hesitation. He knew it was a trap. He knew it was the last trap, the end of this grim campaign— but he knew they had her.

He ran into the station. Tongues of heat crawled across a vaulted ceiling five stories overhead. He was flanked by columns bathed in fire. All was silent but for the crackling of the flames.

Nickel ran at him from the left. He turned and plunged the scythe through the rotter's black heart. Threw the body aside. Too easy.

Eviscerato roared from the other end of the room.

He crouched like a threatened animal, pacing back and forth, Lily clutched against his chest.

"*Let her go!*" Adam bellowed.

The King of the Dead cocked his head and clacked his teeth together: *CLACK-CLACK-CLACK*, like some sort of primitive taunt. He tightened his grip on Lily. She screamed.

"I said *LET HER GO GODDAMMIT!*"

Eviscerato held out his right arm. He shook it violently, then pointed at Adam. The scythe. He wanted it off.

Adam removed the straps and let the blade clatter on the marble floor. "All right!"

The Petrified Man seized him about the waist in a brutal bear-hug, swinging him high into the air and then squeezing his body against the zombie's own bony bulk.

Then he was spinning through the air—a column approached—his back was folded around it for one brief, agonizing moment before he slumped to the floor. The Petrified Man was upon him immediately, smashing his head into the column. He grabbed the behemoth's shoulders and pulled himself up to slug him in the jaw. The zombie simply smashed him into the column again. Adam's world trembled. Bits of flaming plaster fell around him. Now flying again—slamming into the floor. Lily screaming.

Eviscerato hurled her aside and raised his cane over his head. Charged at Adam. The former Reaper lifted his head, and the cane lashed him across the jaw, sending him reeling straight into the Petrified Man's arms. He was turned upside-down and swung into another column. Unconsciousness threatened to overtake him.

Eviscerato drove the cane deep into Adam's gut, piercing his false flesh and churning his insides. Adam howled in agony. Eviscerato snapped his teeth and smiled that dreadful smile of his, that showman's smile. *Watch the fallen angel suffer and die at the hands of a mere human—less than a human, in fact! Nothing more than a rotten corpse, a dancing, capering corpse, meekest of all men —inheritor of the earth! The world is dead and soon she will be dead with us, Reaper. And you will be NOTHING—*

Adam grabbed the cane and snapped it in two inside his body. Eviscerato grunted. Adam plowed his feet into the rotter's teeth.

The Petrified Man grabbed Adam's head and jerked him straight up, bringing him back down on a sharp knee, driving a spur of bone deep into his back.

Adam was pounded into the floor. The Petrified Man stood on the back of his head and started grinding his face down. And somewhere, Lily was still screaming.

He cried out her name. His head was going to be pulped any second, the Petrified Man digging his heel into the base of it.

Then the pressure eased off. The zombie stepped back. Adam was able, painfully, to turn his head ninety degrees and look up. And he saw the Petrified Man standing there, a dull stare on its face, the point of the scythe protruding from its groin.

Lily released the blade and stumbled back. The zombie turned toward her, stiffly, hands grasping at the blade in the small of its back. Then it teetered and came down like a redwood.

Eviscerato spread his arms and roared. He ran at the girl.

Adam caught his ankle and brought him crashing down. Adam leapt onto the King of the Dead's back and locked his arms like a vise around the rotter's neck.

He pressed his lips to the hollow of Eviscerato's ear. "Never again," he growled. And he wrenched with all his might.

The zombie's spitting head separated from his shoulders, and a geyser of foul waste spewed forth from the stump of his neck. His eyes turned white and lolled in his skull, and his mouth dropped open, as if to utter final words. But there were none. He would die, this time, without ceremony.

Adam stood, clutching the head, and gripped it in both hands. He stared into Eviscerato's hateful face. "Never again."

And he knelt over the Petrified Man's corpse and staked the head on the end of the scythe. A grating howl sounded as whatever was inside of the King took leave of his corrupt crown.

Adam fell on his back. Lily threw herself on him. "No!"

"I'm all right," he whispered. "I just need... a moment..."

A pillar of flame passed through the entrance and into the station. Lily shook Adam. "Get up! Hurry!"

Adam rolled over onto his elbows and saw the Omega shuffling toward them, reduced nearly to a skeleton by the fire covering it but still coming, the rage of a thousand million forcing its withered limbs to move.

Adam rose, clutching Lily to his breast.

The Omega stopped a few yards from them. Its head rolled uncertainly on a brittle neck, and a cry of despair emanated from the center of the thing—a thousand million wicked souls consumed by their cosmic failure.

The Omega exploded.

Adam covered Lily in his cloak and closed his eyes to the hail of burning bones. They rained over him, tinkling on the floor; then it was over.

He hustled her out of the station and into the street. Neither saying a word, they made their way back to the Hummer.

Adam opened the back door, and Lily cradled Voorhees' head. "We can go now," she said.

"Are they all dead?" he rasped.

"Those that aren't soon will be," Adam said.

"The people? All the people?"

Adam didn't answer.

"Rome is ash, then." Voorhees' words whistled through bloody teeth.

Adam didn't reply to that either. Something more pressing had suddenly dawned on him.

He was supposed to appoint a replacement, wasn't he? A new sentinel, to keep the order. That the thought hadn't crossed his mind until now told him what he needed to do. He looked at the detective—what was left of him. This world had worn Voorhees down, reduced him to a shade. There was nothing more he could do while bound to this coil.

Adam placed his hand on Voorhees' shoulder. "I have an offer for you. A job, if you're interested."

Voorhees shook his head. "I think I'd rather just die, friend."

A tiny cloud of breath escaped the cop's pale lips. Then no more.

"But..." Adam shook his head. "You were the one. I chose you."

Lily hugged his back. "I chose *you*," she said softly.

He turned to her. "What?"

She was glowing.

A soft aura—like a cloak of white—covered her figure. She smiled up at him, then looked down at her hands in wonder.

"You?" Adam stammered. "But you're—you're—*a child*."

"You were too, once," Lily said. And it all came back to him.

*A kingdom in the east... he a young boy, working in his grandfather's fields. He'd seen her there, the woman in white, and had known she was Death.*

*Terrified at first, he'd told his grandfather and fled to the city. And that was where she awaited him.*

*And she'd told him, and made him understand why it was him, and he now knew what it was that had stirred deep in his soul, had made him restless all throughout his young life. Now he knew why he stared every night at the stars. They had beckoned, as she had; no longer afraid, he had taken her hands in his and accepted.*

"A child," Adam whispered. Lily took his hands in hers.

"I'll always be here," she said, "whenever you need me. Just call me."

"*Lilith,*" he breathed. She nodded with a smile.

He knew she wouldn't remember. Not at first. Perhaps later, with the passing of these strange aeons, they would find each other again, and he would tell her the story—her story.

Then she stepped through him, through space, and went to the place from whence he'd come.

Gaylen crumbled to the earth.

# EPILOGUE / AFTERLIFE

As dawn broke, Jeff Cullen breathed in the cloying scent of death and coughed loudly. Perched in the back of a Jeep, he called to the nearest soldier on the city perimeter. "How long do you suppose we need to stay out here?"

"You can go anytime you want," the soldier muttered. "Your job's done."

"What's that supposed to mean?" Cullen snapped. "May I remind you that I am—"

He was grabbed from behind and thrown to the ground. The tip of a blade carved from bone pressed into his throat.

A charred man in soot-stained robes knelt over the senator. "You did this?"

Cullen started to scream and felt the point of the blade bite into his flesh. "Oh God. Lower your weapons!" he called to the soldiers around him. "Stay back! Lower your weapons!" But not a single one of them had raised his or her gun anyway.

"How many people did you kill today?" Adam snarled.

"I—we had to do it! We did it for the other cities! My job is to serve the greater good! That's what I did!"

Adam came close enough for Cullen to smell his burnt flesh. He turned the blade as if readying to strike. Cullen's rhetoric broke down into senseless babble.

"Resign your post," Adam rasped. "No more. Never again."

The senator nodded quickly. "Yes. Yes! Of course I will. I should. I'm sorry, so sorry..."

Adam rose and was gone.

Soldiers looked down at Cullen with contempt. Surely they didn't take what he'd said seriously, about resigning... but they were walking away from him now, and ignoring his pitiful cries.

Others glanced around in confusion at the man in white's departure. One pointed toward the horizon.

The man in white sat on a pale horse. He raised his scythe into the air, a salute—then rode out of sight.

There was much work to be done.

# AFTERDEAD: A.D. 2007

# 0 / GRINNING SAMUEL

The air was musty and stale, choking Ryland with every ragged breath. Seated on a rickety old chair before a table coated with dust, he imagined he was in the waiting room of a mausoleum. He'd been here two hours. Seemed the Reaper was overbooked today.

Before him yawned the mouth of a maze: a series of catacombs cut deep into the earth. A bitter cold whispered at him from the blackness, further constricting his lungs. In contrast was the warmth of klieg lights on his back; his long face was made longer in shadows cast sharply upon the table. On second thought, this seemed less a mausoleum than a television studio. Backlit like a late-night host, Ryland crossed one leg over the other and tapped his gold wristwatch, waited on his guest. Flanked by the klieg lights at Ryland's rear were his audience, a huddled contingency wearing insect-like night vision helmet, hugging their M4 carbines which would punctuate his words like a laugh track if the guest wasn't being cooperative.

The hush in the entrance of the catacombs was palpable as the mold in the air. His men's breath, filtered through their helmets, was inaudible. Ryland coughed on a mote of dust. The sound cracked and echoed like a rifle report. Then the hush returned.

The hush was anticipation.

Something shifted in the catacombs. Ryland straightened up a bit, as a formality; although what was shuffling through the dirt towards the klieg lights likely couldn't see him, not because of the lighting but because its eyes had long crumbled from their sockets.

Still Samuel always found his way to the table. Sometimes Samuel found his way to other things.

He was attired in a soiled and worn shirt from the colonial era that had once been white, but was now a dingy brown; same with his loose-fitting trousers. Samuel never requested new clothing. He probably only wore these threadbare threads out of habit. If they finally fell from his shoulders, revealing his emaciated husk of a frame, he'd likely not react.

Everyone always noticed his hands first. Ryland's gunmen heard the rusty creaking of Samuel's metal fingers, crude constructs tethered to his wrists with wire; fitted over what remained of his original appendages with an intricate system of antique clock parts housed within the palms. The mechanical hands flexed continuously as Samuel plodded along.

Once interest in the fidgety hands had waned, there was nowhere else to look but at his face: brown flesh-paper so fragile thin, stretched over an angular skull; the holes were eyes and nose had once been to serve purposes now fulfilled by other means; and the jaws. Another mechanism, screwed into the bone and affixed with steel teeth. Ryland stared in wonder, imagining the blind afterdead seated somewhere deep in the catacombs, working with hands that were not his own in order to build his razorblade smile.

"Grinning Samuel" was his full moniker (Samuel not being his real name, no one knew what that was). He settled in a chair opposite from Ryland and placed a small burlap sack in front of him. Stared, eyeless, at the living.

He was uncommonly picky and any transaction with him came with certain rules of conduct. Some had been established from the get-go while others were learned at great cost. Most important was the invisible line running down the middle of the table, separating Ryland from Samuel, a line of principle as effective as an electric fence. No one crossed that line. This cardinal rule was established when Ryland's predecessor had reached out to grab that little burlap sack. In the ensuing melee, all the gunmen had swarmed past the now-screaming-and-bleeding liaison with every intention of dismembering Samuel.

And he'd killed every single one of them. Every one. The liaison had watched and died as blood jetted from the stump of his wrist. Watched and died while blind, smiling Samuel stuffed the gunmen's remains into his stainless-steel maw. He didn't feed often, yet he still thrived down here, in these catacombs beneath a defunct Protestant parish; a walking testament to the potency of the earth around him... the earth contained in that burlap sack.

Opening a briefcase, Ryland turned it towards Samuel. This was the transaction. He slid the case to the center of the table, just shy of that invisible line, and the zombie's mechanical fingers rummaged through its contents. Watch gears, springs, miniature coils and screws. Although whatever it was that infused this accursed earth had kept Samuel from rotting away entirely—he still needed to maintain his most-used joints, his limbs, his appendages, those terrible jaws. They creaked as he fingered a brass cog.

Seemed like it'd be so easy right now to snatch the burlap purse with its pound of dirt and to riddle Samuel with bullets, throwing the table in his face, cutting him to ribbons with automatic fire. To finally storm the catacombs. As Ryland felt his own fingers jumping anxiously in his lap, hr forced himself to picture his predecessor, dying on the earthen floor beside this very chair, dying on his back in a shitty paste of dirt and blood.

Ryland was jarred back to reality as Samuel pushed the sack across the table. His sightless, metallic jack-o'-lantern visage turned slowly from side to side, as if surveying the firing squad flanked by klieg lights. Ryland, never certain whether the afterdead could still hear, mumbled thanks and took the sack. For the first time he addressed his team. "Fall back."

They did, except for Goldhammer who came forward with a hazmat container the size of a lunchbox. Samuel sat quietly as Ryland took a handful of soil from the sack and, like a drug buyer testing the product, sprinkled the dirt over the dark mass in the container. "What's his name?" He asked Goldhammer, who replied through his bug helmet, "Pancake." Ryland smiled wryly and stroked the ball of black fur. Now he felt a rhythmic movement beneath his fingertips; the kitten shuddered, shifted. It was in an advanced state of decay and broken beyond repair by a callous parade of freeway traffic, so there was little for it do now but purr.

"Dirt's good." Goldhammer called back to the others. Another container was brought forth to receive the sack's contents. Ryland closed the first over the cat. It muttered weakly with dead vocal cords. He smiled again. The sack was returned to the table beside the briefcase, both for Samuel to keep. Taking one in each metal fist, the zombie stood up.

The lunchbox in Ryland's hands jerked, and even before the black blur flew past his face and down the tunnel, he knew; even as his legs pumped against his will, sending him past the table and over that invisible line in futile pursuit, he knew. Goddamned crippled cat! Ryland's mind snapped as a clutch of mechanical fingers took root in the center of his chest.

Pulled off his feet by Grinning Samuel and out of reality by the numbing terror in his veins, Ryland head dimly the patter of bullets against Samuel's back. Goldhammer, like a double-jointed ballet dancer, pirouetted off the table and drove a boot into the afterdead's defunct groin. While his legs jackknifed through the air, he planted his M4 against Samuel's temple and got off a good quarter-second burst of fire before the zombie punched through his body armor and yanked out a streaming handful of guts. A spurting, slopping mess that cushioned the soldier's fall immediately followed it.

Ryland had been thrown clear of the battle and crashed into the dirt; having been tossed deeper into the catacombs he saw Samuel as a hulking silhouette against the lights, swaying under a barrage of gunfire. Ryland felt bullets zipping overhead and pressed his face into the earth, tasting that accursed dirt which Goldhammer had just died for.

Died... Christ.

The government had accumulated a half-ton of soil from the parish over the past three decades, and they run a battery of test, burying bodies and clocking their resurrection, administering strength, endurance and aptitude tests. What little intelligence Samuel exhibited was rare in afterdead (except those who stayed near their Source, of course); they usually came up sputtering the last of their blood & bile and clamoring for the nearest warm body, abandoning all higher faculties in the lust for living flesh. Indeed, such was the case with Sergeant Goldhammer, who sat up beside the besieged Samuel and fixed his bug-like gaze on Ryland. His exposed viscera were caked with soil, his back to the other men—but surely they realized what he'd become...

Goldhammer made a wet noise inside his helmet. Ryland heard it over the gunfire.

Pawing through his own innards, the dead soldier came at his former commander. Former as of thirty seconds ago—yes, he was fresh undead, and there was still some basic military protocol embedded in that brain of his, wasn't there, so Ryland threw his out (wrist broken, he felt) and screamed "STOP!!"

Goldhammer did, crouching on all fours with a rope of intestine dragging between his legs. He cocked his head and was the perfect picture of a sick dog. He was trying to recognize the word and why it had halted him in his tracks. Ryland could see the gears turning, like the gears in Grinning Samuel's jaw, and at that moment Samuel ripped into the firing squad and the hail of bullets was reduced to a drizzle. Goldhammer pounced.

Ryland pivoted on his broken wrist with a blinding snap of pain and caught the other between his glassy bug-eyes with a bootheel. Goldhammer grunted, batted the leg aside. They wrestled there on the ground with Ryland kicking himself further and further down the tunnel, all the while aware that soon Samuel would be finished with the others. Backpedaling on his hands and hindquarters, he disturbed a pile of pebbles—no, gears, the strewn contents of the briefcase! Ryland closed his good hand around a fistful of them and, with a half-hearted cry befitting the last act of a dead man, hurled them into Goldhammer's face. Relatively pointless but still an amusing precursor to Samuel's hand sweeping down like a wrecking ball and crushing Goldhammer's skull against the wall. The soldier crumpled to clear a path for the grinning afterdead. His steel maw was painted with rust from the insides of Ryland's men. The zombie knew right where his prey was, and Ryland's situation hit rock bottom as the damaged klieg lights faded out.

"STOP!! STOOOOOOOOOOP!!!" he shrieked. He now knew for certain that Samuel could still hear by the way that his pace quickened. A barely discernable silhouette in the faint remnants of light, Grinning Samuel's grasping fingers squealed as he drew closer. Ryland's back struck a wall. He waited for those fingers to find his heart.

His broken wrist was jerked into the air. He screamed, imagining his entire arm to be gone. But it wasn't, and Samuel wasn't even moving now. With his breath caught in his throat, Ryland just sat and listened in the dark.

And then he heard it...

Tick-tock, tick-tock.

His wrist twisted a little. He bit into his lip while Samuel traced the band of his gold wristwatch. The pair remained motionless in the shadows for what seemed like an eternity, but Ryland counted the ticks and tocks and knew it was less then a minute. Finally, in spite of both terror and logic, he stammered, "it's a Rolex."

The watch left his wrist, and intact arm dropped into moist lap. Samuel could be heard shuffling off into the catacombs, going down beneath the parish churchyard where the mystery of his unlife dwelled. The tick-tock, tick-tock gradually ceased.

Ryland sucked icy air into his lungs and sat there for what really did seem an eternity. There were a few dull spots of light visible down the tunnel. There, he'd have to confront the remains of his slaughtered team; but Samuel did quite the number on them, and none would be getting back up. He pushed his ankles through the dirt until the circulation returned to them and tried to stand. Still a bit shaky, wrist throbbing like mad. And goddamn it was getting colder by the second. He took another breath, sat back down, and listened to the silence.

Then he heard it...

*Meow.*

Ryland smiled just a little, as much as his strength would allow, and reached a blind hand into the darkness.

# 1 / REBIRTH

Hell, from a scientific perspective: the Big Bang spit sub-atomic particles in every direction through the nether. This newborn fabric of existence was torn asunder and sewn back together with every passing nanosecond—a ceaseless quantum storm. Chaos was, in fact, the seed of Order; and even now the matter both inside and out of our bodies is subject to this frenetic cosmic turmoil.

In the very beginning, through an infinitesimal rip that closed almost as soon as it opened—something struck through. Dark matter spewed across the infant universe at a speed beyond that of light, a speed reserved for the supernatural whose laws contradict all nature. Some of these tendrils of darkness were snagged in cooling gas clouds. Some of their dark energy was trapped within stars and planets.

This is a story about one world with this strange energy coiled about its core, leaking through fissures in the crust here and there to manifest chaos. It's a story insignificant in the whole of time; nevertheless, the great architects record these events.

It begins with hot lead punching through the left ventricle of Pete Clarke's heart. The bullet corkscrews through his meat, bounces off vertebrae and chews into bone. He feels its wake in him, a burning tongue lancing his torso, and he falls heavily.

**Democratic Republic of Congo—2 hours earlier**

Another coup, another civil war, another quiet genocide. Guerillas and tribes were clashing in the rainforests, senseless slaughter in which neither side understood the other's agenda. Clarke's team had touched down in the midst of it with mock UN seals adorning both their uniforms and their chopper. Whittaker skirted the makeshift encampment and snuffed a couple of colobus monkeys that had watched their descent from the trees. A veteran of jungle warfare and extreme survival alike, Whittaker took pride in securing the perimeter. His grizzled face was flushed with exuberance uncommon for a man his age. Bagging the monkeys, he slung his rifle over one shoulder and headed back to Clarke's position. The team leader was hunched over a satellite phone setup. "Uplink's not working," he said softly, perhaps not even aware of the other's presence. Whittaker clued him in by dropping the bag into the dirt.

"I said we wouldn't need kickers." Clarke muttered without looking up. "You don't know this region any better than I do," Whittaker replied. "Why not play it safe?"

"You just like plugging the little guys." Clarke smacked the side of the console.

Whittaker grinned. "I don't have any subordinates of my own to abuse, Captain."

Clarke smiled back. He enjoyed the camaraderie among his men, but at the same time felt a twinge of discomfort over their complacency. Bradshaw was coming over now, lugging a few clear plastic cylinders; he guffawed at the sight of the monkey bag. He had a raucous belly laugh befitting an imposing black man, and Clarke had to silence him with a stern look. "Ken," he said to Bradshaw, "see what you can do with the sat phone. I'm gonna go break Harmon in."

Whittaker snorted as Bradshaw took Clarke's place at the console. "Radio's as good as any of this shit." Punching keys, Bradshaw shook his head. "Time isn't gonna wait for you to catch up, Whittaker." He produced a few tiny plastic bags from his vest and tossed them. "Take care of the lanterns while I do this?"

Catching the baggies, Whittaker nodded gruffly and scooped up the plastic cylinders. The old man was efficient, good at following orders, but he longed to be the one giving them, didn't he? Bradshaw watched him tromp away. No one had the heart to tell him that, at fifty-six years, with three decades of service under his belt, he was still a grunt doing busy work.

Harmon, on the other hand, had been charged with prepping the arsenal, a critical task. She didn't view it that way, but no one ever did when it was their first time in the field. At least that's what Clarke was telling her. "Widowmaker's your best friend," he said, perched in the side hatch of the chopper. He was referring to a cleaver-like blade with a molded grip and knuckle guard, a simple yet intimidating piece of weaponry. One was laid out for each team member. "That leads us to Rule One—no headshots. Your firearm is meant as a last resort. Bullet to the brain only kills what little impulse control still exists in afterdead. So if you shoot, aim for the limbs." Taking up a widowmaker, Clarke slipped it into a sheath on his back. "Decaps will render them harmless. You've been trained in close-quarters combat—rely on your widowmaker."

Harmon nodded absently; she'd heard it all before. He felt it bore repeating. Clarke eyed her uncomfortable stance, subtle curves concealed by a defensive posture and eyes shielded behind red hair. She was clearly conditioned to play it low-key and go unnoticed, and seemed quite attuned to it. "Rule Two—bites don't infect. You've been told a dozen times, now believe it." He took the opportunity to roll down the sleeves of his bite jacket: nylon-covered chain mail reaching over the wrists. "Too many assumptions and too little understanding about bites has caused men—and women—to lose it and get killed over a minor flesh wound. Romero-itis," he finished with a smirk.

She frowned at the term. "You mean like the movies? Never seen them."

"Really? Oh, you should. Romero's are the best. Just remember the Devil had different ideas when he made his.

"Three," Clarke concluded, "watch your dead." Harmon looked up at that one. It never made sense until it was too late... she'd know what it meant soon enough.

\* \* \*

Slitting open the tiny baggies, Whittaker emptied freeze-dried bugs into the plastic cylinders. He was setting them up around the perimeter, twelve in all, turning the rotors of the chopper into the hands of a clock face. Pausing at twelve o'clock, he winced. Back was going again. "Goddamn," he whispered. This wasn't a glamorous job—especially these little mop-up exercises—but at least he used to enjoy being in the field. Now he could only try to take his mind off his aching back by thinking about the grueling paperwork that waited back at the base. Bureaucratic horseshit had taken the wind out of his sails and the joy out of his work... no, it was age, and he damn well knew it. The night before, at a debriefing in Zaire, he'd excused himself twice to shake out a few drops of piss. The memory alone made his bladder start fidgeting right now.

The sun dropped below the tree canopy and he hustled to hang the bag of monkeys from a low branch. Done, he glanced over at Bradshaw, still fighting with that sat phone. Bradshaw was a dedicated soldier, one of the developers of widowmaker combat and a tireless jack of all trades. Whittaker liked to think of him as a friend, or at the very least, a good man who rose above his pedigree.

Clarke sat beside the chopper and watched daylight fade. They'd landed a good distance from the local skirmishes; most likely because the guerillas had been scared off by the brutal slayings of their comrades. This forest was rife with afterdead: walking corpses, dead tissue infused with the undefined catalyst that sprang forth from some Source deep in the earth. Clarke was most concerned about the stealth and speed of the reported killings. These afterdead had a pack mentality, which meant a couple of things. First, they had eaten enough living tissue to restore some primitive brain function, and second, they had also probably eaten enough to regenerate their rotted flesh—giving them the appearance of mortal men. It was another case of Romero-itis to assume that afterdead were all decaying relics of past life. The soul had been replaced with a new vitality. And it hungered. In his years leading these outings, Clarke had seen everything from near-skeletons to fully restored men, some of whom among the latter had developed chilling characteristics. The previous summer he'd caught one that had actually relearned speech, slurring something it'd probably heard from its many meals..."Please!"

Please. Did please mean anything to something that existed only to sustain itself? If so—did it understand that same sentiment when uttered by a mutilated victim, only to ignore their shared will to survive? Had the thing truly been begging for release so that it could go on killing?

No point in asking those sorts of questions. There were others assigned to figure them out. He just exterminated them.

Bradshaw called to him from the sat phone and shrugged in silhouette. "No uplink." Harmon sat at the edge of the camp; she hadn't yet forgiven Clarke for weapons prep. She probably thought the new girl had been stuck in the kitchen when in fact he trusted her more than anyone else. Because she wasn't his friend.

Little things had been going wrong since they touched down, but it hadn't yet seemed suspicious to Captain Clarke. Nor did it when the kickers, those dead monkeys dangling in a sack, begin shrieking.

"FUCK!" Bradshaw shouted, leaping up off the ground as his widowmaker leapt into his hand. He glided across the camp and sliced cleanly through both the bag and the monkeys' skulls. "Whittaker!" He snapped. "You're supposed to cut their fucking throats!"

The old man grunted. He was in a fighting stance, eyeing the trees. "See Clarke, the kickers went off before the—"

Four of the twelve cylinders, the ones on the same side of the perimeter as the kickers, bloomed with light. The fireflies inside had resurrected—embraced by the aura coming off of what was likely to be a large number of afterdead. They could be heard now in the trees: shuffling, sniffing, unaware they'd been made. Clarke glanced at Harmon. She had one hand on her widowmaker and the other on her Beretta. "No," he whispered sharply, pointing at the gun.

Like the stage lights coming up on Act Three of a tragic spectacle, the rest of the bug-lanterns bloomed. "Christ." Whittaker backed up. "They're surrounding us." Bradshaw reached into his chain mail for a second widowmaker.

Hell offered a moment of bemused silence before opening its maw. In that second, Harmon discerned a man standing no more than two feet from her, edging through the trees and then accelerating upon eye contact. She fell back, her heels rooted to the ground where she stood, the rest of her body fighting gravity while she tried to raise her pistol toward the naked ghoul.

Its face split like a ripe fruit as Clarke's widowmaker carved into its cheek. He swiped the pistol from Harmon's grasp; his face, gaunt in the lantern light, looked coldly at her, through her, then he finished the afterdead with a decap before spinning to open another's neck.

They attacked all at once, two dozen of them. Bradshaw scissored one's head off, ducking its flailing limb, planted his elbow in the gnashing jaws of another and shattered its neck with a cruel jerk before delivering the killing blow. Whittaker was hacking through them like a madman, mighty swings halving skulls left and right. He whooped when they tore vainly at his bite jacket; bellowed while cleaving into one pinned under his boot. He wasn't the artist Bradshaw was. Dead was dead and technique meant jack when the bodies were all laid out. And they were going down fast, the pack mentality long abandoned. It was only hunger that mattered now. In a way, Whittaker understood them (decapped another), but he understood dogs too. Stifled a laugh as one of them shook his arm in its teeth. Decapped it.

Harmon had backpedaled to the center of the camp and gotten her bearings. The afterdead were native tribesmen, their nude forms almost pitiful as they came at the soldiers. The one thing that reduced her pity and brought her back to reality was their bellies: glistening, trembling, fat with meat. They ate well.

"Harmon!" Barked Clarke. "Secure the bird!" She pivoted towards the chopper and saw an afterdead climbing in. Its back was to her. Easy kill. Widowmaker in hand. With legs equal parts rubber and cement, she ran. The zombie paused in the hatch; she quickened her pace, raised the blade and made a grand arc down toward the base of its neck.

Corporal Bradshaw danced. He danced through the milling undead, taking a new partner with every second step. Pirouette, kick, surprise decap of the one at his rear. Split the chin of the female coming from the side. Her face was young and beautiful. He dashed it to pieces. Thankless work, all of it; the rest of humanity didn't know about afterdead, but he did, and he danced only for them, designed a terrible new death for each of their kind. Spinning in the dirt, he drew closer and closer to the chopper. Cutting a swath toward Harmon.

Clarke turned to see Bradshaw lop her leg off at the knee.

Harmon's blade had been a few inches from the afterdead in the chopper; she frowned as her balance shifted and the blade took its ear off. She kept going forward, into its back, and the two collapsed in a heap on the ground. It tried to roll over beneath her. She tried to get up. Couldn't. Legs numb. She looked down and saw. Then came pain.

Clarke wasn't sure what in Christ was happening until Bradshaw took her arm, the one that might have grabbed her gun had Clarke not slapped it away. And Whittaker, Whittaker was suddenly in the cockpit. The rotors began moving against the stars. Harmon screamed, writhing on top of the afterdead. Bradshaw peppered the ones on the perimeter with bullets. Clarke charged at him, not knowing what he should or could do, only feeling the certainty of the widowmaker in his right hand.

Bradshaw knew his captain was coming and met Clarke's blade with one of his own. The other opened Clarke's groin. The captain's face flushed. He gaped at his friend. "You weren't supposed to see," Bradshaw said quietly, and shot him through the heart.

\* \* \*

Harmon slung her remaining arm over the chopper's landing gear. The thunderous din of the rotors almost drowned out the pain of teeth on her leg's stump. More overpowering was her fear; fear of being left behind. They were lifting off now and her leg was tugged free of the afterdead's mouth.

Bradshaw leaned out the side, steadying himself. He placed his pistol against her ear. "WHY," she shrieked. He didn't reply before firing, and by then it didn't matter anyway.

\* \* \*

The light and sound of the helicopter receded into the distance. Civilization left the Congo, reason left the Congo, and Clarke stirred at the footfalls of the surviving afterdead. They moved slowly toward him, eight left, although he couldn't be sure of his count because his mind was screaming gibberish and images of Harmon's dismemberment clouded every thought.

Struggling to his feet in a thick paste of dirt and blood, he trained his gun on the first comer's kneecap. Wet copper filled his mouth; he choked, stumbled and missed the fucker by a good three feet. They shuffled onward. Feeling one at his back, he spun with the widowmaker at neck level. It bit into the afterdead's jawbone; he wrenched the blade downward, took the head.

Sudden movement on the left. He fired twice. A startled corpse shook its pulped eyeballs from the sockets and staggered aside. Clarke's legs buckled and he actually sagged against one of them. It embraced him hungrily. And now he wasn't breathing right. Too much blood in his throat. Jamming his pistol into the hugger's chin, he emptied the clip. No head left to deal with.

How many remained now—five? Three? How many were there to begin with? Another one caught his wrist. He lopped its hand and head off. They had all closed in around him, even the blind one. Good, he thought, 'cause I can't walk. Bracing himself on the sightless fiend, he decapped its neighbor. Then fingers from behind sank into the bloody ruin of his groin. Pain washed over him like rebirth, reaffirming everything alive in his body, and with endorphins spilling through his tired veins Clarke sawed into the horde.

It was seconds, maybe minutes later when he stopped, realizing he was chopping at the ground. The afterdead were all quartered and lying in their juices. So was he, he saw, tracing with bone-white fingers the flowering gash in his lap. And now he wasn't breathing at all. Clarke accepted it. What else could he do?

A wet sound drew his attention to an armless torso lying nearby. The head was mostly intact, but its throat was cut from ear to ear, opening and closing along with its mouth. Smack, smack, smack went the ragged flesh. The thing wouldn't accept death, even as it starved and fell apart here; instead it stared intently at the fresh meat scant inches away.

Clarke laughed and died.

* * *

A day later, he woke up.

# 2 / CHUMS

"Are you hearing anything I'm saying?" Stoddard barked through his mask. Bradshaw realized he'd been staring blankly into a pile of entrails and blinked. "Nope, not a thing."

"Where's your mind at lately?" Stoddard asked. He steadied himself on his shovel, presumably was scrutinizing his friend's face; Bradshaw couldn't tell thanks to that bug-like filtration mask. Stoddard had never gotten used to the smell, the stench of rot that blanketed the streets and permeated this truck. He used to puke all the time but had started taking caffeine pills to suppress his appetite (along with excessive amounts of Dramamine), and no longer ate while on the job. The glassy visor of the mask hid his eyes. It was unnerving, and Bradshaw was reluctant to talk anything other than shop under such circumstances. He looked back down at the entrails.

They were standing knee-deep in guts in the rear of a refurbished dump truck. The gleaming casings of intestines quivered as they jostled along. Bradshaw worked his shovel beneath a pile of cadaverous tissue. "This whole mope thing," Stoddard called, "it got anything to do with why you're on slop duty?"

Jesus. Did he really not understand? Two soldiers had died on Bradshaw's last field assignment. It only made sense that he'd be confined to the base for a while. Only made sense he wouldn't want to talk about it. Furrowing his brow, he said, "I'm burned the fuck out. I was burned out before what happened in Congo... I wonder if that's why we lost them."

Stoddard shook his bug head emphatically. "If you hadn't been there, no one would have come back. Remember that." It was quite the opposite, actually, but Bradshaw just offered a thin smile. "Thanks, Joe."

"I'm serious!" The truck turned off of the tree-lined access road onto a residential street: all duplexes in bland pastels, typical of a military base. Scooping some viscera into his shovel, Stoddard lobbed it over the side where it splattered in the well-manicured grass. "So much for making it into Better Homes and Gardens." He cracked. The houses looked like shit close-up anyway: walls spattered with rust-colored stains, windows smeared with filthy fingerprints. It was no problem to treat the grass, but no one was going to stand out here cleaning windows. Especially when the afterdead just messed them all up again. Like little kids trashing their rooms, only instead of dirty underwear and spilled Kool-Aid, it was dried-out organs and lost limbs. And here they came; hearing the truck's rumble, the afterdead staggered out of open front doors, past the skeletons of cars and plastic flowerbeds.

It was important to put on the appearance of a real base, just in case some foreign satellite was able to punch through the scrambled signals shielding the area. Offices, hangars, a commissary, a school, a clinic. Traffic lights and trash dumpsters and playgrounds with little shoeprints stamped into the sand. All a brilliant facade—but now was feeding time, and all semblance of normalcy vanished as dozens upon dozens of dead converged on the street.

Bradshaw joined Stoddard in hurling shovelfuls of gore out the back. Those afterdead who were quickest fell upon the first offerings in a defensive posture. The others continued to follow the truck. "It's funny." Stoddard observed. "The runners are always going to get the most meat, and the more they eat, the stronger they get."

"It's not funny, it's Darwin." Bradshaw ignored the putrid rot in his nostrils, ignored the stumbling parade reaching toward him. "Before long those runners are going to be too healthy. We'll have to take them out."

"I look forward to it." Stoddard replied. He reached behind his back to pat the sheath where his widowmaker was stowed. "Have you seen Postman lately?" He tossed another wave of slop. It hit a woman head-on. She collapsed, and Stoddard's hand flew to his mask in shock; after a second, he started to laugh. Several other afterdead knelt to pick the gore off of her thrashing body. "Kinky!"

"Anyway," Bradshaw muttered, "no, I haven't seen Postman. Why?" Postman was one of the oldest specimens on the base. In the beginning, the scientists had suited corpses up in uniforms, to better identify them regardless of physical condition. So you had Postman,

Electrician, Nurse (Stoddard's favorite) and the like. After a while it was determined that specimens weren't around long enough to require such measures. But a few of these veteran afterdead still existed on the base, and Postman was one. He—it, rather—endured because it didn't feed often, which made it one of the weaker and less desirable subjects. The scientists said that Postman had learned to pace himself in order to avoid being targeted. But how the hell would he—no, IT, dammit—know to do such a thing?

"Postman took a headshot last week," Stoddard said. "He tried climbing into Grimm's slop truck, bought himself a lobotomy. Anyway, after Grimm came back and filled out the report, we had to go find Postman and verify it. So we go to the school, and he's in there, but not wandering the halls like usual. He's sitting on the floor with a stick."

"This is one hell of a story." Bradshaw flicked a string of meat off his waders. "Let me finish," Stoddard scowled. "Anyway, Postman's got this stick and he's fishing around in the bullethole. He's trying to get the bullet out."

"How do you know he was after the bullet? Maybe he was just poking around."

"Yeah, sure. They don't get bored, Ken. Anything they do, it's for a reason."

Not true, Bradshaw thought. All they really needed to do was eat. Didn't breathe, didn't fuck. They barely qualified as animals, yet some rotter sticking a twig in his brain justified a twelve-page report in triplicate. More paperwork than he'd had to fill out after two field operatives died. Behind the truck, two males bent and bloated by decay played tug-of-war over a rope of tissue. Bradshaw heaved more chum at them, and the conflict ended abruptly. As more and more feed littered the street in the truck's wake, the afterdead were falling to their knees like supplicants. There was something familiar and troubling about it... Reminded him of Sunday worship as a kid. He'd grown up in a Texas border town, his mother a black homemaker, Dad a Venezuelan preacher. Their very own little white church seemed to absorb the dry heat, and every week Bradshaw would stand in silent awe as Dad cried from the pulpit, sweat running in rivers from his face and fists. Looking back, it wasn't any spiritual rapture that overcame so many in the congregation—it was heat exhaustion. But to the young boy it was a power radiating from his father. Even the walls ran with moisture. It was a local phenomenon, those glistening tearstains that seemed to appear out of nowhere on the walls. Especially on Sunday: as the worshippers swayed in praise, the entire room had seemed to vibrate. Bradshaw would grip his mother's hand, head hot and swimming, the buzzing in his ears swelling to a crescendo, and the walls wept. They wept.

In lieu of a life-size crucifix there was a stained-glass image of the Savior behind the altar, and Dad meticulously polished it every other day. Bradshaw would sit in the pews sometimes and watch. Whenever his father's back was to him, the boy reached out and touched the tearstains. He pressed his fingertips to his nostrils; the smell was sweet, like something from his mother's kitchen. It made perfect sense to a child that Christ's teardrops were of sugar and syrup. His wouldn't be bitter or salty. Lot's wife turned to salt because she disobeyed the Lord, Dad said.

One day, when it reached 110 degrees and dusty winds battered the church, and Dad was cleaning the stained-glass window, Bradshaw had felt the room vibrate again. The walls murmured to him. He pressed his hand to them, felt it. Then he looked up and saw his father's fear-filled eyes fixated on him.

At the joint of the west wall and the ceiling there was a hole and it was from there that the bees poured. Bradshaw made it out, Dad didn't. They said he was allergic. They said that thousands of bees had been nesting in the walls, so many that their honey seeped through when it got hot enough. That day, *Nature* had delivered a judgment against *God*, and that was the day Bradshaw realized He was just a snake-oil salesman, manipulating forces that were already there.

\* \* \*

The lingering odors of slop duty hadn't yet begun to fade when Bradshaw and Stoddard were sent into the bayou to harvest. The corpses seeded the previous day were reviving. There were a finite number of these Sources in the world—places where this strange energy, like honey, seeped through the soil and reanimated the dead—one was here in Louisiana, and so the base had been established. And despite the fact that fresh specimens were returning to life at that very moment, Stoddard was going on in a loud voice about the tattoo he always talked about and never got: "Death From Above" between his shoulder blades with an image of Christ behind the lettering. It was nothing but ironic to Bradshaw considering their occupation. Slogging through a stretch of mud filled with gnarled roots (nothing ever died out here, just kept growing), he ran that by Stoddard. His companion shrugged. "We didn't make the URC, brother, we just plug them into it." URC—Undefined Reanimation Catalyst. Scientific term for "we have no fucking idea."

The first afterdead of the night was chained to a gnarled monster of a tree at the edge of the mud. It stared at them, perplexed. It was male, early thirties, saliva running from its lips and a rank odor coming off its soiled jeans. "He shit himself," Stoddard spat. "Way to go, partner!" He clapped the undead on the shoulder and detached a thick chain leash from the tree. Bradshaw trudged on to the next rotter. "I'm thinking of getting a dog." He told Stoddard as they hauled the lot out of the bayou, through a manned gate and onto a fenced pathway. "Retriever or something."

"You'd keep it on-base?" Stoddard raised an eyebrow. "Why not?" Bradshaw replied. "You know they don't mess with animals. Watchdog's not a bad idea, anyhow." He yanked one of his chains to get a straggler moving. It lurched at him; Bradshaw was ready with the stun gun and knocked it on its ass. He jerked impatiently until the wide-eyed corpse staggered to its feet. "Maybe I'm a little lonely. That's not a crime, right?" Stoddard nodded in understanding. They were forced to make their home next door to these things—and the kicker was, the afterdead had better digs. It was almost maddening to plod through their rosy faux-neighborhoods, to look at that all day and then go back to an 8x8 room in a bunker. Grimm, one of the base's certified lunatics, had decided to "move out to the suburbs" and seize a home from the afterdead. He'd done it, too. Cleaned out a house near the bayou, changed the locks and brought in what little furniture he could scrounge up. He actually slept every night with afterdead pawing at his bedroom windows—but still he slept in an honest-to-God bed, in a real house. Base Commander St. John normally wouldn't have allowed such a stunt but Ryland wanted to see the outcome.

Ryland... shit. Bradshaw realized he was late for a meeting. "Let's pick it up Joe."

After depositing the afterdead in a holding pen and bidding Stoddard good night, Bradshaw walked to the truck yard. His path was protected by a low-voltage electric fence from which most afterdead had learned to stay away. Halogen street lamps cast the deserted streets beyond the fence in a garish light; that light ended at the yard's gate, where he eased himself inside. "I'm late, I know."

"Are you?" Seated on the front bumper of a slop truck, Ryland shrugged. "I lost my watch. How're you holding up? You look exhausted." It was a funny remark coming from him. Bradshaw sometimes thought that maybe, when God was putting Adam together, He wasn't happy with some of the bones He'd rendered from the earth. Some were too angular, too odd, too cruel in appearance alone. So He threw them out, and someone else double-bagged 'em in flesh and here you had Nathan Ryland. Cancerous jowls hung from sharply jutting cheekbones, above which sunken eyes were pitted into an oblong skull. And his face bore a greenish pallor, maybe that was just the lighting. Fish, the guys called him, though not to his face because he was frequently off-base as government liaison, and also because he'd have them castrated. Kneading his gloved hands, Ryland shivered. "So? How are you?" Bradshaw said he was fine and gave his report. The debriefing upon returning from Congo had been short and sweet; he'd been taken off field duty for a month; then ordered into counseling. "Hugs and hand puppets," cracked Ryland with a lipless smile. "I've already spoken with Whittaker. So it was you who shot Clarke?"

Bradshaw raised an eyebrow, but nodded. "I'm sure you had no choice," Ryland told the eyebrow. "Collateral damage. It's a popular phrase with my friends in Washington. It means no more questions. You've got nothing to worry about, Ken."

Bradshaw grimaced in the shadows. "I know that. Doesn't mean I have to be happy about Clarke."

"No one said you had to be happy." Ryland replied. "I'm sorry it took so long for me to get together with you. It's a bad month. I'm flying to D.C. every other day and St. John's on my ass to put in for a budget increase. He thinks I'm a lobbyist just because I don't wear the uniform. But enough about my problems." Standing up, he patted Bradshaw's shoulder. "We're good, okay?"

Bradshaw knew asking would be fruitless, but he did it anyway. "Clarke was a good... a good leader... why him? He didn't need to be out there."

"There's always collateral damage. Remember that." Ryland answered. His presence left the yard, and Bradshaw stood silent in his wake, a puppet without his puppeteer. After a few moments, he gathered up his strings and trudged toward the bunkers. On the other side of the electric fence, a silhouette peeled away from the night: a female, with papery gray flesh and hollowed-out knees giving her a strange falling-forward gait. She stopped a few feet from the fence, the muscles in her face working at something resembling a frown. Bradshaw ignored the thing and kept walking.

* * *

7,270 miles away, the relief organization Our World, based out of Brisbane, had set up a triage in Congo. They were dangerously close to the most recent clashes in the republic's civil war, but Matt Hinzman knew that the needy tribal peoples would stay in their rainforest home—even if it meant running afoul of guerillas. As chief supervisor of the Congo effort, his decision went unchallenged, and even now, lying under a crumpled tent with his right arm gone, he didn't regret making the call.

Sara Lister, a colleague of fourteen years, lay a few yards off. Her eye was pulled from its socket and rested in the hollow of a flayed cheek. Matthew heard feet shuffling at his back, but couldn't turn over. He stayed motionless and hoped they couldn't sniff him out.

The canvas tent pulled away from his body. He was turned to face a man wearing some sort of paramilitary uniform. Thank God! "The tribesmen," Matt gasped hoarsely. "They tore us apart."

The soldier traced Matthew's jaw line with his fingertips. There was a nasty gash just below his chin. The soldier dug his fingernails in and pulled, paying no mind to the terrible screaming, which eventually stopped.

Sitting cross-legged in the middle of the camp, Clarke ate quietly. He eyed his surroundings in search of more meat. There was a half-devoured woman nearby clutching something in her hand. He recognized it: a pistol. He had one too, he thought, and fumbled around his waistline until he found it. The familiarity of it in his hand released a flood of memories, all clouded fragments. But recalling that he himself had been shot made him aware of the dull pain in his chest. Looking down, Clarke prodded the bullet hole. It hurt but wouldn't keep him from moving. The hole between his legs was another story. He picked idly at the gashed tissue hanging out of his pants; more fragments came to him, the lingering memories of sensations for which he no longer had any use. Clarke tugged Hinzman's upper lip off and chewed it for a while.

His brain shuffled his memories into some sort of order. Someone he trusted had shot him. Rules had been broken. He couldn't recall every point of protocol, but he knew it was a mistake to leave him for dead instead of finishing the job. He never would have done that himself. Bradshaw—that was his name, Bradshaw—wouldn't normally have done that, either. Confusing. His mind kept working while he ate. Good soldiers wouldn't leave something like this to chance. They'd come back for him. Staying here to feed would be a risk, but then feeding anywhere would soon become a risk. He'd have to kill them all.

It was a simple decision made in the basest region of his mind. Self-preservation was his sole purpose. Clarke pulled Hinzman's esophagus out with slick fingers. He knew he had to keep feeding in order to stay alert and heal these wounds. He knew a lot of things other afterdead didn't.

# 3 / DRINKS AT DUSK

"I never win," Whittaker grumbled into his Captain & Coke. The Captain was being an unsympathetic prick this fine evening; Whittaker could barely feel the warmth of the liquor in his belly, not with the knot of anxiety that grew tighter with every spin of the roulette wheel.

Spending a furlough in Vegas was always an exercise in pain. Every dollar that came out of his pocket went straight into the casino's, or into his liver—he knew it and everyone around him knew it. They encouraged it. Whittaker was used to rolling with the punches, though. He'd return to the base next week with a few bruises, take some ribbing from his comrades, then it was back to work. In the end, he figured, this yearly gouging in Vegas was better than sitting at home alone getting wasted (although the booze there was a hell of a lot cheaper).

Whittaker watched the last of his chips jump from his hands like he was a leper, then he left the casino-hotel, crossing the street to a strip joint. Ah, warm ten-dollar beer and the plastic smiles of girls whose age was anyone's best guess in the garish crimson lighting. He took a table near the back of the room. Immediately there was a girl striding toward him. "Hi," she said in a half-pert tone. It was early evening; Whittaker wasn't big money. She hadn't even brought along a bottle of champagne to hock. "What're you in the mood for?"

"I..." He scratched his beard, leaned back, looked at the shadowy girl in the red lights. "I don't know. I'm all right. Thanks." She was gone before he knew it. He wiped a layer of sweat from his brow, opened his jacket, and wondered what the fuck was keeping him from putting a gun in his mouth. Christ, his sidearm was in the rental. Right across the street. He could do himself there in the car, no point in going up to his room. *There's a story for the fellas back at work.*

*Whittaker finally cashed out. What took him so long?* He winced at imagined eulogies punctuated by hollow laughter. Fuck that. He knew why he always came out here.

Leaving the bar without a drink or a dance, Whittaker got into the rental car. Like the casino and the strip joint, it smelled of stale cigarettes, and the A/C blew a hot wind across his eyes. He pulled out of the lot and headed north. A/C never got any better; he shut it off and rolled down the windows, cradling his pistol in his lap.

Away from everything, he got off the highway and felt out a spot that seemed right; he stopped and inhaled the air. It was just beginning to grow dark. He reached under the passenger seat for the bottle of Myers Dark he'd kept there. He didn't need it in order to go through with this. It would just be nice. Getting out of the car, he sat himself on the hood. The door popped behind him—he turned, certain he'd shut it, and a dark blur snatched the gun from his hand. He felt it against his temple and that feeling was suddenly the last thing in the world he wanted.

"*Clarke.*"

He looked like he was still alive, by God, he really did. His movement was fluid, his eyes glistened red as the sun went down. But there was nothing, NOTHING in his face. No emotion, no steeliness either. Just nothing.

"Who ordered you to kill me?"

Whittaker swallowed a lump of phlegm. "I won't ask twice," Clarke told him. Same voice, same cadence. He couldn't be undead.

"I don't know," Whittaker breathed. "B-Bradshaw handed down the order. I don't know who told him. But it wasn't you, Pete! Harmon was the target! You were just in the wrong place!"

"I think you're lying," Clarke replied. He took the gun away from Whittaker's head and slipped it into the waistband of his pants. "I'm going to torture you until you tell me what you know."

"I don't—" Whittaker's words and teeth were blown out of his mouth by the liquor bottle. He felt it shatter against his head, a painless, stunning sensation; then fire spread down the side of his face. He reeled and tried, stupidly, to run. Clarke flattened him on the hood of the car and pressed the jagged remnant of the bottle's mouth between his upper lip and any teeth that were left. "So you know I mean it," Clarke said flatly, and he sliced the lip off.

Whittaker howled, beat against his attacker and the car, but Clarke held him down with one rigid arm. That's when Whittaker knew for certain that yes, he was looking at an afterdead. And his entire face was on fire now, hot blood filling his mouth. He spat and whimpered. "Thlease!" He cried. Red flecks misted Clarke's face. Clarke stepped back and stomped, once, and this time the pain was instantaneous. Whittaker's shin splintered like a rotted branch. He was thrown to the desert floor.

Whittaker could only roll from side to side, sobbing and choking, waiting for the next blow. Pain radiating from above his neck and below his waist met in his stomach. He puked his guts out in the dirt, Clarke silent this entire time. "WHY?!" the old soldier bellowed.

"I'm going to kill them before they kill me, again." Clarke didn't see the point in explaining himself, but he had to work through Whittaker's shock to get information. Falling silent once more, he watched his victim paw at the ground.

"How dith you geth here?" Was the next question. "We leth you in Congo!"

"Boat. Stowed away. I'm going to ask you questions now." Clarke knelt beside Whittaker, making a conspicuous display of the pistol. "This wasn't your first hit, was it?"

"N-no."

"You and Bradshaw, you worked together? And you say you don't know who the orders came from?"

Whittaker shook his head madly. Clarke reached down and touched his ruined cheek; blinding pain shot through Whittaker's skull, blurring his vision. It was a shard of glass that Clarke was retrieving from Whittaker's face, and he sucked the blood from it before tossing it aside. "If you don't know anything else, you're useless to me."

Whittaker tried to sit up. He was batted down like a rag doll. He said every prayer he knew and begged for mercy. "Thlease don't!" Whittaker's face darkened. "Thith ithn't about protecting yourselth. It's about REVENTH! You're juth like me! Juth like—" He was still screaming when Clarke put a round through his head. It wasn't a mercy bullet; just easier that way.

Clarke fed, eating around the alcohol-soaked pieces.

* * *

Ryland's office was located in a nondescript storage building. At least that's how it appeared on the outside. Inside was one of the most heavily fortified and upscale structures on the base. Passing through its weathered metal door, the young man who had an appointment was surprised to find himself in what looked like an office lobby. The soldier at the metal detector waved him forward. "Cervantes?"

Nodding, the olive-skinned man stepped through the security checkpoint. The soldier spent several silent minutes reviewing Cervantes' paperwork; he didn't scrutinize the forms, just stared at them. Stalling. Finally, another soldier entered the lobby from the back with an automatic swinging brazenly in his right hand. "Go with him," the first soldier muttered, and handed over the papers.

They moved briskly down a quiet corridor, where the soldier rapped on the door marked ADMINISTRATIVE LIAISON. A murmur from inside, then Cervantes entered the office alone.

"I apologize for the cloak-and-dagger bullshit," was the first thing Nathan Ryland said. Blowing the steam off a cup of coffee, he motioned to a chair on the other side of his desk. He was a stout man in a crisp suit, its soft colors masking the pallor of his tired flesh. "Whenever I bring an appointee onto the base, the brass are especially skeptical. Even the fact that you're military doesn't help. They consider you to be my man, cut from the same cloth as me. Just the same," Ryland smiled, "once you're out there among the rotters, you make fast friends."

Ryland liked to read people by making them nervous. Cervantes knew that the moment he came in. The nonchalant gestures, the thin-lipped smile. Eyes like cold marble, though. This little back-and-forth that Ryland did with newcomers, it was just pretext, the sort of behavior expected from men in black. For all this, Cervantes only went into the man's consciousness for a fraction of a second, and even then, barely dipped his toes in the water. But Ryland knew.

"So, Cervantes, tell me about myself." He folded his meaty hands on the desk. "Why did I appoint you to this post?"

"You believe I can use my telepathy with the afterdead."

"We discussed that at Fort Leavenworth. Tell me something that I haven't *said*."

"I prefer not to dig that deep into someone else's head. Sir."

"That must take remarkable discipline." Ryland replied. "Most with your ability don't make it half as far as you did. I understand that refining one's own subconscious can be... distressing?" Cervantes only nodded.

"Now then, speak from your own intuition. What do you think you can do here?"

"I know there's little sense in reading their thought processes—they seek only self-preservation. There's no motive or intent that isn't visible on the surface. There's no community dynamic. They barely acknowledge one another. But they acknowledge the living."

"And you've been able to affect the perception of others so that they don't see you. Creating a perpetual blind spot."

"Yes—but only for myself, and only against minds of limited function," Cervantes replied.

Ryland nodded along. "That's all we need. See, there are certain areas of the base that are inaccessible, places with high concentrations of afterdead. I'd like to get into these areas and see what they're doing without disrupting them. Commander St. John doesn't agree—but I usually get the last word when it comes to government property."

"You mean the base?"

"I mean the zombies."

Ryland tapped his keyboard for a few minutes. "We have a soldier named Grimm who's been living out in the field, in one of the houses in those mock-up suburbs. He's been sending back a lot of interesting observations about the dead around there. At least he was. It's been two days since we heard from him. Some grunts drove by the house and didn't see anything, but the congestion was too great to risk getting out of the truck."

"You don't think he's dead?" Cervantes asked.

Ryland shook his head. "And even if he was, we'd have to verify it and pull out the remains. What I need you to do is get into that house without disturbing the dead. Can you?"

That had been the question. Cervantes still wasn't entirely sure of the answer, even as he was jostled along in a Humvee on the base's quiet streets. The descending sun turned the afterdead up ahead into opaque silhouettes. The driver, a Corporal Bradshaw, slowed the Hummer to a stop. "I see a couple dozen at least," he muttered. "That's Grimm's house on the right-hand corner. I have to let you out here."

Cervantes nodded. For some reason, he expected a few personal words of encouragement, maybe a clap on the back... nothing. Bradshaw dropped into reverse and looked at him. Cervantes got out.

He slipped a pair of headphones over his ears, fingering the Walkman in his jacket pocket. White noise crept into his ears, and he cleared his mind, watching the afterdead shuffle about in the street. He reached out to them. Their minds were like hollowed-out gourds, with only tendrils of primitive activity, each easy to manipulate. The hunger was extraordinary. For a moment, Cervantes felt saliva building in his mouth; he shook the hunger off and dug into the subconscious of each rotter in his view. Already shambling towards him was a male in a butcher's apron. Underneath was a simple boiler suit, but the apron—caked with solid layers of gore, heavy on the afterdead's shoulders—gave him character. Yet inside each unique mind Cervantes felt the same emptiness. He blotted himself out of their sight, their smell, their hearing. The Butcher stopped in his approach. After a moment, he reversed direction, returning to the horde.

The duplex in which Sergeant Grimm made his home was noticeably different from the rest. The sod had been pulled up and replaced with a generous layer of loam. In the moist clay were planted several large flowers. Each blossom had thick, flesh-toned petals surrounding its red stigma. Cervantes briefly had the impression in his mind of a woman's flayed sex spread before him; then he was assailed by the smell. Jesus! Worse than that of the rotters at his back was the noxious odor from the plants. He recognized them now as *stapelia gigantea*, carrion flowers—the odor lured foul insects to ensure pollination. Maybe, he thought, it kept the zombies from smelling Grimm, too.

He tried the front door. Locked. A newly installed lock, at that. Eyeing the undead, Cervantes rapped sharply. "Sergeant!" A couple of them turned at the sound, but were unable to pinpoint its source. They trod aimlessly through the loam. He knocked again, harder. He could try and reach out to Grimm, but it might mean giving himself away outside. Not worth it, he decided, and headed around back. There was a window slightly ajar; easing it upward, he hoisted himself into a hallway. The air in the house was moist, earthy. Cervantes traced his fingertips along the wall, and they came away stained with mold. He advanced, and almost as soon as reached the end of the hall the smell of feces struck his nostrils.

"Never could get the plumbing working," a voice said from a dark corner, as if reading *his* mind. "Want a drink?" Cervantes' eyes adjusted to the lack of light. The man slouched against the wall was haggard, unshaven, malnourished. His uniform was draped over bony shoulders like a tablecloth. Didn't they feed him... ?

Grimm pushed a box of wine from between his legs. "I don't know you," he croaked.

"I'm the new guy." Cervantes lowered himself to eye level with the man. They had feared for Grimm's safety, but it appeared that his sanity had wasted away long before the flesh. Grimm used his thumb to wipe out the contents of a plastic cup and tilted the box's spigot over it.

"Tell them I'm fine. I really am. You wouldn't think it to look at me, but I am. I like it here."

"What do you like about it?" Cervantes asked. He began probing Grimm's mind. It was an incoherent ruin in there, akin to an attic overtaken by cobwebs. Nightmare images of the undead hordes flashed before him. Bloody meat, grasping fingers. Lips smacking.

Grimm laughed boisterously. "I like the quiet."

"Why did you stop communicating with the base?"

"Radio's busted." Grimm gestured in no particular direction and took a gulp of his cheap wine. "I dropped it outside. They just walked all over it, the pissers. I contemplated smoke signals." Cervantes pushed deeper... Grimm was hiding something within the rotted walls of that attic. Behind a door in this house. He saw the radio, not dropped but hurled to the street. He saw Grimm greedily scooping meat from the street into his arms, stealing it from the afterdead.

"Sergeant, you know you've worried a lot of people. Surely you would have made some effort to contact them if this was all an accident."

Grimm's crusty eyes narrowed. "You don't believe me? You don't know what it's like out here, bud. You don't KNOW. You're on the outside looking in. I sleep with the dead. I—" Grimm stopped himself suddenly. Cervantes tore through the attic wall and saw the horror.

"Oh my god." He was on his feet, moving back down the hall.

Grimm leapt up, spilling the box, and cried "NO! Noooooooooo..." Glancing back, Cervantes saw the other soldier wringing his hands like a child who knew his number was up. He pushed open the last door on the left.

It was impossible to tell she was undead, save for the blood caked around her mouth and on her nightgown. She was very healthy, lovely even. Of course she was—Grimm brought meat home for her. Only her wrists and ankles, where she was bound to the bed, showed signs of damage: flesh had been sloughed from bone, most likely in her struggling. Her eyes lit on Cervantes and she began to twist and lurch.

Between her bruised thighs... Cervantes saw carrion flowers and vomited.

"No, no, no." Grimm paced in the doorway, beating his head with his fists. "It's not... you don't KNOW!!"

*I don't want to*, Cervantes thought, shaking the stolen memories from his head. He felt Grimm's hands on his shoulders, pleading, trembling with sobs, then he was thrown violently into the hallway, and Grimm locked himself in the room with a howl. "Sergeant!" Cervantes shouted, his head ringing from the fall. And now he could hear them: outside, pawing at the doors, the windows... he rushed down the hall to slam shut the window through which he'd come. Just as it came down a gnarled hand shot through. An eyeless face smacked against the glass, spraying pus like a sponge. He'd lost contact with them, and now they were being drawn to the tumult inside. Cervantes looked back at the locked door.

Inside, Grimm knelt beside the female and pulled a jackknife from his boot. "Ryland put me out here, he made me stay out here," he called, sawing through the afterdead's restraints, "because I KNOW. I know what he did and what he's going to do. Ryland's the bad one, not me! Not—"

Cervantes shut his eyes tight and willed away Grimm's screams, the snapping of bone and the voracious roars of his former lover.

# 4 / DARKER FLAMES THAN THIS

"Clarke, Harmon, lost in Congo. Grimm, committed suicide right here on the base." Commander St. John rattled the death list off as if he was reading sports scores. His team had lost.

Behind his great desk, littered with medals and keepsakes from his years in the battlefield, the old hawk loomed like an angry father, white hair meticulously-groomed over steely gray eyes. Those eyes were locked onto Nathan Ryland. He glared silently, expecting something.

"These things happen," the other man finally said, gloved hands folded.

"'These things happen'? You've been given too much pull around here," St. John growled. "It was your idea to let Grimm play out there with the rotters, and he cracked. You pushed for an expedition to Congo and two good soldiers are dead as a result. Hell, now Whittaker's been AWOL for a week. He's a combat vet, a hero, and lately I've seen him following you around like a goddamned puppy. Have any idea where the hell *he* is?" St. John grasped his temples, wincing: migraine. Suits like Ryland sauntered into military operations from their "classified backgrounds" and fucked up the whole works. Ryland was like the executive branch's little spy, carrying out the silly whims of armchair warriors and putting St. John's boys in the dirt. He sighed. "Bradshaw takes Clarke's place as leader of the field unit. And he selects his new teammates. Not *you*, Ryland, *him*."

"Fair enough," Ryland replied. His pale, fatty jowls made his smile all the more repulsive. He was soft all over, wasn't he? St. John just shook his head. "Get out."

Bradshaw met Ryland outside the administrative building. Ryland clapped a hand on his back. "I didn't even have to bring it up.

He promoted you. Now, I only ask that you put Sergeant Cervantes on the team. His assigned duties aren't important, I just want him out there."

Bradshaw nodded, and they walked along the electric fence separating their world from that of the afterdead. A few rotters milled around in the grass, probably in search of overlooked chum from a previous feeding. "Who else will you choose?" Ryland asked.

"Stoddard and Thomas," Bradshaw replied quickly.

"I see you've been thinking about this," Ryland grinned. "Captain."

Bradshaw offered an insincere smile in return. He'd just flown up the ranks to a critical leadership position—all because he was a killer, and worse than that, a lackey. He still didn't know the reason why he'd shot Pete Clarke through the heart. It would have made as much sense at a backyard barbecue as it did in Congo. And Ryland... something was wrong with him. His face was more sunken and pale than usual. He carried his bulk with an awkward gait. Looked like a..."Ryland, I've got to get down to the warehouse for a pickup. Talk later?"

"Of course." The pale man nodded curtly and wandered back to the administrative building.

Joe Stoddard was already stationed at the warehouse. Bradshaw had Cervantes and Thomas meet him there as well. Thomas was an older woman, hard, not a feminine bone in her body. What hadn't been drilled out of her when she transferred to the base had been washed away at the sight of the lunging rotters (Bradshaw wondered if it was different for a woman, seeing new life created, but from death). She'd stopped wearing her bite jacket long ago, and both her arms bore scars as a result; nonetheless she'd definitely be an asset in field missions. As for Cervantes... Bradshaw hadn't seen much of him since Grimm's death. There were murmurs that Cervantes was some sort of psychic, the sort of nonsense the Defense Department had messed with fifty years ago. Maybe they were still messing with it. Hell, Bradshaw had seen stranger things.

"I appreciate your choosing me," Cervantes said.

Bradshaw decided against saying *you're welcome*. "We've got a truck coming in five minutes."

Stoddard barked from his post, "It's already here!" and opened the main loading door to admit the semi's refrigerated payload.

Bradshaw slapped a button to start the conveyor belt that led from the warehouse to the scientists' underground compound.

"Let me ask you something," Cervantes said. "What do they do down there? What tests do they run on the afterdead?"

Had he just been reading Bradshaw's mind? The captain crossed his arms and gave Cervantes a stony look. "It's not my jurisdiction. I've learned not to ask."

Stoddard slapped Cervantes' back as the truck opened. A steel box came out on rollers and they guided it onto the conveyor belt. There were five more inside, each coated with ice, electronically sealed; and within each, a fallen soldier who would be inducted into the undead population. Somewhere, Stoddard knew, there were graves with empty coffins upon which grieving mothers placed tiny flags. But these boys were still serving their government, in a way. *Whatever helps me sleep at night.*

"Seal's broken!" Thomas snapped, banging on the lid of the next box. Stoddard came around and hoisted the lid up to look inside. Though the body was in a clear bag, he wasn't able to tell if there was any putrefaction. "You think it matters?" he asked Bradshaw.

"Dead is dead," came the reply.

Stoddard forced the lid down and pushed the box onto the belt. "Can't argue with that logic, boss."

"Don't call me boss." Bradshaw tried to grimace, but Stoddard's expression teased a hint of a smile from the corners of his mouth.

\* \* \*

Ryland locked his office door and sat on the edge of his desk. His breathing was growing more shallow with each passing day. It didn't hurt, it wasn't uncomfortable; he was just afraid someone might notice. Good thing a yearly physical wasn't required of him. He dropped into his chair and turned on his computer, entering several encryption keys before he could get into his files. Despite all that security—and a few extra measures he'd added himself—he knew that there was always someone reading his e-mail. That's why his most precious files were in paper form.

Unlocking the bottom desk drawer to produce those files, Ryland checked the contents. All there. Could never be too careful. A medical report, written up by one A. Harmon, dated seven months prior. Blood work results. Digital photographs of his right hand.

Removing his glove, Ryland saw the ugly scars. He tried flexing his fingers. There was stiffness and pain, only the pain seemed strangely distant, and even as the skin cracked and bled he continued closing his hand into a tight fist.

The URC, the energy in the earth that revived the dead, was never intended to be weaponized. Maybe in some horror movie, a corrupt military lab would try to turn URC into a contagion, but the real government understood the possible consequences. Still, factions within were sparring over what to do; and several months ago, Ryland had led a group of private contractors to New England to check out another Source. And... he began to laugh uncontrollably at the memory, the goddamn absurdity of it. "Fucking cat," he gasped between giggles.

The cat's love bite shouldn't have had any effect, but Harmon had discovered an anomaly in Ryland's blood when he returned to the base for stitches. He knew immediately what had happened. The URC had bonded with some virus lying dormant in the feline's system. Some thought it possible. Now he knew it was. And just like that, it was a contagion. A cosmic roll of the dice, a sick twist of fate. All these hundreds of thousands of years, and only now had it happened... and to Nathan Ryland.

It took a few months of watching his arm die before he made the decision to transfer Harmon to the field and silence her. Grimm had been another story altogether...

Though the tissue in Ryland's body was dying, he didn't feel much discomfort. The infection was turning him undead piece by piece, yet he retained all his mental faculties, even if there was a cold hollow growing inside of him as his soul was forced out. Thus he had reasoned that, like the afterdead, he could maintain a healthy appearance and a clear head if he fed. The afterdead's chum was trucked in biweekly and stored at the ass-end of the base where the smell wouldn't offend. So Ryland had gone out to the storage building, walked in, shut the door, and promptly vomited at the sight of the festering meat spread before him. Dropped to his knees, dry heaving, arms shaking until he was prone on the floor in his own puke. "I-I can't," he had whispered, fighting the urge to keep retching. He looked at his dead hand. It felt so detached, like it wasn't really part of him. It was almost surreal to see it scooping up a handful of rancid medical waste. He forced it down, stuffing his fingers into his throat and trying not to taste it. But the smell hit him again. He spewed chum all over his pants.

Then Grimm had walked in. He looked through the visor of his gas mask at Ryland's bloody mouth and hand and clothing, Ryland sitting on the floor with a blank stare, like a boy caught playing with himself. Two days later, Grimm was living out in the neighborhood with the afterdead. Ryland had figured no one would believe the story if Grimm told them, but why take any chances?

Most of his body felt dead, somehow, and even though he was now able to eat chum and keep it down, there were still signs of it. If he sat in his chair too long he'd get mottled purple spots all over his buttocks, legs and back. Sometimes at night he'd wake up to discover his bladder had emptied itself. Trying to get out of bed, he found himself paralyzed by what seemed like rigor mortis. And Jesus Christ, he farted all the time, expelling the noxious gases of internal decay. He couldn't eat nearly enough to stave off such things; he couldn't risk being caught shoveling chum into his mouth again. St. John was already on his ass for three deaths.

Day by day, Ryland was growing accustomed to the spreading infection, and so was his ego. He decided it wasn't chance, but that he'd been *chosen*. He would be the first true afterdead—not some soldier who took shrapnel in Lebanon and had his dead body dumped in that accursed swamp. No, Ryland was willingly giving himself over to the other side. There had only been one more test to pass, and that was Cervantes. The telepath hadn't sensed Ryland's condition at all. He was now confident that he was not dying, but *evolving*.

He longed to go out among the afterdead and see how they reacted, if at all. Would they attack him, or consider him one of their own? He chuckled at the thought. They were senseless animals without purpose. The scientists spent all day and night cutting the dead into pieces, burning them, pulling out their organs. They only sought to define the afterdead, to put it all in books and file it away, then they could sit back and relax knowing that humanity was still top dog. Insecure fools. He alone would know death firsthand, experience it in a conscious way.

*Chosen.*

He dug into the base's historical archives—information suppressed from the general public—researching the ways that tribal peoples around Sources had explained the phenomenon. Of course, they had decided that dark gods were responsible. The gods were long gone, perhaps dead, but their leavings endured—including strange words that had probably been made up by the savages but were purported to focus and direct the chaotic Source energy.

He had been studying these words. His extensive education gave him a leg up on the military historians who'd catalogued and promptly forgotten these silly fables. He was beginning to understand the lost tongues of the old gods, and he was beginning to believe that he might be able to do greater things with the plague-energy that coursed through him.

Somewhere beyond death, off this mortal coil, lay godhood.

\* \* \*

It was a long drive to Whittaker's house. The rental car was running on fumes; Clarke had used Whittaker's credit card to refuel, but it wasn't long before he exhausted the remaining credit. Holding the dead man's ID against the steering wheel, checking addresses as he drove, Clarke finally came to a small frame house with an unkempt yard. The first key he tried opened the front door.

The interior was almost bare. There had been feeble attempts to decorate: a generic print of an elk in the woods hung on the wall. The leather couch had two end tables covered in magazines. Clarke pushed aside the top magazine, a year-old issue of *Newsweek*. The one below it, and all the ones below that, were porn.

As expected, Whittaker had an impressive gun collection in the bedroom. Some of them were modified arms from the base, illegal to have in the home. Clarke opened the glass doors of the gun case and began pulling weapons out, setting them on the bed for further scrutiny. Opening the closet, he kicked aside a few pairs of jeans lying on the floor and found Whittaker's Army fatigues neatly folded. Knowing Whittaker's fondness for his days in combat, he wasn't surprised to see the uniform in pristine condition. It would be a bit loose on Clarke's frame but that didn't matter. He pulled it on over his soiled clothes.

There was a pickup truck in the garage, and for that Clarke also had a key. He pulled out with a satchel of weapons beside him in the passenger seat. A memory was stirred in the recesses of his mind... nearly a decade before, when he'd been a young officer and had just been brought onto the afterdead project.

The first corpse that the government had resurrected was an unpleasant character named Louis Brownlee. In life he had been locked away in a federal prison for fatally shooting two DEA agents during a bust. Small-time hood made notorious by capping a couple of undercover agents. A chain smoker, cancer had claimed him early during his double-life sentence. Brownlee's body had quietly been shipped to the Louisiana base and seeded in the swamp. The URC infused his tissue, and a group of soldiers watched in horror as he rose from the muck and fixed yellow eyes on their warm living flesh.

The military were eager to explore the possible applications of the undead. Could Brownlee be made to obey the living? Could he fight? Could he infect? Clarke sat in smoky rooms, with celebrated generals and Defense Department officials yelling at each other, as the afterdead began to appear less and less useful. Finally, Brownlee was placed under restraints and brought into one of the meetings. The officials stared blankly at him. He returned the look. A colonel named Richard St. John took a long drag off his cigarette and met the creature's gaze without fear. Brownlee's withered lips opened and closed, a weak sound emanating from his throat. "What is it saying? What does it want?" A man asked. Standing up, St. John approached Brownlee. "His file said he was a smoker." And he placed his cigarette in the zombie's mouth.

The stiff, pained stature of the afterdead relaxed. Brownlee leaned his head back and exhaled. He was still addicted.

Not long after that, Clarke and a small team were flown to a facility in Puerto Rico, Brownlee brought along in chains. The secret prison there housed a few terrorism suspects, and these prisoners were strong. They didn't talk under burning lights, they didn't weep in the face of brutal torture or even sexual humiliation. A religious fervor possessed them and made them more than men, at least in their own minds.

Clarke wheeled Brownlee into an interrogation room on a dolly. An Arab, sitting in a lone chair, narrowed his eyes.

The CIA interrogator was leaning against the rear wall. He spoke in English. "Salim, this gentleman is here to make sure you answer my questions." Clarke released the straps holding Brownlee down, and the afterdead stepped into the middle of the room. Clarke stood away from him and held up a carton of cigarettes. "Play nice, Brownlee."

The next hour was a nightmare. Clarke fought to stand still and watch, his knees knocking. Even the interrogator was shaken by the end of it; he could barely issue the order for Brownlee to finally kill Salim. Together they rushed from the room and let the zombie feed in peace. And on closed-circuit monitors in another room, the remaining prisoners watched in terror. They were much more compliant after that.

Brownlee's addiction to nicotine seemed to be the only leverage that his handlers had. After devouring a captor, he would sit on the floor in a pool of gore and light cig after cig, staining them red with his fingers and lips. He allowed himself to be chained and flown around the world, always with Clarke holding a fresh carton before him. Over time, they noticed that he seemed to become healthier if he ate frequently. His eyes almost began to look human again. Unnerved, they cut back his food supply.

Brownlee's last assignment took him to Arlington, Virginia, and the interrogation of a CIA officer accused of selling intelligence. Clarke tapped Brownlee's chest with a carton. "You know what to do." Brownlee nodded slowly and entered the room where the officer was waiting. They gave him twenty minutes, then went in.

He was only supposed to have bitten off a few fingers, eaten them in front of the subject and sat quietly. But the subject was headless, all four walls covered in her blood. Brownlee tugged strings of muscle from the stump of her neck and stuffed them into his mouth. Clarke drew on him. "Get away from her," he snapped, trying to mask his fear. Brownlee looked up at him, reached out a crimson claw for the pack of cigs. "Smoke?"

Clarke dropped his gun and pissed himself. Other team members swept past him to lash chains around the afterdead, who sat calmly, his eyes never leaving Clarke's. They brought him to his feet and pushed him toward the door. His rancid breath was hot on Clarke's face as he said "I'm a good dog," in his guttural monotone.

He was never seen again after that. The government discontinued that particular program.

Clarke thought about the role he'd played before his murder. He had been a good dog too. So had Whittaker and Bradshaw. Now it was time to learn who their master was.

# 5 / THE MAN COMES AROUND

He lay quietly and stared upward into nothingness. His legs jostled a bit, as did his sidearms. In his mind he saw a rough schematic of Fort Armstrong's layout. He'd been on the road for several hours now, not breathing, not smelling the faint decay of his skin nor the freshness of Whittaker's borrowed fatigues. A bit of plastic was pulled tight across the tip of his nose; he was wrapped in a transparent body bag inside a steel coffin, and the only little bit of light afforded him was from the fracture he'd made in the lid's lock sometime during the journey.

It was ice cold. Hours had gone by, how many he couldn't say. He didn't daydream, nor did look ahead to the tasks that awaited him. This was the idle mind of a dead man.

Most questions had been answered. Ahead was only the goal of self-preservation, self-preservation assured by the execution of his executioner. The endgame lay with he who had turned Whittaker and Bradshaw against him. Clarke still had some of Whittaker's gristle in his molars. He didn't wonder what Bradshaw would taste like (*right turn, slowing down—Armstrong's west security gate*), nor did he yearn for the man's dark meat. There would be no particular satisfaction in killing Bradshaw, the one who had slit open his satchel and spilled his manhood onto the dirt. Bradshaw had also shot him through the heart, whispering some apologetic sentiment that Clarke couldn't recall. He couldn't recall the words, but was keenly aware of the bullet's location in his meat. It festered there and corrupted the other meat around it, though Clarke had no use for that anyway (*truck coming to a stop—coffins jostling slightly*).

There was talk outside. Clarke wondered if he might be recognized; not that they bothered to identify each corpse that came into Armstrong, but he was a former team member. Shouldn't he have a nice little plot in Arlington, they'd ask? Or maybe it's better this way, they might say, that he takes his secret knowledge back to its secret grave.

The lid moved. "Another broken seal," a female snapped. Light entered the coffin, and Clarke stared straight ahead, knowing his pupils might have some small reaction.

The female leaned over him, eyed him through the plastic. *Thomas*, his mind said.

Would she say "Clarke" to him?

She didn't say anything. The lid slammed shut. Yelling. Then, rolling. Down, down into the earth, beneath the base where the scientists justify all of this. A seed of curiosity was born in Clarke's mind; for the genuine corpses, one of whom he'd swapped places with, this was a new birth. Stirring in the womb—shaking off swamp mud, chains buckled about your hands and feet, tethering you to one of the gnarled old trees thick with crud and in the air a thousand million insects humming. An insufferable place, the Source, its ever-womb teeming with abscesses of grubs and vines and God only knew what else. They were bound for the swamp, but first they'd be opened up and picked at by the scientists, who'd pull on their masks and aprons and slave over the new flesh; removing troublesome shrapnel and cancer tissue, setting broken bones. Assigning nicknames. Clarke felt his box clattering down a conveyor belt at breakneck speed and wondered if they made bets on the number of vertebrae broken during this cruel descent.

Then he was being ferried along a vertical belt, and stopped rudely, and the lid was opened once again.

Clarke lay perfectly still, sidearms tucked beneath his thighs. A face cloistered in goggles and antiseptic materials, resembling a giant insect, stared down at him.

"Hello," said the zombie to the bug.

Clarke kicked himself out of the steel coffin with arms akimbo, squeezing off a volley of bullets before hitting the floor and rolling underneath the conveyor belt that had brought his corpse into this neo-Hell. As he did, he got his first good look at the underground lab: a huge, garishly lit cavern crowded with cables and monitors. And scientists, each one paralyzed with confusion.

Clarke rose and let fly a hail of bullets that sent a storm of sparks into the air as monitor after monitor exploded. He saw the scientists diving for cover and screaming for the soldiers to come down.

The bug-like doctor lay at Clarke's feet, trembling. Clarke slurred his words: "I want Bradshaw. Sergeant Bradshaw."

"It's Captain now," came the voice at his back.

Bradshaw vaulted over the conveyor belt and hacked into Clarke's kneecap with a widowmaker, sliding out of harm's way just as the afterdead put the soldier in his sights. Gunfire peppered a computer console and sent another fountain of sparks toward the rock ceiling.

Clarke felt his knee coming apart. It had been a clean shot from Bradshaw, always the master with the blade. The bug-like doctor was crawling away, sobbing. Clarke dropped down and caught his ankle. Raising him up as a shield, the zombie rounded the sputtering console in search of Bradshaw...

Who was racing up the service tunnel to the receiving warehouse, his mind outpacing his feet as he panicked: *the gunman's an afterdead. The afterdead is Clarke.* Bradshaw, who had understood little about his covert assignment under Ryland, was now certain that he understood nothing at all.

* * *

Above ground, every available serviceman was speeding toward the warehouse. Waves of Jeeps whisked past fences where the base's afterdead lingered, curious.

And Nathan Ryland, sitting in his office, heard the alarms sounding and his heart began to palpitate... and then it stopped. He shuddered in his chair, slipping forward just slightly so that his gut nudged the edge of his desk, and he died.

The soul departed the body. Ryland jolted in his chair, this time sending the computer monitor crashing to the floor, and he sat up undead. The tissue in his head and hands and haunches was suffused with a dark, creeping energy, and he stood.

A soldier opened his door and leaned in. "Sir, there's an emergency in the research facility. I've been instructed to remove you from the base in the event—"

Ryland, nodding, came around the desk and tore the soldier's throat open. He eased the young man's automatic to the floor and took in great, gluttonous mouthfuls of flesh.

* * *

Clarke threw the bug-like doctor to the floor of the concrete tunnel. "Enner ashess code…"

"A-access code?" the terrified scientist asked. Clarke nodded. The doctor opened the door allowing Clarke into the receiving warehouse.

A spurt of gunfire threw the doctor back. Cries of surprise and outrage were heard from the other side of the door: "What the fuck are we dealing with?!"

"It's Clarke." Bradshaw said grimly, watching the door from behind the massive wheel of a dump truck. Stoddard just stared at him. On the other side of the captain, Thomas was reloading her M-16 and cursing herself for shooting the doctor.

"Explain," Stoddard said. "Ken?"

"I fucked up." Bradshaw counted the beads of sweat rolling down the side of his head. "Me and Whittaker, we fucked up. We killed Clarke and Harmon."

"Wait a minute…" Thomas started to back away.

Bradshaw turned and said, "You're not part of this. Go." And she did.

"I'm staying," Stoddard whispered.

"Joe, this isn't your fight."

"If it's your fight then it's my fight, brother."

"No time for this bullshit!" Bradshaw hissed. Stoddard just shrugged.

Thomas edged toward the receiving bay, where she'd be able to leave the warehouse and join the soldiers scrambling outside. A cold hand closed over her throat.

"No sound."

She cocked her head a quarter-inch to the right and saw her dead comrade, Pete Clarke. He wasn't a zombie horror; the only indication of his lifelessness was the empty look in his eyes and that raspy monotone. He stared at her, through her—then she smelled the gas.

She spun away from him, finger on the trigger, and he popped her through the head before she got off one shot. Pulling himself onto the receiving bay, he fired a second round into the spilled gasoline he'd liberated from the trucks.

\* \* \*

The warehouse exploded. Soldiers heading for the entrance were thrown back.

Stoddard rose from the grass outside, coughing violently. He and Bradshaw had each gone through a window. Before he could orient himself, soldiers poured through the clouds of smoke to grab him. "Wait! Ken! Ken!" He bellowed.

Bradshaw staggered through a column of darkness into Clarke's arms. He shoved the afterdead off, and turned to see no escape route, only piles of flaming debris surrounding them; he'd chosen the wrong window and the wall had simply come down around him.

"Whooo?" moaned the afterdead.

"Ryland," Bradshaw answered, drawing his twin widowmakers. "I don't know why. I don't know why it had to happen, and I don't know why I did it. I'm sorry Pete."

He leapt at Clarke, going straight for that wasted knee—the afterdead buckled, and Bradshaw scissored off an ear and most of one cheek. He hit the ground ready to pivot, sending his other blade into the meat of Clarke's waist.

Clarke whirled to face him; Bradshaw knew that the damage dealt to his opponent meant nothing—there was no pain, no shock—quickly, he planted a widowmaker between Clarke's eyes and jerked his head sharply downward. The neck broke. Clarke's eyes rolled in their bloody sockets and he pawed at Bradshaw's uniform. "I'm sorry, so sorry," Bradshaw was whispering, as he freed his blades, stepped back and prepared to decapitate the undead.

Clarke could not offer the same sentiment. He felt nothing as he shook the pistol from his pants leg and shot Bradshaw through the heart.

For the first time in a long time, things made sense for Ken Bradshaw, including his own demise, and as he fell forward he thought that, maybe now, all things would return to their proper state and the corruption he'd helped sow would wash away. It was a foolish notion, but comforting in death.

* * *

Base Commander St. John beat his knuckles against his desk as he listened to radio reports of the havoc on the other side of the base. All they knew at this point was that a shooter had breached the labs, and the receiving warehouse was in flames.

Stoddard's voice came over the radio. *"He's an afterdead! Bullets won't stop him!"* How was one miserable rotter causing such a panic? It was the men on the ground, they needed to pull themselves together and assess the situation with level heads. He grabbed his radio to issue just such a decree when the intercom on his desk squawked. "Commander! It's Ryland—he's coming up, he's—he's attacking everyone! Just about took my finger off!"

"What in the Christ." St. John yanked open the drawer at his right hand and roused his Desert Eagle from its foam bedding. He walked out of his office and into the hall.

Ryland was tugging on a staffer's arm, teeth gnashing scant inches from her ear. St. John fired a shot into the ceiling. Ryland released the terror-stricken girl, and then he was alone with the commander.

"Somehow I sense, Nathan Goddamn Ryland, that you're the one responsible for all of this. Am I wrong?"

Ryland said nothing. As his eyes adjusted in the hallway, St. John became aware of how blood-soaked the liaison's suit was. He also became aware of a repugnant, gagging odor. Decaying tissue. "You're... you're dead. Undead. *You're* the rotter? What have you done?" St. John roared.

Ryland spat a mouthful of someone else's blood onto the floor.

St. John fired two rounds into Ryland's chest, kicking him to the end of the hall where he crumpled. The base commander took no chances as he approached the body; standing at arm's length, he emptied the Desert Eagle into Ryland's bloated corpse.

This was the end for Fort Armstrong, St. John realized. The entire base, like the files stored within, like the bodies lying on the floor—it would all have to be razed and the ashes scattered to the winds. And all because of this miserable snake in the grass—

Ryland bit into St. John's palm. The commander kicked him away with a snarl and watched blood swell in the wound. "You're dead! Son of a bitch!" St. John clasped his hand to the belly of his uniform and staggered away. At least there wasn't any risk of some sort of infection.

* * *

Clarke slipped behind the wheel of a Humvee. Full tank of gas. He knew that Ryland was likely to be just across the base, though it wasn't so simple as a straight line from point A to point B.

He decided to simplify, and drove through the electrified fences separating the living from the dead.

Soldiers scrambled to put up a roadblock, but the fencing came down like a curtain, folding into the dirt, the afterdead walking right over it even as their toes burst into flames. Every soldier in Fort Armstrong was sure they couldn't become infected, each was sure that they were dealing with little more than sedated dogs, each saw the afterdead converging with renewed speed on the fallen fences.

Some of them fired, but they all ran.

\* \* \*

Esteban Cervantes awoke from a nightmare. In the nightmare, he was alone on a desert road. An old man dressed in black approached him. "*A causa de los gatos, ya en Egipto,*" the man rasped. His eyes were not human and boiled with shapeless larvae. But it was the sound of the man's leathery tongue over his rotten teeth that drove Cervantes from sleep. Then he heard the alarms.

A flurry of panicked thoughts and prayers assailed him. He was generally able to phase out others' thoughts, but this crisis had put everyone's psyche into overdrive. Between all the nervous breakdowns and the bottled-up rages looking for something to shoot, Cervantes wasn't sure where he'd be of most use.

As he jogged out of his quarters, a Hummer ran up the curb and stopped. "In!"

He complied without hesitation, and paid no mind to the faint small of rot—but then his mind's eye saw into the other and there was NOTHING.

"I can't..not... drive good," Clarke muttered, motioning to his ruined knee. "Take me to Ryland and I will... won't..not shoot you."

"All right." Cervantes slipped into the driver's seat, probing Clarke's skull with telepathic tendrils. There were only patches of memory, a few pages from a book... but he saw enough to know why Clarke had come back. As for Ryland's involvement..."I don't know why I'm saying this," Cervantes began; he figured the zombie's promise not to shoot him was the closest thing to honesty he'd ever heard, as the undead were incapable of lying, and wanted to return the favor. "Something's wrong with Ryland. I'm not sure what it is, but there's something unnatural about him. And if that has to do with you, Captain, then maybe you already know, but—"

An arm smashed through the window and grabbed at the wheel, followed by a head. Cervantes knocked both away, but he felt the bite, teeth raking through his flesh, and as he jerked the wheel to the side, caught a glimpse of Ryland's face—

\* \* \*

Stoddard led the charge against the loosed afterdead. They were run down with dump trucks, then those left standing faced the blades of standard-issue widowmakers. Stoddard let out an *"OOH-RAH!!"* as he dashed a rotter's head against the side of a truck. He tried not to think about the Clarke situation—the mere fact that there *was* a Clarke situation—

One of the administrative staffers came hurtling toward him. Stoddard chopped away groping hands and tripping limbs and escorted the woman over to an idle dump truck.

"God, you got bit." He rummaged through his uniform, as if he still carried a First Aid Kit on his person. "Nathan Ryland bit me!" The woman exclaimed. "Then all these others—I'm bleeding everywhere—feel faint –"

"Wait, *Ryland?*"

The woman slumped to the ground. No pulse.

"Oh my God," Stoddard yelled, "could somebody — AYYEAAGGHH!!"

He kicked the woman's teeth away from his thigh and drew his pistol. "Are you alive? Say something!"

She rose, pushing out her breasts, licking Stoddard's blood from her lips—

Giving the gun and its owner one last look, she took off. Self-preservation before hunger.

"FUCK!!!" Stoddard sat down, waited for his pulse rate to drop a little, then looked at his wound. Well, this was bad. A new bad. Someone would come up with a better name for it later. All Joe knew was that he was going to turn into a zombie.

That's when one of the base's rotters lunged around the truck and tore his throat out, and he was spared that last pain in the ass.

# 6 / AN END; AND, A BEGINNING

Ryland stared curiously at Clarke as they circled one another on the roadway. Cervantes stayed down in the Humvee, not bothering to peer out the window; instead he reached out to their minds and mapped out their movements in his own, translating the simple impulses of their zombified brains.

Ryland stopped. His mouth struggled to form words. The memory was there, in his nerves and muscles, and if he could just get the thoughts from his brain to his lips..."Clarke," he said finally, and something resembling a smile crossed his face.

"Is thish why?" Clarke couldn't help his slurred speech now, with his cheek mangled, but he got the point across. "Is thish why you killed me?"

"Yes," Ryland answered. "I am not like you. I am a new afterdead. I am the birth of a plague."

He gestured towards an older zombie, one of the base's experimental subjects, as it staggered across a field a few hundred yards off. "I have spread it to many, living and dead. They all carry the plague now."

"Why?" Clarke asked. There was no bitterness or longing in the question; he asked only because that was his mission, to know why he had been killed. To understand, so that he would not be killed again.

"Because," Ryland answered, "I wanted to see what would happen."

An unsatisfying answer, perhaps, to the living beings that were now being infected with this new plague, but good enough for Clarke.

Ryland came at him then, and despite Clarke's condition, it was easy to fend off the inexperienced fighter's attacks. Clarke smashed a

259

bony fist through Ryland's teeth, and the other made to swallow the fist, seizing Clarke's arm with both hands and gnashing the jagged nubs of his teeth on Clarke's dead skin. Clarke felt tendon and muscle being torn away and, planting a boot on Ryland's groin, jerked his hand free.

Ryland staggered back, snapping his jaws like a mad dog, ragged sheets of gray flesh dangling from his broken teeth. "No good. Dead meat." Though undead, he seemed to be somehow relishing every new experience of his afterlife, the proud parent of the contagion and a new flesh. In the Humvee, Cervantes felt disgust for Ryland, disgust that boiled in his throat and threatened to make him retch; meanwhile Clarke, who felt nothing, raised his shredded fist and rejoined the fight.

He stabbed two fingers through Ryland's eye socket, pulping the orb as if it were nothing and sinking knuckle-deep into the cold jelly of the dead brain. Ryland grunted, then made a sound like a laugh. He swatted at Clarke's various wounds without effect.

Clarke hurled Ryland to the asphalt and knelt on his neck. There was a snap, and Clarke grabbed Ryland's hair and jerked his head to one side. Another satisfying snap.

Ryland gurgled, tried to speak, but Clarke put all his weight on the man's throat, and wrenched at his head as hard as he could, and before long there were no more words left to say.

Ryland's head, a chattering, pulpy mess, rolled to the curb and was forgotten. Clarke stood up, looked back at the Humvee.

Within, Cervantes' mind was suddenly assaulted by a crushing force that blinded his inner eye.

"My lucidity is... different from yours," Ryland's head whispered. Clarke whirled to see Ryland's body writhing, churning in time with the words of the disembodied head. His chest rose and fell with something that wasn't breath; ribs and flesh snapped apart. There was something inside of him.

"I used every resource at my disposal to try and understand what was growing inside of me. What I was becoming. And I found the words of the old gods who left their dark energy here on our little insect-world... I found that I could be much more than just the plague..."

Tentacles erupted from Ryland's body and snaked across the street to caress his head. Ryland moaned; Clarke watched as his brains were pulled out through the bottom of his skull, watched as the tentacles withdrew with their prize and settled in the cavity of Ryland's headless torso, cradling his brain there.

Clarke heard Ryland in his head now, as if the man had become pure thought. The brain pulsated as Ryland spoke.

*Ia! Ia!*

Ryland's body rose with the brain nestled in a bed of throbbing tentacles. He began stalking toward Clarke.

*I am more than a new flesh... I am a new being... a new god...*

Cervantes rolled out of the Humvee, clutching his head, blood streaming from his open eyes. He rose to his knees and saw the horror Ryland had transformed into.

He raised an M16 and let loose.

A hail of bullets shredded Ryland's body, sending him staggering back, his exposed brain jolting about as the tentacles exploded outward in an effort to contain it.

*No! NO! You can't kill me! I am—*

*I—*

A trio of bullets sailed through the night and punched into the meat of Ryland's brain. It flew apart like so much refuse.

*I...*

Ryland crumpled, tentacles flopping weakly on the asphalt. Cervantes' head cleared, and he was able to think again: *so much for the gods.* He knew they had no place in this terrifying new world.

Clarke turned. Cervantes aimed the M16 at him.

Clarke considered this situation for a moment; here was meat, meat that had helped him in his mission but meat nonetheless. Yet, that meat had a gun. And something else was curious about that meat, something special about him that Clarke's bruised mind couldn't pin down.

He turned from the soldier and walked away.

Cervantes looked at the bite mark on his wrist. He could sense that something was wrong, very wrong, that this wasn't a typical bite. Just as Ryland, whose disembodied head continued to gnash its teeth, was not a typical zombie. Something coursed through his veins and took hold of the cells in his blood.

*God... I'm infected.*

He turned away as well, away from the fight, from Ryland's remains, and walked. He would need to tell others, on the outside. He'd need to tell the world that its end had finally come.

# VALLEY OF THE DEAD
## THE TRUTH BEHIND DANTE'S INFERNO

Working from Dante's *Inferno* to draw out the reality behind the fantasy, author Kim Paffenroth unfolds the horrifying true events that led Dante to fictionalize the account of his lost years ... For seventeen years of his life, Italian poet Dante Alighieri traveled as an exile across Europe, working on his epic poem, *The Divine Comedy*. During his lost wanderings, Dante stumbled upon an infestation of the living dead. The unspeakable acts he witnessed--cannibalism, live burnings, evisceration, crucifixion, and dozens more--became the basis of all the horrors described in Inferno. Afraid to be labeled a madman, Dante made the terrors he experienced into a more "believable" account of an otherworldly adventure filled with demons and mythological monsters. But at last, the real story can finally be told.

THE TRUTH BEHIND DANTE'S INFERNO

VALLEY OF THE DEAD
*Kim Paffenroth*

ISBN: 978-1934861318

# *Autobiography of a* WEREWOLF HUNTER

It takes more than silver bullets to kill a werewolf.

Sylvester James knows what it is to be haunted. His mother died giving birth to him and his father never let him forget it; until the night he was butchered by a werewolf--the night a full moon ruined his life. Alone in the world, a Cheyenne mystic trains the boy to be a werewolf hunter. As Sylvester follows his vendetta into the outlands of the occult, options become scarce. And he learns it takes more than silver bullets to kill a werewolf ...

To kill a werewolf, it takes a hunter with a perfect willingness to die.

"IF YOU PICK THIS BOOK UP YOU WILL NOT BE ABLE TO PUT IT DOWN."
—HORROR SOCIETY

*Autobiography of a* WEREWOLF HUNTER

BRIAN P. EASTON

ISBN: 978-1934861295

MORE DETAILS, EXCERPTS, AND PURCHASE INFORMATION AT
# www.permutedpress.com

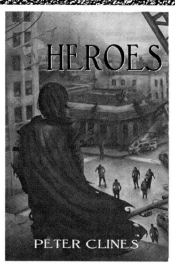

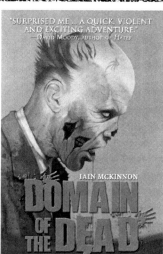

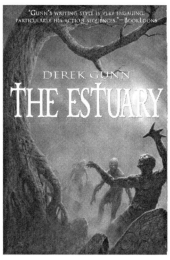

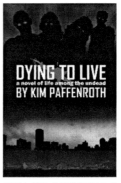
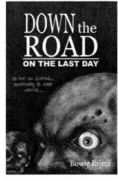

### BY WILLIAM D. CARL

Beneath the dim light of a full moon, the population of Cincinnati mutates into huge, snarling monsters that devour everyone they see, acting upon their most base and bestial desires. Planes fall from the sky. Highways are clogged with abandoned cars, and buildings explode and topple. The city burns.

Only four people are immune to the metamorphosis—a smooth talking thief who maintains the code of the Old West, an African-American bank teller who has struggled her entire life to emerge unscathed from the ghetto, a wealthy middle-aged housewife who finds everything she once believed to be a lie, and a teen-aged runaway turning tricks for food.

Somehow, these survivors must discover what caused this apocalypse and stop it from spreading. In their way is not only a city of beasts at night, but, in the daylight hours, the same monsters returned to human form, many driven insane by atrocities committed against friends and families.

Now another night is fast approaching. And once again the moon will be full.

ISBN: 978-1934861042

### A ZOMBIE NOVEL BY TONY MONCHINSKI

Seemingly overnight the world transforms into a barren wasteland ravaged by plague and overrun by hordes of flesh-eating zombies. A small band of desperate men and women stand their ground in a fortified compound in what had been Queens, New York. They've named their sanctuary Eden.

Harris—the unusual honest man in this dead world—races against time to solve a murder while maintaining his own humanity. Because the danger posed by the dead and diseased mass clawing at Eden's walls pales in comparison to the deceit and treachery Harris faces within.

ISBN: 978-1934861172

MORE DETAILS, EXCERPTS, AND PURCHASE INFORMATION AT
# www.permutedpress.com

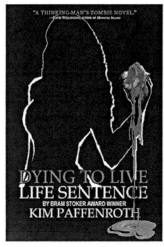

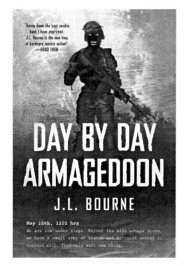

9 781934 861738